# NEVER TRUST A LADY

*Suzanne Robinson*

BANTAM BOOKS • NEW YORK

2011 Bantam Books Mass Market Edition

Copyright © 2003 by Lynda S. Robinson

Published in the United States by Bantam Books, an imprint of The Random House Publishing Group, a division of Random House, Inc., New York.

BANTAM BOOKS and the rooster colophon are registered trademarks of Random House, Inc.

Originally published in paperback in the United States by Bantam Books, an imprint of The Random House Publishing Group, a division of Random House, Inc., in 2003.

ISBN 978-0-553-58423-3

Cover design: Lynn Andreozzi
Cover illustration: Aleta Rafton

Printed in the United States of America

www.bantamdell.com

2 4 6 8 9 7 5 3

Bantam Books mass market edition: March 2011

## Also by Suzanne Robinson

*To my dear friend*
*Barbara Sanders*

# NEVER TRUST
# A LADY

# PROLOGUE

❧

*Mississippi, March, 1861*

DUSK FELL ON the sleepy town of Natchez perched on high, fern-covered bluffs over the west bank of the mud-laden Mississippi River. A gentleman planter stood on a promontory holding the reins of a mahogany Thoroughbred. The horse nickered and lowered his head to graze while his master gazed across the mighty river to the green-carpeted lowlands of Louisiana. Farther south the gentleman glanced at a series of mounds, the reputed haunts of an Indian tribe whose very name was lost to the passage of centuries.

He thought of the man who had just left, his friend. The one upon whom everything depended. Not everyone in the South was as farsighted as they were. Most of their friends didn't realize that Lincoln was deadly serious about fighting to save the Union. Likewise, after so many years of threatening secession, the North never believed that the states of the Deep South would leave the Union. Even now certain elements on both sides sought compromise. They were a minority. The North had done nothing yet, but it would soon. And then the killing would start, or as his friend was fond of saying, "The Mississippi will turn red with blood."

His friend had said good-bye, for his work ordained a different path than the gentleman's, a journey north into the capital of the enemy. Few knew his friend's real name, and for many months the gentleman planter had been in the habit of thinking of him by his code name—Iago. Only a half dozen of those in power in the South knew Iago's real name or the nature of his work for the Confederacy. The work was of a particular kind, that of going among the enemy, seeking out secrets, observing strengths and weaknesses and taking advantage where opportunity offered. Such talents made his friend unique, and they were the reason for the meeting tonight.

Under the auspices of the new Confederate government the gentleman and his influential friends had formed a group whose task it was to examine the position of the South with a realistic eye, and then to evolve strategies taking that position into account. The planter and his friends saw beyond Southern bravado and the immediate problem of an anti-slavery president. As John C. Calhoun of South Carolina had foreseen, the stately, rural South had lost control of Congress to immigrant-ridden, brash Northern states, and she might never get it back. Now that the North was in charge, she would make laws regarding slavery and tariffs that would ruin the South.

There was no choice but to fight this strong, uncompromising enemy, and Iago was one of the South's weapons. He moved freely in and out of Washington. He visited the houses of Yankee generals and cabinet members. He watched movements on the railroads and secretly read government plans for the navy and army. He trained others in such work and sent them north. And like all Southern gentlemen, he was as familiar with revolver and rapier as he was with saddle and rifle. But unknown to most, Iago also possessed a chameleon quality—one moment a cultured gentleman, the next a calculating killer who prided himself on being so skilled in the art of murder that he could slit a man's throat without spilling a drop of blood on himself.

The gentleman devoted a last fond thought to his friend, then mounted and guided his horse back to the red dirt road. The sides of the road were bounded by old rose hedges, and from these borders soared live oaks with their trailing draperies of moss. The trees stretched their branches toward one another, forming a gently swaying rooftop as the road wound away from the town, past the borders of cotton plantations. Here and there the rider passed a carriage, to which he tipped his hat with respect. More often he met trudging black field hands wearily homebound after a day's grueling labor. These he did not acknowledge.

At last the gentleman turned down an even smaller road almost invisible in its thick shroud of grapevines and pine trees. After carefully picking his way in the growing darkness, the rider glimpsed a broad avenue formed by ancient oaks. At the end of the avenue stood a three-story redbrick house with a pedimented front portico and Doric columns. The windows behind the colonnaded galleries were dark except for a glow in one of the first-floor windows. No groom came to attend the rider as he approached the mansion. The gentleman could hear the distant sound of singing from the slave cabins, but these were some distance from the house. The only other sounds were the scraping of branches against the roof and the gentle hissing of oak leaves rustled by the March wind.

Tethering his horse, the gentleman entered the silent house. Without knocking he walked inside. It appeared deserted, but the gentleman barely glanced past the fluted columns that supported a plaster arch to examine the darkened elliptical staircase. He turned immediately to a door on his right and knocked lightly three times, paused and knocked once. The door opened to reveal a room crowded with upholstered rosewood furniture, French gilt mirrors and unlit crystal chandeliers. A marble and rosewood table bore a single silver candleholder that provided the only candle in the room. Around the table sat four men holding cigars or glasses of bourbon. Silent nods greeted the newcomer, who took up a glass of bourbon and downed it swiftly.

Replacing the glass on the marble tabletop, the newcomer spoke quietly in a soft Mississippi drawl. "Each of you has signaled your agreement with my views on the situation between our new Confederacy and the North by coming here tonight. Gentlemen, we know our beloved South is rich in land, in cotton, sugarcane, tobacco and rice. We also know it is not rich in railroads, steel mills, manufacturing plants or numbers of citizens when compared with our enemy."

Only one window was open in the parlor, but a soft, cool breeze fluttered the candle on the table.

The speaker's gaze caught that of each man listening to him before he continued. "Honor, righteousness and our grand military traditions will go only so far in aiding our cause. But with God's help and our own conviction, we will prevail." The speaker was used to oration and his words came easily. "The North doesn't think we'll fight to preserve our way of life."

Here a chorus of agreement interrupted him.

"And they have elected to the presidency that abolitionist ruffian Lincoln, a man with no formal education and certainly no administrative experience, who is antislavery and anti-South. It is an insult, gentlemen."

"A damned insult!" cried one of his listeners.

"Indeed," said the speaker. He paused to light a cigar and blow out a long stream of smoke. "The views we've discussed must remain secret, gentlemen." He leaned on the marble table and lowered his voice. "With the funds we've gathered, we'll be able to carry out a daring design and end this conflict, hopefully before too much blood is shed. It's a dangerous plan, but the result is worth the risk. We agree that the Confederacy badly needs the recognition of the major European powers, especially Great Britain, but Great Britain will wait for us to prove that we're able to remain independent of the North before she commits herself. If we can influence the British government to recognize the Confederacy, the North will back down."

"Or face the threat of war with England," one of the men added.

"Exactly." The speaker sat in a vacant chair and drew it closer to the table. The listeners leaned toward him. "Gentlemen, I have met with the agent known as Iago, and from this meeting has come a grand purpose. We must give Great Britain a push in our direction."

"Bring her over to our side irrevocably," chimed in another gentleman.

"Yes. We must force an irreparable rift between the North and Great Britain. To do that we must create a quarrel between them so grave and so violent that nothing can overcome the resulting animosity."

The speaker continued in an even lower voice. "Assassination, gentlemen. The details must be left to our friend. Iago is considering arranging for a fanatical abolitionist to be blamed for the death. Everyone knows they're mad."

"But not mad enough to risk war with Great Britain," said a listener.

"You're deceived," said an older planter. "Haven't you been listening for the past twenty years and more? The abolitionists will stop at nothing and say so plainly in everything they publish. Why, I can remember what that Garrison fellow wrote in that trash he calls *The Liberator*. He said he wouldn't equivocate, he wouldn't excuse, he wouldn't retreat a single inch."

The speaker nodded. "Some of you have to remember what he wrote in that public letter to Henry Clay. Called slavery 'the sum of all villainies.' Said it was 'concubinage, pollution, theft and kidnapping.' Garrison and the abolitionists have been thirsting for our blood for decades. They're convinced they're on a holy mission to redeem America. Damned crusaders."

A voice whispered, "And the British target? I suppose it should be a member of the government, a cabinet member perhaps."

A smile widened the speaker's mouth. "Indeed, sir. As you say, it should be someone extremely high in the British government." He leaned even closer to the others and whispered a name.

There was a shocked hush. The men exchanged fearful glances, but the only sound came from a rush of wind that whipped up the white lace curtains in the parlor and blew out the only light in the room.

# CHAPTER ONE

❧

*Natchez, Mississippi, 1861*

SHE WAS ALONE and far from home, and if she wasn't careful, she could get caught in the middle of a war. Eva Sparrow walked through the darkness between rows of lush magnolias and inhaled the scent of recently turned soil in the flowerbeds of Eastman Hall in Natchez, Mississippi. She must leave America soon. She wouldn't be here when the trees bloomed or see the magnificent explosion of camellias that lent such charm to the warm Southern nights. But even if there was no war coming, nothing could keep her here in this land where, from the comfort of a graceful white mansion, she could hear the crack of the lash and the cries of slaves being whipped.

After exploring America from New York to Texas and back, she would go home. At home people led uneventful lives secure in the knowledge that they lived in the most powerful country in the world. At home her family and friends all knew the same people, did the same things year after year. In April they returned to London from their country houses. In

May the Season began. For months they rushed from dinner to ball to luncheon to dinner and to the next ball. In July they went to the Henley Regatta and the cricket finals. In August after Parliament adjourned they went north for grouse season. Thus began the season for shooting things and hunting—partridge, pheasant, fox. Then came Christmas, and soon it was time to go back to London and do it all over again, and again, and again. Eva had long ago realized that the sheer busyness of the social calendar did little to make up for its tedium and emptiness. So she had stopped being busy. At least, the way everyone she knew was busy.

Her relatives wouldn't believe the things she'd done—traipsing through swamps outside New Orleans, learning to ride a quarter horse, driving cattle down the Chisholm Trail. Had they lived, her parents would have been shocked. Her friend Winnie, with whom she was staying at the moment, was shocked. Eva didn't know whether Winnie was more alarmed by Eva's adventures or her sun-browned complexion. The only members of her family who weren't shocked at Eva's new life were her great-aunt Lettice and uncle Adolphus. Aunt Lettice would have liked to go along on Eva's journeys if she weren't so frail, and Uncle Adolphus admired everything Eva did. Having been something of a reprobate in his youth, he saw a little of himself in his niece.

Her brothers disapproved most of all. They were both older than she was. The oldest spent most of his time in his country house, having inherited his father's earldom. The younger relished his career in the admiralty. Conforming and comfortable in their places in British Society, neither had ever had occasion to question its tenets. Eva had once been as compliant as they, and it had taken her a long time and much maturing to abandon her dependence upon the approval of her family and social set. Now that she'd succeeded, she was enjoying her freedom.

Eva went up the steps, between the soaring columns of Eastman Hall, and walked down the veranda. The upper and lower porches extended around the entire circumference of the house. She glanced inside to see the Negro footman Josiah and Betsy, the cook, clearing away the remains of this evening's meal. Even in March, Eastman Hall sat in the midst of lush greenery, a stately colonial house bearing classical fixtures and an air of refinement. Various Eastman ancestors had brought Greek statuary from Europe and placed it among the azaleas, ivy and willow trees. Last summer Eva had seen the house wearing roses, gardenias and azaleas like some grand aristocratic lady.

She passed the windows of the music room, smiled and nodded at Winnie and another dinner guest, but didn't linger there. Once she had envied the Honorable Winifred Broome for her dashing, handsome young husband and especially for her chance to travel to a new and exciting country. Then she'd come for this visit. She'd lived for weeks here and at the Eastmans' plantation, Fairfield, and witnessed the enforced servitude of hundreds of people. And the consequences.

Eva would never forget that first morning at Eastman Hall, how Winnie had appeared at breakfast gowned in splendid yellow muslin with her face as pale as the white lace on her dress. Her husband, Cyrus, had come into the dining room shortly after, and a lovely young Negro woman had appeared on his heels. She'd scurried into the kitchen, her head down, her face grim and anxious. Eva's gaze had darted from the slave, to Cyrus' cheerful countenance, to Winnie's drawn features, and she'd come to the most likely conclusion. In all the time they'd spent together she and her friend had never spoken of that morning, but the truth was there between them, an open secret and secret shame.

Being in the South had made Eva realize that despite her unconventional ways—her traveling without a chaperone, her adventures in the American West and in the Middle East—her life had no more meaning that it had had before. Thousands upon thousands of people suffered here while she saw the sights and visited. She wanted her life to matter, but she wasn't sure how to make it so.

Swinging her crinoline around the wide corner of the veranda, Eva took the exterior stairs to the next floor. She had reached the back of the house, where a particularly tall magnolia tree grew outside the doors to her bedroom. She liked to lean on the porch rail and lift her face to the soft southern breeze. She should be inside making conversation with the other houseguests. Winnie had invited newspaper publisher Lorenzo Ward to meet Eva as well as two local planters and their wives. Another planter from Texas, Stephen Nash, represented Winnie's only attempt at matchmaking, not for Eva, but for a local belle named Adele Hunter. But soon into the evening Eva had realized there was another purpose to this gathering. The men were all rich and politically prominent and had participated in forming the new Confederate States of America last month.

Ambrose Vickery had chortled to his wife, Grace, "I declare, Mrs. Vickery, I do wish these matters would come to a head. Otherwise I will have raised a company of soldiers for nothing and will have no chance to knock the heads of those damned Yankees."

At other times during the evening the men had gathered together to speak quietly in shadowy corners, and if she drew near, they would all bow and smile and change the subject of their conversation. Eva still didn't know what they had been talking about, but she had read concern and bitter determination in every face.

Shaking her head, Eva leaned against a corner post, delaying a few more minutes her return to the party. There were at least two eligible men inside, but Eva had no interest in them. Thank goodness Winnie knew better than to try to matchmake for her widowed friend. Eva had lost her much-older husband several years ago and was in no hurry to replace him. After a marriage stifled by convention and propriety, she was reveling in her freedom.

Soon she would have to return to the house even though she disliked the air of conspiracy that prevailed there. Even the ladies seemed on edge, whispering, casting anxious glances at the huddled men, shushing one another when Eva or one of the slaves passed. Eva felt like telling the poor creatures she had no interest in their secrets. The things that bothered her were blatant—the contrast, for example, between the gracious manners and lifestyle of these people and the conditions in the quarters behind the screen of moss-draped oak trees at the back of the garden. Clutching her shawl about her shoulders, Eva sighed. For once it would be good to go home.

She turned to go inside, but a small click in the silence of the garden drew her back to the railing. She looked down to see light from an open door spread onto the lawn. Someone closed the door and silently slipped over the banister. As he left the dim light Eva glimpsed the tall form of a Negro man. Then a whispered conversation began, and Eva realized that two people stood under the branches of the giant magnolia and were concealed by the wide, waxy leaves that formed an impenetrable screen to her. She turned once again, but one word froze her. She thought she heard one of the speakers say "secession."

They were keeping their voices low, but Eva heard more phrases. First the word "summer," then "get north" and "Fort Sumter." Finally came a last exchange.

"Come with me."

"No!"

Leaves rustled on the grass, and Eva thought she heard a retreat toward the slave cabins. A lithe shadow whisked back into the house, and all was silent again. Frowning, Eva considered what she'd heard. One of the slaves seemed to be planning his escape. She didn't blame him, even though his chances of success weren't good. Once his absence was discovered, Cyrus would offer a reward when he published the slave's description throughout the South. He would also hire slave-catchers to pursue his property. Everyone would be on the lookout for the slave. Cyrus might even allow the use of dogs to run down the escapee.

Eva shuddered and pulled her shawl around her neck. She would keep silent. Her own fruitless efforts at freeing slaves had taught her the value of circumspection. After leaving Natchez for Texas she'd thought of a plan to purchase slaves, take them north and free them. She'd gone to a horrible auction house in New Orleans; her presence in a place where no lady went had caused a furor. The owners of the auction house had gawked at her when she put forth her request to purchase an entire family of Negroes. They had refused, of course. Their reasons had been twofold: First, she was a woman, and second, she was British, and would take the slaves out of the country. She could have asked for no clearer proof of the fixed intentions of the wealthy planters of the South. Negroes were property, and they would remain so.

"Frightful," Eva muttered to herself. She went into her bedroom, which was illuminated by gaslight that made the ivory damask bed canopy and comforter glow.

"I don't like his chances at all, and it's a thousand pities," she whispered to herself as she went to the mahogany dresser and fished in a drawer for a fresh handkerchief.

She paused with her hand on an embroidered square of fine lawn as she recalled the other phrases she'd overheard. The slave had wanted someone to go with him—a woman, if Eva was correct about the second voice. Perhaps he intended to escape this summer, and perhaps he'd been encouraged by recent events. In November the Republican Abraham Lincoln had been elected president of the United States. South Carolina had seceded from the union the next month. In January Texas had seceded, and in February seven Southern states had formed the Confederate States of America. The whole country was now in turmoil. Hundreds of army and naval officers from the South were resigning their commissions, leaving the North bereft of its finest military leadership. Many government forts had fallen into Southern hands, and the few still manned by the Union in the Deep South were running out of supplies. Everyone knew that Lincoln would soon have to resupply Fort Sumter in South Carolina or risk its surrender.

Gloom settled over Eva as she contemplated the plight of any slave who chose to try to escape in this political climate. Pulling the handkerchief out, Eva shoved the drawer closed and left her room. She hurried downstairs and paused for breath in the music room, where Adele Hunter was showing off her skill at the piano. The young lady finished to polite applause, and Cyrus Eastman immediately came to Eva and kissed her hand. His red-gold hair flowed in romantic locks over his forehead; he was quite proud of it.

"My dear Lady Eva, your absence has deprived us sorely."

Eastman gave her a courtly smile, which Eva returned more because of his manner of speech than the words themselves. Cyrus drew out most one-syllable words to two, barely touched consonants and spoke with habitual graciousness. Like most Southern gentlemen, he was chivalrous to the point of violence and was easily offended when he thought his honor had been questioned.

"Thank you, Mr. Eastman. I was enjoying your lovely gardens. I shall miss them dreadfully when I return to England."

"And we shall miss your delightful self, Lady Eva."

Her host conducted her to a seat by the fireplace, settling her beside Winnie and his mother, Dolly Eastman. Dolly still affected the sausage-curl ringlets and narrow skirts of twenty years ago. The footman Josiah came in with a silver tray bearing coffee and cups. The room was as fine as any Eva had seen in England. Indeed, many of the fixtures at Eastman Hall had come from Europe. The fireplaces were of

Carrara marble; the wallpaper and curtains were French, the furniture English. Eva's feet rested on an Aubusson carpet, and over the mantel hung a painting by Constable. In this elegant room warmed by the glow of gaslight and the flames from the fireplace, lulled by the tinkle of silver spoons against china, Eva tried to forget the desperate whispers she'd overheard on the veranda.

The low, booming voice of the silver-haired Lorenzo Ward intruded on her thoughts. A natural gossip, Mr. Ward was cursed with rheumatic problems that swelled his joints, but his health never interfered with his lust for scandal. Eva resigned herself to listening to the men's conversation, for as usual Cyrus and Mr. Ward dominated it.

"Have you heard the latest news?" Ward asked, standing in the middle of the room waving a glass of sherry.

Cyrus replied, "I doubt it, sir, since everyone knows you're the first to hear everything."

Josiah offered a cup of coffee to Eva.

"Why, the sheriff has arrested one of those confounded Underground Railroad conductors."

Eva's hand touched the china cup Josiah offered and felt it slip. She caught it silently before it slid off its saucer. Josiah was looking at Lorenzo Ward. His dark eyes had flashed wide open, then he jumped as Eva pressed the cup and saucer into his hand to keep it steady. He caught his breath and glanced down at Eva, who smoothly removed the china from his grasp. His startled gaze held hers for a moment before Eva looked pointedly at Winnie to remind Josiah of his task. The young man recovered himself and went back to the serving tray. The ladies were clamoring for more details.

"Do tell us who was arrested, Mr. Ward," pleaded Dolly Eastman.

"You will hardly believe it," Lorenzo said. "It was Mrs. Eliza Summer."

"No!" Winnie and her mother were incredulous.

Eva watched Josiah freeze at the mention of Mrs. Summer's name. Luckily, everyone else's attention was on Lorenzo Ward.

Ward addressed Eva. "You know what the Underground Railroad is, Lady Eva?"

"Excuse me, Ward," Cyrus said. "Josiah, that will be all."

The young man's expression transformed into a wooden mask. Once the footman was gone, Cyrus continued. "Forgive me, Ward, but one mustn't bother servants with things they don't understand."

Ward nodded. "Or we don't wish them to understand. Indeed, Eastman. Well, my lady, the Underground Railroad is an organization bent on depriving legitimate owners of their rightful property by helping our servants abscond. They harbor runaways and send them on to the next house and the next until they get them to a state that doesn't allow slavery, or to Canada."

"I see. Thank you, Mr. Ward." Eva sipped her coffee to avoid further conversation, but she needn't have bothered. Adele Hunter and the planters were consumed with curiosity and demanded a full accounting.

"Who would have guessed," Adele said. "Old Mrs. Summer. Why, she has three slaves herself."

Dolly Eastman nodded so vigorously the feathers on her headdress nearly flew off. "I don't know what's gotten into folks these days. She must be demented."

The speculation and gossip continued for over an hour before the evening ended. Eva said good night to her hosts. She ascended the curved main stairs and went down the hall to her room. She was about to open her door when she heard someone whisper her name. Around the darkened corner that led to the servants' stairs she glimpsed the footman Josiah.

"Psst. Miss Eva."

Looking over her shoulder to be sure she wasn't observed, Eva hurried around the corner to join the young man. Josiah was tall, too thin for his height, with great dark eyes and close-cropped hair. He seemed to be all hands and feet. He was shifting from one giant foot to the other at the moment. He tugged at the starched collar of his formal servant's uniform.

"What is it, Josiah? Is anything wrong?"

"Miss Eva, why d'you help me, back there in the drawing room?"

"You were about to drop the cup."

"You the one tried to buy them folks from the auction house, ma'am?"

"How did you— Yes, Josiah, I am." Winnie had told her that slaves seemed to have their own informal methods of communication. Eva watched the young man struggle with some inner turmoil. His features contorted with a mixture of anxiety, apprehension and uncertainty. Finally she spoke again. "You were planning to escape with Mrs. Summer's help."

Josiah gasped, then said, "Don't tell, Miss Eva!"

"Shh. I'm not going to tell. What a frightful thought. But you've no one to help you now. You must be terribly careful, Josiah. People are stirred up because of secession. These Southern planters think Mr. Lincoln is going to try to free you, and they're furious. They're certain to be more alert than ever for anyone trying to flee north."

Shaking his head, Josiah whispered fiercely, "It don't matter. I got to go north. I got to, and now the lady that was to help me has been arrested."

"I'm so sorry."

"So I thought maybe you would help, seein' as how you tried to do such good for my kind before."

"But what can I do? I've no way to hide you."

Josiah suddenly dropped to his knees. "Please, Miss Eva. Get Mrs. Winnie to let you buy me."

Eva gaped at the young man on his knees in front of her. "Get up!"

Josiah regarded her with solemn, dark eyes and rose gracefully to his feet. "Will you help me, Miss Eva?"

That was it. He had stated his request, tried to show her how desperate he was, and now he simply waited. Eva wondered what would happen to this strong-willed boy if she left him here.

"Are they cruel to you?"

"No, ma'am. But I'm grown. I'm a man, and I got to be a free man or die. One way or the other, I'm going north."

Eva saw the conviction in his face, the certainty that shone from his eyes. This young man was going to run, whether she helped him or not.

"You know what they'll do if you run," Eva whispered.

"Miss Eva, you must've got an idea of what it means to be bought and sold, or you wouldn'ta done what you did. Mistress only bought me 'cause my maw was grievin' for me. You know Cook, Betsy, she's my maw. Master Cyrus won't care, and I got no one to turn to, ma'am."

Images of this earnest, proud youth being torn

apart by dogs and whipped until he had no skin raced through Eva's mind. "I'll speak to Mrs. Eastman, make up some story about needing a strong young servant to help me on my travels. I don't know if she'll consent, Josiah, but I'll try. If she agrees, we'll leave in a few days for Washington."

Relief brought tears welling in Josiah's eyes. He let out a long sigh.

"Thank you, Miss Eva."

"No one else wishes to come with you?"

The young man's expression grew shuttered. "No, ma'am. There ain't nobody goin' to come with me. Maw says she's got to stay 'cause of my brothers and sisters."

"I'm sorry."

"Thank you, Miss Eva. I won't forget this, ever."

# CHAPTER TWO

HE GRIMACED AT the taste of the chewing tobacco lodged in his cheek, but he didn't spit the stuff out. It was part of his costume, along with the chaps, the wide-brimmed hat, the bandanna and the quarter horse. Nobody would take much interest in a scruffy cowboy riding into town among the hundreds of newcomers attracted by the prospect of money to be made off the coming conflict. Ryder Drake walked his mount across Long Bridge over the Potomac, toward Washington, D.C., after a long and agonizing trip from Texas. Behind him he'd left a prosperous ranch, many friends and—unknown to anyone—a string of newly acquired spies for the Union.

Ryder guided his horse around a line of wagons loaded with boxes of ammunition and left the bridge, heading toward Pennsylvania Avenue. It was April, but there had been a dry spell that had reduced the city's normal mugginess. Carriage and freight traffic swarmed in all directions, stirring up dust and making more noise than Washington had seen in a decade.

A sleepy Southern town populated mostly by Virginians and Marylanders, the capital seemed to Ryder to be the opposite of the elegant cities of Europe. Although it boasted an impressive setting among the wooded hills and panoramas of the Potomac River Valley, it consisted mostly of scruffy wooden and brick buildings and dirt streets. The capitol dome was unfinished; chickens and cattle roamed the vacant lots and roads, and the sun-blasted, humid summers fostered mosquitoes, flies and noxious smells from primitive sanitation. The swamps of the Potomac harbored typhoid, wasting sickness, malaria and dysentery. Ryder knew for a fact that foreign governments considered Washington a hardship post. And soon it would be the center and prize of a civil war.

He turned up dusty Pennsylvania Avenue, wincing at the way his horse had to pick its way over the ill-laid cobblestones. The capitol was ahead of him in the distance now, and on either side behind lines of trees sat low buildings—stores, hotels, boarding-houses. A horsecar rattled by ahead of a cavalry unit resplendent in dark blue uniforms and gold braid.

Ryder's pace slowed because the avenue was crowded with shoppers and vendors hawking candy, oysters, soap and pies. He heard music and watched an organ grinder for a moment, then passed on to a group of street singers caroling "Dixie." Three weeks ago the whole city had been on edge and hissed with rumors of assassination as Abe Lincoln rode down the avenue to his first inaugural ceremony. Ryder wished he could have been there, but the new president had made it clear that his mission in the South was more important.

In the intervening time the South had organized itself into the Confederate States of America and had taken possession of many military outposts within its borders. Ryder had been furious when General Twiggs had surrendered to the Rebels all the outposts under his command in Texas. What was worse, Fort Sumter in South Carolina would run out of supplies any day now. The president was being forced to make a decision—resupply it and provoke a war, or withdraw, which would encourage the rebellious states and go a long way toward ensuring recognition of the Confederacy abroad.

Ryder's troubled thoughts dwelt on this prospect as he worked his way down the avenue. He didn't envy Lincoln, who had come to the White House inexperienced in presidential administration. He would have to feel his way through the complexities of running a government while the entire nation was disintegrating around him.

At last Ryder came to a decrepit old house next to a vacant lot on the south side of the avenue. Spitting out his tobacco, he fished in his pocket for a piece of peppermint candy and stuffed it in his mouth with relief. He tethered his horse to a hitching post, watching to see if anyone noticed him. He crunched the candy, swallowed it and eyed a group of men who were laughing and talking across the street. They clapped one another on the back and strolled into the lobby of a hotel. Ryder pulled his hat down over his eyes and left his horse.

People streamed around him as he stepped onto the porch, and with a glance behind him he slipped inside through the creaking front door. The door swung closed, shutting out sunlight, but there was an oil lamp sitting on a couple of vegetable boxes stacked one on top of the other. A man stood beside the door, his hand on a pistol stuck in his waistband. Ryder removed his hat, thrust his fingers through his hair and nodded.

"Afternoon, Webster."

"Afternoon, Drake. I didn't think you'd make it on time after so long a trip."

"No fighting yet."

"True." Webster nodded toward another door across the room. "They're in the back. I'll keep watch."

"Thanks."

Ryder knocked on the door and opened it to reveal two men, one vastly tall and lean, the other wiry but short. The taller of the two broke into a smile when he saw Drake.

"You see, Pinkerton. He made it. Welcome back, Drake."

"Thank you, Mr. President." Ryder shook the president's hand and then Alan Pinkerton's. Pinkerton was the president's chief intelligence gatherer.

Lincoln folded his long frame into a chair and indicated another. "Sit. You look as exhausted as a squirrel in a pecan orchard in fall."

"I'm a mite tired, sir."

"All the more reason for us to hear your report quickly," Pinkerton said with his soft Scotch accent.

He wore a neat beard and mustache. His red hair was thinning on top and streaked with gray. His beard and curly hair emphasized his large ears and high forehead. He had a long, thick nose and folds in his cheeks. Altogether he seemed an unimpressive little man, considering he ran the most famous investigative company in the nation.

Lincoln's appearance was just as incongruous, considering his exalted position. His great height and craggy face, his expressive eyes and gangling frame lent him an almost comic air. Ryder had yet to meet anyone who could laugh at the man once he knew Abe Lincoln. He knew many that hated Lincoln, mostly Southerners, and hardly any of them had met the object of their hatred. Ryder was astonished at the change in the president in the short time he'd been gone. Lincoln seemed to have aged two decades. His face seemed worn, his eyes haunted, and he was thinner than ever. The impending decision about Fort Sumter must have weighed terribly on him. No president had ever been forced to decide to go to war against his own people.

Pinkerton slid his chair between the president and Drake, and Ryder dragged his thoughts back to the reason for his visit.

"How many agents did you recruit?" Pinkerton asked.

"Eleven," Ryder said. "Eleven spies for the Union. I'll give you a list as soon as I get home and can write down all the details."

"What are things like down there?" Lincoln asked. "Is there any hope they'll see reason?"

"No, sir. They look upon your election as a threat to their liberty and their way of life. They are sure you mean to destroy them."

Lincoln shook his head. "I've said over and over that I will do nothing about slavery in their states."

"But you also say that slavery is an evil that must be allowed to die a natural death, which means no more new slave states, no slavery in any of the territories," Ryder pointed out. "Besides, sir, they don't believe you, and nothing you can say will convince them you're their friend."

"I'm a friend of the Union."

"As am I, Mr. President," Ryder replied.

"Indeed," said Pinkerton. "Now tell us what you've learned of their preparations."

Ryder spent almost an hour describing the activities of the rebellious states. He listed the numbers of men he'd seen volunteering for military service, the amount and types of ammunition being shipped. Pinkerton took notes while the president listened gravely.

"If there's a fight, it will be a hard one," Ryder concluded.

Pinkerton shrugged. "They can't win."

Lifting one eyebrow, Ryder said, "Aw, hell, Pinkerton, the South has a long tradition of military service, and it's a big place. Texas alone is about the size of France. And just you wait till your Yankee boys start traipsing through the swamps of Louisiana."

"Gentlemen," Lincoln said. "We won't settle these differences here."

Ryder bowed in his chair. "No, sir. But there is one more problem."

"Just one?" Lincoln said with a little smile.

"While I was in Richmond I visited James Chestnut and his wife, Mary. They're quite influential among the Southern politicians, and James was talking about getting allies for the Confederacy. They're going to appeal to Great Britain to fight on their side. They're counting on the British need to maintain the supply of cotton to their Lancastershire mills. If war comes and we blockade the South, the British mill owners and workers will suffer greatly. They'll howl at their government to do something, and Palmerston is the kind of prime minister who might relish a fight. That's what Chestnut and Jeff Davis and the others are counting on."

Lincoln and Pinkerton exchanged looks.

"We can't have that," the president said. "If Britain enters the war, we might as well give up. Why, most of the army is in the West keeping peace on the frontier. I haven't even called for volunteers yet. We sure can't fight the British Empire along with our own rebels."

Ryder sighed with weariness and said, "Exactly, sir. It's something we must avoid, and it is my opinion that we should begin to cultivate the goodwill of the British government at once."

"I know nothing of foreign affairs, Drake." Lincoln shook his head. "And the secretary of state hopes that if it appears that we're threatened by a foreign power, the rebellious states will rally around us to fight a common enemy."

"That's madness!" Pinkerton cried.

Lincoln shrugged. "Seward is desperate to hold the Union together."

"Mr. President," Ryder said, "I think we should seek the help of an intimate of someone high in the British government—informally, of course. Such an influential person may serve as a conduit by which understanding and peaceful intentions can be communicated."

Lincoln furrowed his bushy brows as he thought. "Who is this influential person?"

"I don't know yet, sir."

"Attend to it, Drake. I've matters of more pressing concern to deal with. I've decided to resupply

Fort Sumter. The fleet has already sailed and should be there tomorrow."

Now Ryder understood why Lincoln looked like he hadn't slept in weeks.

"There was no other choice, Mr. President," Ryder said softly.

The three men sat in silence, contemplating a bleak future. Then Lincoln grunted and stood, and the others rose as well.

"Send word when you've developed a plan regarding Great Britain," said the president.

"Of course, sir." Frustration and grief at the coming ordeal made Ryder burst out, "You know I'll fight to the death to save the Union."

Lincoln cocked his head to the side. "You remind me of a story, Drake, about a young man who was about to go to war. His sisters made him a belt, and on it was embroidered the motto Victory or Death. 'Oh, no,' the young man said. 'Don't put it quite that strong. Put it Victory or Get Hurt Pretty Bad.' "

Ryder blinked, then burst out laughing. Pinkerton and the president joined him.

"Indeed, Mr. President," Drake said. "I take your point."

Lincoln was suddenly grave. "My dear Drake, I may be the humblest person ever to be elected president, but with the Lord's help, I'm going to save this Union." With that, Lincoln left.

Pinkerton shut the door behind the president and turned to Ryder. "The responsibility for saving a nation rests on his shoulders."

"It's tearing him apart."

"Yes." Their eyes met, each man contemplating the enormity of Lincoln's burdens. Then Pinkerton continued. "You've done well, Drake. I'm sending

Tim Webster south along with a few others to permeate the most powerful groups of Southern firebrands. They can contact the people you recruited." He offered Ryder a cigar, and Ryder refused. "So, did you convince your mother to go to Baltimore?"

"No. She said she'd risk staying in Charleston rather than live in a city full of Yankees and turncoat Southerners."

"I'm sorry to hear that. I know you will worry about her."

"Yes," Ryder said. He didn't want to dwell on the subject of his mother.

"She raised you in Virginia, didn't she?"

Ryder nodded stiffly, not liking this turn of conversation. His relationship with his parents had never been easy, and now that his father was dead and his mother retired to Charleston, he wasn't any more inclined to discuss them. He searched for a way to change the subject.

"I reckon you keep an eye on who's coming and going in this city, Pinkerton. Heard of any British visitors who might be of use to me?"

The detective eyed the glowing end of his cigar and frowned. "Washington is hardly a favorite resort of the British politician. The prime minister, Lord Palmerston, favors the South, you know."

"Yes, as does Lord Russell, the foreign secretary." Ryder suppressed a yawn. He'd been riding since daybreak, and the dinner hour was approaching. "I must find someone who can help us make them understand what we're fighting for."

"You can't go to Lord Lyons, the British ambassador, if you want this to be private and informal. A few speculators have arrived from London, but they'd be no good to you." Pinkerton put his foot on the seat of a chair and propped his arms on his knee. "Hmm, I don't recall— No." The detective snapped his fingers. "No, that's not true. There is one person, a relative of Lord Adolphus Tennyson, who is Lord Russell's particular adviser. Tennyson would be of great help. His opinions are listened to in the British cabinet, and the queen is fond of him."

"Excellent. Who is he, and where is he staying?"

"It isn't a man. Her name is Lady Eva Sparrow."

Ryder shook his head. "Hold on a minute. We can't go bringing a lady into this. What if she's a pampered Society miss whose most difficult decision is picking out the right lace for her next ball gown?"

"She's not a miss, Drake. In fact, she's a widow, and she shares a London house with her uncle, Lord Adolphus Tennyson. He dotes on her, and if what I hear is correct, she's not at all what you'd expect."

"Look," Ryder said, "few women have experience in public affairs, or with handling a matter as grave as this."

Pinkerton eyed him. "You aren't married, are you, Drake."

"No, but—"

"You may have a poor opinion of the female character, but one of my best agents is a woman, Kate Warne."

"I know that. I have great admiration for Miss Warne and for all the brave American ladies on both sides of this mess who get precious little credit for their contributions to our civilization. But there's a confounded minority to be found in the upper reaches of society who are absorbed in nothing more challenging than figuring how many changes of clothing they'll need for the next country house party. Those are the women I'm talking about, and the British seem to turn them out in larger numbers than we do. It's as though all the sense and gumption has been bred out of them." Ryder sighed and shook his head. "Besides, I have a feeling this business could get bloody, and I can't abide the idea of endangering a lady."

"Well, if you're against the idea, so be it. Let me know if you change your mind."

Ryder headed for the door. "I won't. I'm dead certain of that, but thanks all the same. Now, if you'll excuse me, Pinkerton, I've a hankering for a hot bath and a big dinner with all the fixin's."

"Did you know your Southern accent gets stronger when you're agitated?"

Surprised, Ryder stared at the detective. "I'm not agitated."

"Tired, then. I've made a study of Southern accents of late. Yours is an interesting mixture of Virginia and Texas."

"If you say so. Good afternoon to you, Pinkerton."

"And to you, Drake. At least consider Lady Eva Sparrow. She's perfect for your purpose."

"I doubt it, but I'll keep her in mind," Ryder said as he left.

The door closed behind him, but he heard Pinkerton snort. Webster saluted him as he left, and Ryder emerged once more into the din of Pennsylvania Avenue. Mounting, he turned his horse in the direction of the house he'd rented near the presidential mansion.

He tried to throw off the disgruntled feeling Pinkerton's needling had provoked. He had no intention of justifying his decision not to use a lady to act as intermediary with the British cabinet. That would involve exposing events in his past best left alone.

However, as he rode past a group of men gathered around a shoe-shine boy, Ryder couldn't help remembering why he had so little patience with Society ladies and others who frittered their lives away in wasteful and meaningless pursuits.

His mother, Felicita Drake, formerly Felicita Locke, was from a Virginia family prominent since pre-Revolutionary times. It was from her that Ryder inherited his black hair, dark green eyes and lithe body. Through Felicita he was related to blue-blooded families with names like Randolph, Custis and Washington. A belle of Virginia Society, Felicita was the only daughter of wealthy parents who owned a great deal of rich farmland in the state. Miss Locke knew her worth, and early on decided that no ordinary planter would be worthy of her. Thirty-four years ago, when she was seventeen, she went to England, where she met and quickly married Lord Simon Villiers Drake.

The new Lady Drake imagined herself to be marrying the classic English nobleman with castles, town houses and treasure chests to spare. What she got was a man whose pockets might as well have had holes, so fast did money fall through them. Lord Simon used Felicita's money to pay his debts but quickly ran up even greater ones. Dashing Felicita's hopes of being a leader of British Society, Lord Simon took his wife back to Virginia to save on expenses and escape his creditors.

Beautiful and self-involved, Felicita had no patience with failure and no intention of altering her lavish lifestyle to accommodate a reduced income. She criticized her husband but offered no solutions to their money problems. They spent the rest of their married life locked in a vicious battle to see who could blame the other for problems they both caused. Felicita expected her husband to provide for her without recourse to the Locke family wealth. Simon had the British aristocrat's attitude that whatever property his wife possessed became his upon marriage. In addition, he had a nobleman's casual view of money in general. No matter what happened, it would always appear when he needed it.

Ryder was born into this household of internecine, toxic recrimination. Both selfish and relentlessly focused on themselves, his parents would criticize Ryder and make hurtful comments to him, treating their only child no better than they treated each other. When they weren't criticizing him they confided in him. Each would complain to Ryder about the other, thus putting him in the middle and tearing him apart. To survive, Ryder soon learned to keep to himself and to behave correctly and decorously in order to avoid his parents' vitriolic carping. He grew up the opposite of his father and mother— grave, responsible, concerned about others. He left for school as soon as he could and earned a degree from Oxford in England. After finishing school he lingered in Europe and then traveled around the United States, in no hurry to settle down, especially if it meant living near his parents. He was called back home twelve years ago, to find his father gravely ill and—of course—in debt.

Felicita was glad to have Ryder home. Now she could shove all her responsibilities for her husband's care and finances onto her son. To Ryder it seemed that even the barest show of concern toward Lord Simon was beyond this woman. She no sooner entered the sickroom and greeted her husband than she was ready to leave it. When she did stay, her conversation revolved around the hardships Simon's illness caused her.

As for his father, Simon was anxious to see Ryder alone so he could tell him that he suspected Felicita had been hoarding money and that she had bought a new house in Charleston, South Carolina, to which she planned to retire when he was gone. Ryder was horrified to again be swallowed up in this endless, sick game. When his father died, he discovered that Felicita had indeed been squirreling away cash. She departed for her house in Charleston, leaving Ryder to deal with his father's tangled affairs, and his own grief, alone.

One of the few advantages to his mother's abandonment was that Ryder was able to free the family slaves since Felicita had no interest in how he handled the estate as long as she was kept in luxury. Ryder had conceived a horror of slavery from an early age. Not only did he abhor the idea of one person's owning another, he had also witnessed firsthand the way his father and other planters took advantage of female slaves and how black families were split when sold. It took some time and most of the assets of the Drake English inheritance, but he was able to give the slaves what should never have been taken from them in the first place: their freedom.

This accomplished, Ryder took his diminished inheritance and moved to central Texas, where he staked a claim to vast acreage and spent the next decade building a ranching empire, with no slaves. He had made a success of himself after nearly going bankrupt freeing the family slaves. Now he had a chance to do more, to help get rid of the institution of slavery forever and thus free his country of a great evil. Saving the United States from a conflict with

Great Britain was a vital mission, and he wasn't going to trust the success of that mission to some spoiled noblewoman who was no doubt very much like his mother.

"Lady Eva Sparrow," Ryder muttered to himself. "Probably has the brains of a sparrow as well as the name."

Nothing on earth would make him trust the fate of the Union to such a person.

# CHAPTER THREE

❧❧

EVA LOOKED OUT the window of her sitting room at the budding branches of the trees that surrounded the old Georgian town house on H Street in Washington, D.C. It was April, and she was staying with her friends Horace and Rosalie Blair. She could hear the muffled din of traffic coming down Pennsylvania Avenue, a few Union troops, freight wagons, carriages and herds of cattle. In her hand she held Josiah's freedom papers, and she was worried. On the trip from Natchez she had gotten to know the young man, and in spite of his determination to be free, there was a great deal he didn't know about the world. In the past few weeks the situation between the North and the South had exploded, and war was coming to America.

"A terrible pity," Eva murmured as she watched a nurse wheel a baby carriage down the street in the late-afternoon sunlight.

She would sail for England in a few weeks, and she was worried about her American friends on both sides of the conflict. Like Cyrus Eastman, her Southern friends were certain they would whip the Yankees in a short time. Her friends from the North voiced equally optimistic views of their ability to defeat the enemy in a week or two.

She glanced at the county seal on the bill of sale from Winnie, then perused the manumission documents. Going to a Boule secretary, she took up a pen, then hesitated before signing. She would wait for Josiah; he would want to witness this event. He would be free, but he was to remain in her employ until he could find suitable work in the city. There was a knock.

"Enter."

With an air of solemnity, Josiah came in. He was wearing the new suit he'd purchased with a portion of his wages. He struck a pose with one hand behind his back and the other tucked in his coat, his chin lifted high. Eva smiled and straightened the cockeyed ends of his tie.

"Don't you look elegant."

"Thank you, Miss Eva." Josiah tried to look down at his tie, but gave up and said, "You sent for me?"

"Your papers arrived."

"Papers!" Josiah's dignity vanished. He gawked at the documents Eva waved at him. Then he whispered, "They're here. I never thought I'd see 'em. I been waitin' ever since I can remember."

Eva danced over to the secretary, beckoning to Josiah. "Come look at them. Mr. and Mrs. Blair will be up any minute to serve as witnesses."

Josiah touched the stiff paper. "Look at that. Such fine paper and such fancy writing. Does that really say I'm free?"

"Of course." Eva pointed to a word. "You can read that."

"It says my name."

" 'The slave called Josiah, formerly owned by Mrs. Cyrus Eastman of Natchez, Mississippi, and currently owned by Lady Eva Sparrow of London, England, is hereby and henceforth a free Negro.' "

Eva watched as the stunned look slowly left Josiah's large eyes. Then they grew wet, and Eva turned away. Knowing he set great store by his dignity, she shuffled the freedom papers while Josiah blew into a handkerchief. Another knock signaled the entrance of the Blairs with a bottle of wine. The signing proceeded, and there was a hushed moment as Eva's pen skimmed over the manumission document. She finished the last letter with a flourish, blotted the paper and handed it to Josiah.

He said in a voice roughened by emotion, "I ain't never gonna forget what you've done for me, Miss Eva."

"It was my duty and my privilege to be of service," she replied. "Slavery is a sin."

The Blairs congratulated Josiah and left. Eva drew an envelope from the secretary and handed it to the young man.

"You will need something with which to start your new life."

Josiah opened the envelope; his eyes grew wide, and he thrust the envelope back at Eva. "No, ma'am. I can't be takin' this from you."

Eva put her hands behind her back, refusing to accept the envelope. "Now, Josiah, it would mean a great deal to me if you took it."

Josiah grew serious, cocked his head to the side and asked, "Why?"

"Because I have more than enough wealth for myself, and it's not Christian to just sit on it and not do good with it. The Lord would want me to make things better for my fellow men." Eva smiled at the young man. "Now, you wouldn't deny me my place in heaven by refusing to let me do good, would you?"

Josiah shook his head and slowly put the envelope in his coat. "Most would argue with you about that, Miss Eva. Most would never say we're the same as whites."

"Well, don't you believe them," Eva said.

There was an uncomfortable silence. Then Eva cleared her throat and sat down by the window. She indicated the chair opposite her, but Josiah refused to take it.

"It's not fittin', Miss Eva. Servants don't set with masters—I mean employers."

"Very well," Eva replied, "but I'm only agreeing because my other servants would refuse as well." Eva sighed and got to the point. "Josiah, I'm quite concerned for your situation. You know Fort Sumter surrendered on the thirteenth."

"Yes, I know."

"And Mr. Lincoln has called for troops from the states, but the border states like Kentucky have refused. I want to be sure you understand what is happening, because I know you plan to try to bring your family to Washington."

Eva continued to outline the events that had occurred since the failed attempt to resupply the troops at Fort Sumter. When President Lincoln had called for 75,000 volunteers, the states of the upper South had seceded—Virginia, North Carolina, Tennessee, Arkansas. He had also proclaimed a state of insurrection. A center of secessionism, the state of Maryland teetered on the brink of rebellion. Southern sympathizers had destroyed railroads and bridges linking Baltimore with the North and cut the telegraph lines. There was civil unrest in the state. On April 19, less than a week after the fall of Fort Sumter, the Sixth Massachusetts militia had passed through Baltimore on its way to Washington. A mob had begun to throw stones and bricks, and the troops had fired. Fighting had erupted, and twelve civilians and four soldiers had been killed.

Tension in the capital had mounted as word of the violence spread. Hundreds of pro-Confederate officials and military men had resigned and left for the South. It was as if the government was bleeding. The city expected an attack any day, and it was certain that the thousands of Southern sympathizers still living in the capital would rise up and fight the invaders.

"They expect more reinforcements at any time," Eva said. "But it's been only two days since the secessionists attacked the Massachusetts militia. You must not go south just now, Josiah. It's too dangerous. You know if you're caught down there it won't matter that you have your freedom papers."

Josiah had been watching Eva with his intense, dark eyes. He appeared to think over her words, then nodded.

"You're right, Miss Eva. It's time to lay low. At least for a while."

"I'm glad you understand." She rose and shook Josiah's hand. "Some people say that the secessionists are going to attack and burn Washington, but I don't think that's going to happen. Not yet."

"Thank you, Miss Eva."

"Would you send in my maid? It's time I began to dress for Secretary Seward's dinner party."

As she washed and dressed Eva thought about Josiah and what he would do when she was gone. She feared for his safety, but he would only accept so much advice from her. He was determined to be the master of his fate, and sink or swim on his own merit. She understood this desire, having repeatedly rebuffed her brothers' attempts to govern her life after she was widowed. Eva only had a few weeks before she left for London. In a way she would be happy to go home. She missed her uncle, Lord Adolphus Tennyson. They shared a town house now that Eva's parents had died.

Her maid, Antoinette, laced Eva into a black silk dinner gown studded with jet, pearls and lace. Sitting in the midst of billowing skirts, Eva applied a bit of perfume to her wrists while Antoinette rolled her long, unruly tresses into a bun at the nape of her neck. Her hair had a life of its own; it curled and frizzed and twisted like thousands of snakes if she didn't keep it subdued. What was worse, it was the color of an Irish setter. When she was little she'd lamented that she'd been born with dog's hair. Her mother had replied that she resembled her Irish ancestors in coloring and temperament—rebellious and unruly.

Eva's shortcomings had been one of the few things upon which her parents agreed. She had been born Eva Elizabeth Spencer Tennyson, daughter of William Edward Tennyson, Earl of Southgrave, and his wife, Marie Louise. Like most aristocrats their marriage was an alliance between two noble families, and like many such, the two partners had nothing in common. They produced two sons and a daughter and went their separate ways. When Eva was twelve Marie Louise fell in love with the earl's best friend. Making Eva her confidante, she used her daughter as the bearer of love notes to be posted in London or in the village near their country house. Torn between loyalty to her mother and love for her father, Eva suffered terrible guilt for her part in the affair.

Then one day her father intercepted Eva on her way to post one of Marie Louise's missives, and the secret was exposed. Eva still cringed at the memory. She was crossing the long, dark entry hall at Southgrave Park, her footsteps echoing on marble tile, loud little taps from the heels of her walking boots. Suddenly a shadow detached itself from a wall. Her father loomed over her, a scowl disfiguring his face.

"What have you got there, Eva?"

Eva's fist clenched around the envelope in her hand. "Nothing, sir."

"That looks like your mother's handwriting. Give it to me."

"I'm—I'm supposed to mail it straightaway in the village, sir."

The earl's face reddened, and he shouted, "I said give it to me, damn you!"

Eva jumped at the sudden violence that flared from her father, thrust the envelope into his hand and ran. She scurried beneath an arch and hid behind a column. From there she peered at the earl as he opened the envelope. Tears blurred her vision, but there was no mistaking the stream of obscenities that burst from his mouth as he read the note. Eva hid her face in her hands and sank to the floor, trying to make herself small enough to vanish. She whimpered when the earl thundered past, shouting his wife's name.

Certain that she had betrayed her mother and earned her father's hatred, Eva fled the house. She hid under a pile of leaves in the deer forest that surrounded Southgrave Park. It took most of the night for the servants to find her. The whole family was in an uproar, and her father in no mood to look after a runaway child. Her mother was hysterical. Weeks passed in which Eva floated about the place like a flame-haired, pale little ghost while she waited for her parents to pronounce her doom. It came soon enough, and doom it was. She would go to a boarding school in France while her father proceeded to divorce his wife.

Banished, lonely and stricken with guilt, Eva accepted her fate as just punishment for her crime. She went to France and studied obediently and hopelessly. Months later she learned that the family had prevailed upon Southgrave not to divorce Marie Louise and ruin them all. Instead, he banished his wife to France with orders not to return to England. Eva waited for Marie Louise to come to visit her, but that visit never happened. Marie Louise joined her lover in Paris, then together they took a house on the Loire, where they lived in contented disrepute.

Eva never gave up hope that her mother would renew contact with her, but as the years passed, hope faded to a glimmer. Her eldest brother, Ashton, grew to manhood secure in his position as heir to Southgrave. Sydney, the youngest, excelled in the royal cavalry. Eva rarely saw either of them. In her exile she tried to be good, to become the perfect young lady of whom her father and mother would approve. Perhaps if she was very, very good, they would forgive her. Eva tried hard to atone for her wrongs and regain her parents' love. By the time she was seventeen she was a paragon of boarding-school train-ing—prim, modest, conforming. That year she obedi-ently married Lord John Charles Sparrow, a staid and proper man of fifty, because her father had arranged the match. Deep down she knew that Lord John Charles was about as interesting as a cheese wheel, but it didn't matter. She had to be good. It was the only way she could make up for what she'd done.

She had tried her best to love John Charles, but she had failed. To her young eyes he appeared an-cient, but she soon realized that his age didn't matter. What made it impossible for her to love him was his character. Poor John Charles suffered from a com-plete lack of imagination, which interfered with his ability to sympathize with the unfortunate or anyone who differed dramatically from him. This unhappily included Eva.

Having imagined that marriage would bring free-dom to be herself, Eva learned that her husband wouldn't tolerate the idea. As a young wife Eva de-veloped a knack for curbing her high spirits. She kept silent if she agreed with any philosophies or political ideas that were, as John Charles called them, "damned liberal." These included any extension of voting rights, education reform or even the renova-tion of London's antiquated and dilapidated sanita-tion system, which harbored diseases like typhoid and cholera.

So Eva devoted herself to playing hostess for her husband, making sure that their dinners, luncheons and country house parties included the best people. The best people, according to John Charles, were those who could further his ambitions in govern-ment. While she was doing this, Eva acquired a wide-ranging knowledge of the workings of government and politics. Spongelike, she absorbed the ideas of her husband's colleagues. As time went on, she found herself disagreeing with them. Not that she ever said anything. She was a good wife and kept her mouth shut. Now Eva often wondered if she could have kept it up if John Charles had lived.

She sighed at the thought of her married life as she rose from the dressing table and went downstairs to meet the Blairs. It had taken her a long time to understand that the blame and the guilt for her parents' troubles belonged to them, not to her. There was no use dwelling on the unhappy past. She was free now, and that's what counted. Free of guilt, and free of people who wanted to fit her into the stifling mold of an English lady.

Horace and Rosalie awaited her downstairs. Horace was round-bellied, with the florid appearance of a hearty eater, a receding hairline and a perpetually shiny forehead. His manner was jovial when in the company of ladies but could be autocratic among his fellow bankers, possibly due to the fact that he was one of the richest financiers in the country. Rosalie was much younger than Horace and lovely in a pale blond, wasting sort of way. Convinced that her husband was a genius, Rosalie Blair had a hidden vein of iron in her character that impressed Eva. She'd met the pair two years ago in Cairo in the market, among the displays of saffron, myrrh and frankincense.

The drive to the Secretary Seward's home was short, it being north and slightly east of the White House. Eva got out of the Blair carriage after her hosts, accepting the gloved hand of an officer in dress uniform. Inside, a small orchestra was playing a waltz as they entered. Eva followed Rosalie and Horace to the reception line, where she was introduced to the sixty-year-old William H. Seward.

"It's a pleasure to make your acquaintance, Lady Eva," said the secretary. "I had the honor to be introduced to your uncle when I was last in London. A fine man, Lord Adolphus."

"And he was equally honored to meet you, sir."

Eva glided after the Blairs and accepted a crystal cup of punch. She watched Secretary Seward greet his guests and repressed a smile. The man was slight and stoop-shouldered, with a small neck, so that his head seemed to pop out of his jacket and collar like that of a tortoise from its shell. His ears were gigantic, his nose was sharp and prominent and his lower lip stuck out a bit, giving him a petulant appearance. Both Seward and his wife were ardent abolitionists, and Eva had heard that they'd helped Harriet Tubman and the Underground Railroad by hiding fugitive slaves in their home in Auburn, New York. She admired them tremendously for their efforts. It would be an excellent idea to recommend Josiah to Mr. and Mrs. Seward before she had to leave.

And it was going to be hard to leave. She liked America and felt at home here. There was something about its newness, its scrambling, raucous informality and independent attitudes that excited her. People weren't enclosed and bound up in ancient codes like they were at home. Eva could go about on her own, visiting sites and friends and attending functions, without inciting the censure and shock that she would have in England. Women weren't treated like slightly intelligent horses here. They could divorce, run their own businesses and generally run their own lives without anyone trying to interfere. How much simpler it would be if she could live in New York or

Washington. But Uncle Adolphus would never forgive her if she didn't go home. She had promised to spend the spring and summer with him. He was lonely since his wife had died four years ago. His sons were in India and Siam, and his daughter's husband had been posted to South Africa. More importantly, he'd written her that if she didn't come home soon, he would come and fetch her. He was certain she was going to dally so long she would get caught in a battle.

Eva sighed as she contemplated returning to London. She'd promised to serve as Uncle Adolphus' hostess, which meant receiving the many guests he entertained as an influential member of the government. She would have to give dinners and balls and make conversation with many people without really saying anything. Sometimes it was hard to curb her tongue, and often she would make some acerbic comment that got her into trouble. She'd rather face a flash flood in the Texas hill country than a room full of people who thought she was misguided and eccentric. Especially the gentlemen.

Eva frowned and took a sip of her punch. English gentlemen especially disapproved of her, but after years of conforming her behavior according to her husband's dictates of propriety, she was through worrying about what men might think. She knew the difference between silly social rules and good Christian conduct. She was certain the Lord didn't begrudge her a life filled with interest and meaningful pursuits as long as she did good for her fellow man. There wasn't anything on this earth that could make her return to that old life, because it made her feel useless. To feel as though you were superfluous, a mere piece of lace on a gown, a dried flower under glass, that was like being buried alive. She feared that feeling now, especially since she'd been able to help Josiah.

Blinking suddenly, Eva smiled as an idea popped into her head. She might have to go home, but she could leave funds with someone in America to help finance the relocation of Negroes. They were bound to be displaced in the coming war, and they would need money to start new lives, just like Josiah did. She wished she could be here to help set up facilities for refugees, but it couldn't be helped. Perhaps Mr. Frederick Douglass would know what to do. Of course. She would write him. Eva was still smiling to herself when Rosalie joined her, looking more bright and excited than she'd seen her all evening.

"Oh, Eva, you must come and meet someone. He's simply the most charming and beautiful young man in all creation, next to my Horace, of course. He's a bit severe, but I'm sure it's only because of this terrible secession business."

"Now, Rosalie, you should introduce him to some of your young Washington ladies. I'm sure he won't be interested in a widow and foreigner."

Rosalie caught Eva's arm and began pulling her across the room. "That's all you know. I overheard him talking to Horace just a while ago about being interested in meeting British citizens."

"Whatever for?"

"Who cares? Smile and be your lovable self."

Rosalie chattered to her as they walked beneath the gas candelabra. They joined a group of gentlemen talking by the fireplace. A man with his back to them was speaking.

"Yes, the president has ordered a blockade of the

Southern ports, but he needs more ships suitable for such work."

The man must have sensed their approach, because he hesitated. Then he turned to face the ladies, his mouth shut on whatever he'd been about to say.

Eva almost tripped over her own feet as she caught her first uninterrupted view of him. This man was impressive. He had that distinct look of many American men—broad shoulders, narrow hips and imposing height. Yet unlike many of his fellow countrymen, he seemed at home in evening dress. He wore his stiff shirt and high white collar with ease. The fingers that held a crystal wineglass were long and tapered. The only thing about his appearance that hinted that he might be more than a gentleman of leisure was the tan. His face was brown from the sun, as if he'd spent weeks or months in the open. In addition his black hair seemed to have a mind of its own. Long strands curled away from his face in disarray. Eva suspected that he'd recently taken scissors to it himself. When he met her gaze briefly she caught a glimpse of startling green eyes made cold by evaluation. The chilly stare was gone before she could be certain it was even there, and instead Eva encountered smooth politeness and superficial friendliness.

Horace greeted his wife and made the introduction. "Lady Eva Sparrow, may I present Ryder Drake." Horace clapped Drake on the back. "Drake here is what you might call a special assistant to the president. He's real familiar with the West, especially Texas. Got a big old ranch out there in the wilds."

"Lady Eva." Drake bowed over her hand and dropped it immediately. "Blair, I'm sure we're boring the ladies with all this business talk."

"No, indeed, sir" Eva heard herself say. She

sounded breathless and tittery. She cleared her throat. "I've been visiting a childhood friend who married a gentleman from Natchez, so I've been in the South."

Horace laid a finger on the side of his nose and said, "Our dear Lady Eva is the niece of an influential government official."

Drake gave Blair a look of alarm that caused the older man to burst into laughter. "Here you were searching all over for someone who could introduce you to the British cabinet, and she's right here in this very room! You should see your face, Drake."

"Oh, Mr. Blair," Eva said weakly, "for shame."

Eva watched Ryder Drake's face close up into a fierce expression, which for some odd reason made her insides tingle. Unfamiliar feelings stirred, and she found herself staring at the man, flustered, fluttery and blushing so hotly, she had to ply her fan. Drake was still eyeing her, unsmiling and obviously irritated with the effervescent Horace Blair. Anxious to distract them both from this embarrassing moment, Eva latched on to another topic.

"You're from Texas, Mr. Drake. I was there recently, and I must say that part of the country seems boundless. No doubt it takes several days to ride the boundaries of your ranch."

Drake's eyes narrowed. "You're right, Lady Eva, but that doesn't make me a wealthy man. It makes me a man with a lot of cattle to track down."

"And it must grieve you that Texas has chosen to secede from the Union when your sentiments are the opposite."

Drake nodded stiffly. "Blair, perhaps the ladies would like some punch."

"No, thank you," Eva said.

"Then we must be keeping you from your friends," he continued. "No doubt you've many acquaintances in the city. Washington is a very social town."

"It is," Eva replied, "but at the moment everyone is so tense. What is your opinion, sir? Will there be an attack on us?"

There was a pause in the conversation as everyone waited for Drake's reply. Drake lifted an eyebrow and pressed his lips together. With a curt nod he turned his back on Eva and left. Thus deserted, Eva was left staring at Ryder Drake's black-clad shoulders as they moved away. Nothing like this had ever happened to her. The color drained from her face at the humiliation. Rosalie was clucking at the effrontery, while Horace and the other gentlemen in the group looked embarrassed for her. The men quickly found excuses to be elsewhere, but just then one of Rosalie's friends joined the two women. She was Mrs. Samuel Purbright, a leading Washington hostess.

"I declare," she said. "I saw that from the other room. What rudeness. Mr. Drake has been among the savages too long." She patted Eva on the arm. "Don't you think a thing about it, my dear. We all saw it, and you're to be pitied."

Eva stuffed her humiliation away and raised her chin. "Nonsense, Mrs. Purbright. We British are used to encountering all sorts of savagery, what with the empire and all." Several other ladies joined them, and she raised her voice, hoping Drake would hear. "Perhaps Mr. Drake's rudeness is caused by a case of dysentery from the frontier."

There were shocked gasps and then titters. The ladies spread out and whispered to others. As Eva watched, word of her remarks spread from group to group. She turned to watch it travel out to the dining room and caught sight of a pair of broad shoulders below wild black hair. Someone whispered in Drake's ear, and Eva saw the shoulders stiffen and the tanned neck grow red. Smiling grimly to herself, she swept away to join Secretary Seward and his wife. Whatever had possessed her? She had become a blushing schoolgirl at the sight of a pretty man. She had never done that before, and there was no reason to do it now. Drake had an enticing appearance, but his character was abysmal. He seemed to think she was interested in the size of his ranch for how much wealth it implied. He also seemed to believe that ladies shouldn't be allowed to discuss politics or business. She had enough of that kind of attitude at home in spite of the fact that history provided many examples of women who could handle both. What did Mr. Drake know, anyway?

Eva glanced over her shoulder at her new enemy's stiff back. Two of his friends were teasing him, about the dysentery, she hoped. He would think twice before insulting her again.

# CHAPTER FOUR

❦

IT WAS A week later when Eva was handed into a shiny black carriage to join her hosts and Treasury Secretary Salmon P. Chase. The vehicle moved down H Street, then along Fifteenth past the incomplete Treasury building with its myriad columns and sandstone façade. Mr. Chase was a stately-looking man of great height and breadth, but the most imposing of his features was a massive head with a receding hairline that emphasized its domelike appearance. They turned onto F Street while the secretary described the evening's entertainment to his guest.

"Lady Eva," Chase said, "you're in for a treat, a rare luxury in this young country of ours. Tonight we're to see Mr. Edwin Booth in *Hamlet*. I'm afraid a great many of our actors are merely loud and bombastic, but Mr. Booth is subtle and approaches his art with great insight into character."

"I shall be most delighted to see Mr. Booth, sir. His reputation has spread all over my country."

In truth, Eva was more interested in asking the secretary about Mr. Lincoln and the coming war than she was in seeing a play. Only the day before the Seventh New York regiment had arrived to relieve Washington of the threat of invasion. Tension in the capital had eased a bit, and the regiment's commander, General Butler, had quelled the riots in Baltimore.

"Tell me, sir. Is it true that the president's boys keep chickens and a nanny goat at the White House?"

Chase gave her a rueful look. "I'm afraid so. We're not quite as civilized as we could wish."

"Nonsense. Why, our own queen swears by the virtues of a simple life and retreats to her country homes as often as possible."

Rosalie Blair spoke up. "Ah, but Balmoral is a far cry from a country cottage, Eva."

They all shared a quiet laugh as the carriage pulled up in front of Ford's Theater on Tenth Street. As Eva left the carriage, helped by the secretary, she looked up at the rather plain redbrick building in front of her. The first floor contained an arched loggia through which they went on their way to the state box. On Mr. Chase's arm, Eva climbed the stairs to the dress circle. The state box was to the right of the stage and was reached through a narrow corridor. Eva stepped to the box rail and attracted a great deal of attention from the audience until they realized the president wasn't with her. The box itself was furnished with a small sofa and comfortable chairs, one of which creaked when Horace Blair lowered his substantial weight onto it. Eva took her place between Rosalie and Secretary Chase. The box was decorated in red, white and blue, with a portrait of George Washington mounted above it on the central pillar. Eva noted a rocking chair in the shadows looking out of place amid the formal furniture.

The theater itself seemed small and cramped to Eva, who was used to the grand theaters and opera of London, but as the play unfolded, she realized that Edwin Booth was in fact as compelling an actor as any at home. She was engrossed in the story in spite of having seen the play several times. Hamlet had just begun talking of Yorick when she was overcome with a strange sensation, as if invisible fingertips were walking over the skin on the back of her arms and her shoulders. Eva glanced around and encountered a fixed green stare beneath lowered brows. Ryder Drake was two boxes over, and he was glaring at her as if she'd committed some mortal sin. Behind him she caught a fleeting glimpse of a smaller man with curly red hair before he slipped into the shadows at the back of the theater box. Drake was still glowering at her. Eva's gaze shifted back to his, and rather than break contact, she turned in her chair, folded her arms across her chest and stared back at him. Drake blinked as if coming awake from a trance. His eyes widened, then he broke his angry surveillance and turned his attention to the play.

"How rude," Eva muttered to herself as she looked back at Edwin Booth. It was clear she hadn't embarrassed the man at all. He'd simply dismissed her from his thoughts without any sign that he'd been caught in a faux pas.

Really, the man was incorrigible. Eva frowned as she realized how often his attractive image had flitted through her mind during the week since their meeting. Usually she easily dismissed unpleasant people from her thoughts, and they stayed dismissed. Mr. Drake kept reappearing like some beautiful apparition, but her imagination gave him no voice, all the better to avoid any rudeness the handsome vision might utter. Eva stiffened at the thought that she might be enamored with this man even though he'd treated her so boorishly. She wasn't the kind of woman who groveled after domineering, contemptuous men.

"I'll regress after all my progress," Eva whispered to herself.

"What's wrong, Eva?" asked Rosalie.

"That impossible man was glaring at me. I hardly know him, and he was staring at me as if I'd shot his favorite hound."

"Who?"

"That Drake person."

Rosalie craned her neck to see past Eva, then plied her fan to hide a smile. "My dear, the man is probably smitten."

"Don't be absurd," Eva snapped. "He thinks I'm an addle-headed Society creature."

"I'm sure that's not true. Ryder Drake is half English himself. You probably remind him of his second home."

"Shh. I'm trying to hear Mr. Booth."

Eva fumed until intermission. Then they stood to stretch their legs, and the gentlemen left to fetch the ladies something to drink.

"Secretary Chase says there aren't enough ships to blockade all the Southern ports," Rosalie told Eva.

"If they do stop movement in the ports, Great Britain will suffer." Eva waved her fan. It was stuffy in the crowded theater. "The Lancastershire mills use enormous amounts of cotton, and the owners and laborers will pressure the government to side with the Confederacy. This could grow into a very dangerous situation."

"I know. That's why I'm glad you're here. You must

tell your uncle and his associates in the government that we are fighting to end slavery. That aim is greater than the temporary loss of trade."

"I agree, but that doesn't mean Lord Palmerston will. I'll try to—"

The box door opened and Ryder Drake stepped in. He strode over to Rosalie and bowed. "Mrs. Blair, it's a pleasure to see you again so soon."

Rosalie gave Eva a knowing glance and said, "Why, Mr. Drake, what a surprise. I didn't know you were here."

"I can't stay long. Late meetings and such. But I wanted to pay my respects." Drake inclined his head at Eva, his posture stiff. "Lady Eva, it's a pleasure to see you again as well."

"Is it? Ouch!" Eva rubbed her side where Rosalie had elbowed her. "I mean, how kind of you to visit, Mr. Drake."

"It is my honor." Drake's gaze flitted over her face, then he bowed slightly. A slight flush swept over his cheeks. "I— Allow me to be so bold as to say how privileged we American gentlemen are to have the chance to meet so lovely and charming a visitor from abroad."

Eva eyed Drake with distrust. "You're too kind, sir. I'm hardly a match for all the beautiful American belles I've met."

"You greatly underestimate yourself," Drake said, his posture as rigid as when he'd first entered. His gaze met hers fleetingly and darted away in what Eva refused to believe was shyness. The flush on his face deepened. He cleared his throat. "Enough pleasantries. I need to talk to you privately."

Eva bristled at his sudden change from gallantry

to tactlessness. "Indeed." What could this ill-mannered man possibly have to say to her?

"Oh, look," Rosalie chirped. "There's the senator from New York, and Miss Harris. I must say hello to them."

"I'll go with you," Eva said hastily.

Rosalie pressed her firmly into her chair. "No need at all. I won't be a moment. Hardly any time at all."

"Drat," Eva muttered.

"I beg your pardon?" Drake said.

"Nothing."

Drake moved to stand nearer her chair. He stood with one hand behind his back, his posture as stiff as a railroad tie, his manner grim. Eva deduced that whatever he had to say would be unpleasant. His jaw twitched, and Eva eyed him warily. Now that they were alone he seemed most unwilling to speak, and she thought she knew why.

"Is there something you wished to say, sir?"

Stiff nod.

Eva's patience wore out. "My faith, sir, if making an apology causes you this much pain, please desist."

"An apology?" he repeated blankly.

"For your uncivil remarks the other night, sir."

Drake furrowed his brow. "Oh, I wasn't even thinking about that."

"Is that so?" Eva said, drawing herself erect in the chair. This was the most discourteous person she'd ever met.

Mr. Drake appeared not to notice her growing anger. He seemed preoccupied. "Yes. I wanted to speak to you about—"

"Here we are!" Horace Blair and Secretary Chase bustled into the theater box, followed by waiters bearing trays of refreshments. "The poor fellows were having a time getting through the crowd until we formed an escort. Ah, Drake. It's good to see you. Where's Mrs. Blair?"

"Hello, Blair, Mr. Secretary. Mrs. Blair is visiting friends. I was just having a conversation with Lady Eva." He turned to her. "I have a request to make of you. May I call upon you tomorrow to make it?"

Still fuming from his earlier rudeness, Eva picked up her fan and began tapping it in her palm in a staccato beat that revealed her mood. She pulled her lips into a parody of a smile.

"Of course, Mr. Drake." He also managed a stiff smile. "After I hear that apology." The smile vanished. A typhoonlike expression darkened his face.

"Are you making dictates to me, my lady?"

"Yes, sir. I am."

His jaw working, Drake glared at her and muttered something under his breath.

"I'm sorry," Eva said with a sweet smile. "Was that your apology? I couldn't hear."

Turning crimson, Drake whipped around and strode out of the theater box without another word. Eva's fan snapped against her palm. *Tap, tap, tap, tap.*

"My faith, does that man always present his back to a lady?"

Secretary Chase stared after Drake, then recovered himself and offered Eva a glass of sherry. "I've never seen him like that. He's usually such a gentleman."

"I apologize for my fellow countryman, Lady Eva, my dear."

Eva waved her fan, struggling to control her anger. "Think nothing of it, Mr. Blair. I happen to adore American manners on the whole, so easy and free of the rigid doctrines that stifle Europeans."

Blair shook his head and buried his nose in his sherry glass. "I don't know what's got into Drake."

Two days after the debacle at Ford's Theater, Ryder Drake was getting ready to attend a ball at which he would once again try to approach Lady Eva Sparrow. He'd bungled it terribly the last time, but how was he to know she wanted an apology for some imagined slight? The country was about to plunge into civil war, and her high-and-mighty ladyship was concerned about etiquette.

Yet something had happened to him that night when he saw Lady Eva in the theater, first glimpsing that burnished hair that curled so provocatively around her little ears and at her neck. She hadn't seen him, and he'd been able to watch her for a few moments. Lady Eva was like an exquisite, magical fairy, so small and delicate, and she had enormous eyes of a startling gray. They caught the light and reflected it back so that they seemed brighter than diamonds. Just as remarkable was her lack of a ladylike pallor. Eva Sparrow wasn't afraid to brave the sun a bit, although she obviously took care of her skin. It was smooth, and he could imagine how supple it would be to the touch.

Drake blinked at himself in the dresser mirror. "You stop that right now. What do you think you're doing mooning over an English Society belle? Anyway, she doesn't like you."

God, he wished he hadn't been forced to involve Lady Eva, but every other contact he'd sought out had fizzled. Many British had left once the firing started at Fort Sumter; others refused to get involved, knowing Lord Palmerston's pro-Confederacy stance. Pinkerton had tried to help and ended up repeating his first recommendation that night at the theater. Drake must appeal to Lady Eva. She was the most highly placed person outside British government circles available to them, and time was running short.

That was why he was going to the ball given by Secretary Chase in honor of General George B. McClellan, whom many considered the nation's most promising military leader. Winfield Scott was General in Chief of the Army. He was a hero of the War of 1812 and the Mexican War. His experience and guile commanded almost universal respect, but he was aging and in poor health. Nevertheless, the valiant old soldier had been at the meeting from which Drake had just returned, where they'd discussed Scott's plan for the conduct of the war.

The general's strategy was far-reaching and would demand great resources. It was, indeed, daunting to many who heard it. Drake considered it excellent, even if some were derisively calling it the Anaconda Plan because of the slow, squeezing effect it would have on the Confederacy. General Scott planned a complete blockade of the South's ports from the East Coast to the Gulf of Mexico. At the same time armies would thrust down the Mississippi River to split the states of the Deep South in two and isolate them from cattle- and grain-rich Texas. In this coordinated effort, federal land and naval forces would strangle the Confederacy.

The plan would require a larger military force than the United States had ever had. President Lincoln was going to call for more volunteers to enlist for three years. Secretary Welles would have to expand the navy dramatically. But more troubling than the scale of the forces needed was the fact that several European powers were already amenable to recognizing the Confederacy as a belligerent. In the twisted and nitpicky world of diplomacy, because Lincoln had blockaded the Southern ports rather than close them, foreign governments could get away with legitimizing the South. Secretary Seward was furious and blustered about war with Great Britain. Lincoln was too preoccupied to bother with the niceties of state relations. Drake was afraid Seward would make some blunder that would bring the British into the fight.

Alan Pinkerton barged into Ryder's dressing room as Ryder was putting on his white tie. "There you are. I've been looking for you all afternoon."

"I was in that meeting with General Scott."

Pinkerton waved a leather strap at him. Drake dropped his tie and grabbed the strap, noting the three closely spaced knots that had been tied on it. This was the sign of one of his agents in the South, one he hadn't expected to hear from for months. It was the signal that the agent had come to Washington to report important news.

Drake rounded on Pinkerton. "When did you get this?"

"It was tied to the hitching post at the place on Pennsylvania Avenue. I just happened to have a meeting there today. No telling how long it's been there. I haven't been to the house in over a week."

"You left instructions?"

"I left the sign for a meeting tonight at eleven at the usual place."

Drake picked up the ends of his tie and started

tying it again. "Aw, hell. I have to go to Chase's ball tonight."

"You're slipping into your Texas accent again."

Giving Pinkerton an irritated look, Drake said, "Look, it's too soon for any of my agents to know anything. After all, I just set the network up. He's probably lost his nerve and bolted. You meet him."

"He won't trust me. You have to meet him."

"Oh, all right, but I'll have to slip away from the ball. I have something I've got to do."

Pinkerton grinned at him. "You're going to try that little British lady again? Christ, Drake, you made a real mess the last time."

"It's not my fault," Drake said through clenched teeth as he struggled with his tie. "She's impossible. More concerned about etiquette and apologies than the great events taking place right in front of her. If I'd been able to find anyone else of use, I wouldn't have to approach her."

"Anyone would think you hated women."

"I don't hate women. I dislike useless women who fritter away their lives in pursuit of inanities. They certainly don't belong in government affairs, especially secret government affairs."

"I told you, this lady isn't like that, but no matter. You're as stubborn as Mr. Lincoln, so I'm not arguing with you." Pinkerton picked up the leather strap. "Find a way to hide your attitude. We don't have much time, and we need Britain to keep out of this."

"I know, I know." Drake finished with his tie and began searching for his top hat. "It's not my fault she's a blamed Society featherhead. Come on, Pinkerton, I'm late for the confounded ball."

Half an hour later Drake stood in the ballroom of Salmon Chase's grand town house, one of the largest in Washington. He paused beside a painting of Marie Antoinette and her children, gave the queen's enormous hair and headdress a disgusted glance and continued searching for Lady Eva. The room was painted and plastered in white, with French wallpaper and crystal chandeliers. Crimson velvet curtains draped the tall French doors that opened onto a balcony. Unfortunately, the secretary had yet to install gas in this room, and candle wax dripped from the fixtures onto the floor and some unlucky guests. Nevertheless, Mr. Chase and his guests whirled around the room to the accompaniment of a Strauss waltz. Beyond the ballroom lay a feast worthy of Buckingham Palace in its abundance of French dishes and silver service.

Ryder shouldered his way around the great wheel of dancers, trying to see if Lady Eva was among them. He glanced at his pocket watch and realized it was later than he'd thought. His arrangements would fall through if he didn't find the blamed woman soon. He'd finished an entire circuit of the ballroom in frustration when he saw Lady Eva enter on the arm of an old school friend of his, Lucian Bedford Forrest. Lucian was a scholarly sort, perhaps on account of his fragile health. He had a biting wit that matched his razorlike intellect. A wealthy Virginia planter, Ryder's friend refused to be drawn into arguments about slavery or secession. He'd never succumbed to Drake's arguments for emancipation, but he also never contributed to the defensive and suspicious atmosphere so rampant in the politics of his home state.

Ryder began to make his way toward the couple. Lucian had soft blond hair, pale skin and a lean, ascetic build. Lady Eva was wearing a gown of black lace and teal satin that Ryder was sure wouldn't be fashionable in America for another year. It had probably cost more than Secretary Chase's silver service, and she looked better in it than any woman he could think of. How could such a lovely woman be so exasperating?

Approaching the two, Ryder steeled himself to be charming and weasel his way into Lady Eva's good opinion. It shouldn't be too hard. He'd give her that confounded apology she set such store by and compliment her on her beauty. What could he say? She was a short little thing. He loved her burnished hair and cultured manner of speech—when she wasn't being sly and insulting. She had a tempting figure—best not start thinking about that. Taking a deep breath, Drake plastered a smile on his face and touched Lucian's shoulder.

"Forrest, I haven't seen you in months." He bowed low. "And the charming Lady Eva. I'm so glad you're still with us."

He received a curt nod. This would be slow going.

"Drake, old fellow. Where have you been?"

"Arranging my personal business in Texas, as much as I could."

Lucian gave him a lazy smile. "You should take my advice and hand everything over to a business manager. Tell me, do you expect your backwoods president to engage the South soon? I want to know how long I have before I must leave for Europe."

"He's not just my president, Lucian, and you'd be surprised at his wisdom and education."

"I'll take your word for it," Lucian said with a skeptical look.

Ryder turned to Lady Eva. "You may not know it, but Lucian here reserves his passion for the study of ancient Greece and Rome rather than politics.

He'd rather read Cicero than the Lincoln-Douglas debates."

"All this war talk makes it impossible to conduct a civilized conversation," Lucian replied.

Lady Eva had been staring coolly at Ryder, but when she glanced at Lucian her gaze softened. "There is much we can learn from the classics, Mr. Forrest." She cocked her head to the side. " 'Force without wisdom falls of its own weight.' " Eva ignored Drake's openmouthed stare.

"Ah," Lucian relied. "A lady of taste and acumen who knows Horace." He kissed Lady Eva's hand with a flourish. " 'The man who is tenacious of purpose in a rightful cause is not shaken from his firm resolve by the frenzy of his fellow citizens clamoring for what is wrong, or by the tyrant's threatening countenance.' "

Just then Ryder heard his name bellowed and saw his cousin, Hamilton Locke, coming toward them.

"Oh, no," Lucian said. "The rabid abolitionist approaches. Please excuse me, Lady Eva, Drake. I have no wish to listen yet again to an earsplitting harangue on the evils of slavery."

"But slavery *is* evil," Lady Eva said.

"Yes, my lady, but Locke is so self-righteous about it, he puts me off my food. Until later."

Lucian Bedford Forrest slipped away as Hamilton Locke joined them. "Ryder, I see you've met our charming English rose. I have had the honor only this evening, and she has broken my heart by telling me she's going home next week."

Lady Eva's cheeks grew pink. "Mr. Locke, you mustn't say such things."

Drake lifted an eyebrow. "You're not accustomed to our Southern gallantries, Lady Eva?"

"I hadn't expected them in Washington, sir."

"But Washington is in the South," Ryder said. "And my cousin and I are both from Virginia originally. However, we sought our fortunes elsewhere. Hamilton here has had the opportunity to invest in a couple of railroads."

"There's only one railroad that interests me at the moment," Locke said. "The Underground Railroad. You've met Frederick Douglass and Harriet Tubman. You know the work we've done." He rubbed his hands together. "Soon we won't need to do it at all, and those who have supported slavery will suffer the consequences. God will condemn them to hell-fire and—"

"Ham, watch your language in front of Lady Eva."

"Oh, I beg your pardon."

Ryder listened to his cousin's apologies and checked his watch. It was time. He would have to get rid of Hamilton if his plan was going to work. He caught Hamilton's eye and jerked his head. Locke understood and excused himself to go in search of refreshment. Lady Eva was eyeing Ryder with distrust and moving away.

"I must find Mr. and Mrs. Blair."

"Wait!"

"I beg your pardon."

"Confound it, I didn't mean to raise my voice." Ryder drew closer and spoke quickly before she could withdraw. "My dear Lady Eva, I was most discourteous the other night, and I regret it. I'm afraid the pressures of our terrible political situation have made me ungentlemanly."

"Hmm."

Gritting his teeth, Ryder ignored Eva's skeptical

expression and plunged on. "I must humbly beg your pardon for my conduct. I—uh—I behaved like an ornery no-account churnhead."

"My faith, sir. What is a churnhead?"

"An idiot, my lady."

Lady Eva tilted her head to look up at him, her gray eyes sparkling with humor. "It would be most ungracious of me not to accept such a, shall I say plainspoken, apology. Thank you, sir."

"And I hope you accept a small surprise I've arranged to show my repentance."

"There's no need."

Ryder bowed to her. "Please, my lady. It's important to me."

"But—"

"Surely you won't refuse to meet the president."

He had indeed surprised her. He could see it in the way her eyes widened.

"Bless my life. You're serious."

Ryder nodded and offered his arm. Lady Eva stared at it for a moment, then gingerly placed her hand on it. Ryder conducted her out of the ballroom and into a long library off the entry hall. They went through a door concealed in a bookcase and ended up in a small study. There was a fire snapping and flickering in a fireplace, before which sat a deep leather chair. As they entered, a tall form unfolded itself from the chair, and Ryder smiled at Abraham Lincoln.

"Mr. President, may I present Lady Eva Sparrow."

# CHAPTER FIVE

❧

EVA HELD OUT her hand to Abraham Lincoln and tried not to look as startled as she felt. She had only seen the president from a distance, and he was an unusual sight. Over six feet in height, he was so lanky he looked even taller than he was. His head was long, his forehead high and narrow. With dark, almost black hair that floated wildly if not subdued by a brush, he appeared unkempt even in his evening clothes. This was because his coat hung loosely on him and his pants bagged at the knees. The angles of his face were sharp, his eyebrows bushy and his nose large and slightly askew. His skin was sallow, dry and wrinkled, his cheeks leathery. His ears were extremely large and stuck out from his head. Eva watched her hand disappear into the president's and met his sparkling gray gaze.

"Miz Sparrow, what an honor it is to meet such a lovely young lady from over the ocean."

Eva blinked at the unusual form of address, but

recovered and curtseyed. "The honor is mine, Mr. President."

Lincoln guided Eva to stand beside the fire and glanced at Ryder Drake. "My young friend here tells me that your uncle is a man of consequence in the British government, Miz Sparrow."

"My uncle is Lord Adolphus Tennyson, and he has the honor to hold a position under Lord Russell, the foreign secretary, sir."

"And what do you think of this conflict we're about to begin?"

"War is the curse of mankind, sir. I regret that the United States may suffer from it. I have come to appreciate this country and its freedoms."

Lincoln watched her for a moment, and Eva began to detect a trace of humor in his gaze.

"I think, ma'am, that you would make an excellent diplomat. I've asked you several questions and you've managed to refrain from committing yourself to anything controversial."

"You're too kind, sir."

"I wish our Southern brethren were like you. But there's no middle ground south of the Mason-Dixon Line, it seems." Lincoln clasped his hands behind his back and bent down to her. "And what do you think of the South's 'peculiar institution'?"

Eva pressed her lips together. "Slavery is illegal in my country, sir."

"But what do you think of it?"

"Mr. President, if I could, I would abolish it at once. It is an abomination."

"Indeed," Lincoln replied as he watched her closely. "You remind me of a story, Miz Sparrow. When I was a young congressman from Illinois I had rooms in a boardinghouse here in Washington at which there were several Negro servants. One evening these young men were waiting on us boarders at dinner when a party of lawmen burst upon us and grabbed one of the waiters. It seems that the poor man was working to pay for his freedom. He had but sixty dollars left to pay, and his master had changed his mind. Just like that. Only sixty dollars, and he would have been free forever." Lincoln's gaze grew distant and troubled. "We tried to get him back, but the owner wouldn't budge. I often wonder what became of that young man."

Eva sighed. "A heartbreaking story, sir. I've been to the South and have seen things that cause me nightmares. I don't understand it. It's not as though the majority in the South own slaves. Why do those who don't have slaves support slavery?"

"Ah, well, you see, there's the thing. The idea of owning slaves is right seductive to thoughtless persons. They think that someday they too will own slaves, and slavery is the most ostentatious manner of displaying wealth. You see, ma'am, you can have all manner of wealth—cattle, stocks, railroads and such—and not a soul will suspect that you're rich. But if you've got a Negro trudging at your heels, everyone sees him and knows right away that you own slaves."

Eva shivered. "Then the dream is always there in front of every farmer, tanner and blacksmith."

"Exactly," Ryder said from his place beside the president.

"What do you think is going to happen, sir?" Eva asked.

Lincoln's bushy eyebrows drew together and his shoulders drooped. "Ma'am, I've said before, a house divided against itself cannot stand. I truly believe this government cannot endure half slave and half free. And the Southern states have taken from me any choice I might have had."

A short silence ensued while the president's words echoed in Eva's mind. This man had a simple eloquence that suited him, and a sharp mind that belied his humble appearance.

"Miz Sparrow, my friend Drake here has a favor to ask you on my behalf. I wonder if you would do me the honor of listening to him and perhaps see your way to doing me that favor."

Taken off guard, Eva looked at Mr. Drake, whose countenance revealed nothing. This meeting had been a trap all along, a plan to back her into a corner where she couldn't do anything but agree to Mr. Drake's request. He hadn't meant his apology; if he hadn't wanted something he would still have been as rude as ever. Eva felt a pain in her chest, the pain of disenchantment made more painful for her never having suspected she'd been enchanted by this beautiful and severe man. Stifling the pain, Eva managed a stiff smile at Lincoln.

"Mr. President, I can think of nothing in my power that would be of help, but I shall certainly listen to Mr. Drake's request."

Lincoln chuckled and put a hand on Drake's shoulder. "There, you see what she did? She made it seem like she said yes, when she only agreed to listen. This young lady is right clever."

"I'm beginning to appreciate that, sir." Drake gave Eva a polite smile.

"Thank you, ma'am, for listening. It was an honor to make your acquaintance." Lincoln bowed awkwardly. "Now I must take my leave. I promised Mother I'd be back soon."

Eva curtseyed again as Drake showed the president out of the room. He returned and offered her a seat, but Eva declined. She wanted to be able to get out of the room quickly. Instead of asking his favor right away, Drake rested an arm on the mantel and gazed into the fire. The flames turned his eyes to burning emerald and danced over the smooth, taut skin of his cheekbones. Suddenly he glanced up, catching her watching him, and gave her the first genuine smile she'd seen from him. His face was transformed, and she glimpsed gentleness and lively good humor she'd never suspected, so easily did he conceal his feelings. Eva experienced a profound regret that for some unfathomable reason he'd never bestowed his goodwill upon her.

"Don't be fooled by Mr. Lincoln's awkwardness and mild manner, my lady," Drake said. "I've heard it said that men who take him for a simpleton soon end up on their backs in a ditch."

Eva nodded curtly. "I think anyone who cannot see the greatness in Mr. Lincoln is the simpleton."

"Many don't share your opinion," Drake replied.

"It's easier to belittle someone who disagrees with you than to admit he might have greater vision."

Cocking his head to the side, Drake said, "Well put, my lady. I admire your perception."

At this compliment Eva almost lost her composure. The man could be charming when he wanted something from her. "I must return to the ball, Mr. Drake. What is it you wished to ask me?"

"Very well, my lady, I'll try to be brief. You may not be aware that your country has recognized the Confederacy as a belligerent."

"Of course I am." Really, did the man think she went about with blinders on her head?

"And Secretary Seward is angry about that. He's blustering and making threats when the president has no wish to offend Great Britain."

"That is wise of Mr. Lincoln," Eva replied.

"The president thinks it would be of great help if I were to represent his opinions to Lord Russell and Lord Palmerston through some interested party outside regular diplomatic channels. So we would like to ask you to introduce me to your uncle, who might perform such an office."

Eva studied Drake, noted his closed expression and the stubborn glint in his green eyes. She hadn't heard the whole story.

"Mr. Drake, you got me here under an insulting ruse. No doubt you thought me as simple as Mr. Lincoln is reputed to be. But I am not as light-minded as I appear. I have no intention of compromising my uncle by introducing someone to him who has been less than honest with me."

"Confound it!"

Eva turned to go, but Drake rushed to block her way.

"I'm sorry, my lady. Please, please don't go."

Eva took a step back and looked up at him. "Mr. Drake, I fail to see the use in what you propose. You can make your president's views known through the United States' ambassador to the court of St. James."

She tried to walk past him, but he moved to intercept her.

"Aw, hell."

"I will be obliged to you, sir, if you refrain from uttering obscenities in my presence."

"Sorry! I'm sorry. I apologize. *Sorry.*" Drake dodged around her as she headed for the door and got in front of her again. "I didn't think you'd be interested in the reasons why I need this favor."

"I knew it," Eva snapped. "You do think me a simpleton."

"Not simple, exactly."

Rolling her eyes, Eva planted her hands on her hips and sighed.

"All right, all right. I'll tell you. Jefferson Davis is the president of the Confederate States of America, and he and his government have embarked on a campaign to convince Great Britain to support them in the war. They're going to try to persuade Palmerston and the cabinet to enter the war on their side." Drake rubbed the back of his neck and began to pace. "The British could use their naval power to protect Rebel shipping and supply routes. We know Palmerston's interested in helping so that the South can supply the British textile mills." Drake stopped pacing and met Eva's gaze. "Britain is the most powerful country in the world. If she enters the war on the Rebel side, the United States is doomed."

"I see." This was indeed a matter of the utmost delicacy. She had never involved herself in so grave a situation.

"You needn't be bothered with all this," Drake said, approaching her.

"What do you mean?"

"All you need do is give me the introduction, and you'll be out of it. You can attend the Season without another thought about it. I'm sure a lady like you has more pressing matters to attend to."

Eva folded her arms over her chest. "Such as?"

"Oh, I don't know. Paris fashions, country house parties, going to the opera."

Smoothing her hands over the front of her gown,

Eva said, "I see. So it's your opinion, having conversed with me for a total of a few minutes, that I would be more interested in fashion and parties than in great world events."

"Well, English ladies—"

"You repellant toad."

"Hey!"

"You presumptuous, overbearing, conceited man."

"Now, look, Lady Eva. I was being polite. It's not fitting for a lady to be burdened with more than I've confided in you."

"Oh, so now I can't be trusted to keep secrets." By now Eva was nearly beside herself with anger. This man had assumed all along that she was self-indulgent and shallow. His entire attitude was insulting and belittling. And on top of that, he assumed she would undertake a mission of critical delicacy in the relationship between their two countries without even thinking it through. His attitude was as bad as that of most Englishmen. He was an American; he ought to know better.

"What in blazes is wrong with you?" Drake was saying. "All I want is—"

"All you want is for me to meddle in the foreign policy of the most powerful nation on earth!" Eva stomped around him and opened the door. "No, sir, I will not. I respect Mr. Lincoln and wish him well, but I'm not fool enough to interfere in matters about which I know so little. This discussion is at an end, sir, and I will not enter upon the subject again."

Eva whipped through the door, turned and slammed it in Drake's face as he came after her. She happened to glance down as the door closed. There was a key in the lock. She turned it.

"What in blazes? You open this door, Eva Sparrow."

Eva marched away, a satisfied smile about her lips. She had no doubt Mr. Drake could get out of that room easily, but at least she'd be able to lose herself in the ballroom before he could pursue her with his importunities.

"Hey, open this door!"

Sailing back into the ballroom, Eva was met by Hamilton Locke, who swept her onto the dance floor in a waltz. Soon she was breathless and smiling, for she had always favored this waltz above all others. She loved the swirl and rush of hundreds of yards of lace, silk and transparent tarlatan, the sound of the men's heels on the floorboards, the swelling of the music. The excitement did much to restore her good humor, and when the waltz was over she accepted Hamilton's invitation to partake of a glass of chilled punch. As he handed her a goblet of cut crystal Locke complimented her on her graceful dancing.

"I feel obliged to apologize to you, Lady Eva, for the barbaric conduct of my fellow Americans of the South." Locke had his cousin's dark hair, but it fell over his forehead, and he was always shoving it out of the way. His angular face was pale, and his dark eyes blazed with conviction. "I'm afraid we can never advance as a civilization until we rid ourselves of this abomination of slavery."

"You needn't apologize, Mr. Locke. The institution was set long before you were born, and you're trying to end it now."

"We've tried to do that for years," he replied. "But the Southern states have always thwarted our efforts. They got Texas in as a slave state in '48, and

Kansas might as well be one too. Slave owners ought to be shot."

"Surely there is a way short of violence. Could the government not compensate the planters for the cost of freeing their slaves?"

"Why should we do that? It would be like paying someone not to sin."

"But to prevent bloodshed..."

Locke was fishing inside his coat and brought out a small portfolio. "We're going to have to trounce them, my lady. There's no reasoning with people who would do this."

Eva took the portfolio and opened it. Inside were several daguerreotypes, all of the same Negro man. He was shirtless, with his back to the camera. His back was one huge mass of puckered scar tissue. In the second picture his hands were visible, and every finger had been broken and healed crookedly. In the third the man was dressed in plain homespun. He faced the camera, his head held high, his eyes alight with the defiance that had no doubt earned him his injuries. Eva quietly closed the portfolio and handed it back to Hamilton Locke, feeling sick.

"That poor man."

"His name was Daniel," Locke said as he studied the pictures. "He didn't have a surname until he chose one for himself. He picked Carpenter. He said if Jesus was a carpenter, it was good enough for him. He had a fine wit, had Daniel Carpenter. He died last year. He was only thirty years old."

While Eva listened to Hamilton she was reminded of the plight of so many slaves she'd seen on her travels in the South. What horrors would Josiah have endured had she not helped him to freedom? And what would happen if Britain sided with the Confederacy?

Dismay overwhelmed her as she contemplated the consequences. Still queasy from looking at Hamilton's portfolio, Eva began to regret her hasty refusal to help Mr. Drake.

In the years since she'd become a widow, she had grown independent and intolerant of male prejudice against her sex. But if truth were told, she was nervous around Mr. Drake because she felt so attracted to him. Indeed, he was the kind of man whom she had always considered dangerous and at the same time beyond her ability to interest. So when he behaved rudely, it was much easier for her to take offense and retaliate than to try to charm him. Yet she couldn't in good conscience allow her shortcomings and fears to prevent her from doing something to help the suffering slaves in America. After all, if she was discreet, no harm could come of an introduction to Uncle Adolphus. This was her chance to be more than she could ever be back home. Having experienced a mild form of enslavement herself, she felt a vast sympathy for the noble people suffering so harshly in America. She could tolerate Mr. Drake and his ridiculous opinions long enough to help in her small way. Meanwhile, she could ask the Blairs to transfer some funds to Mr. Frederick Douglass. Mr. Douglass could put the money to work where it was most needed.

Hamilton Locke was shaking his head. "I apologize, Lady Eva. I get carried away, as Ryder often tells me. Your glass is empty. Please allow me to refill it."

"You're most kind, Mr. Locke."

"Eva! Eva, where have you been?" Rosalie Blair arrived on the arm of Secretary Chase. "You missed the president. He stopped by, but now he's gone."

Eva tried to look disappointed. "What a shame. Mr. Secretary, have you seen Mr. Drake?"

"A moment ago, Lady Eva. Ah, there he is. He has his hat. It looks like he's leaving. Come, Mrs. Blair. This is our dance."

Eva waved at Rosalie as the pair moved onto the dance floor. She tried to find Mr. Drake, but she was too short to see over the crowd. She threaded her way around the ballroom and gained the entry hall only to find that Mr. Drake wasn't there. He must have gone outside. Dashing into the room used to hold cloaks, she donned hers and hurried outside.

Drake wasn't on the steps or in the carriage that had just pulled up. She glanced up and down the street and spied a tall figure passing beneath a gas streetlamp down the block. Not wanting to shout at him, Eva lifted her skirts, ran down the steps and rushed after her quarry. She quickly lost her breath because of her tight stays and had to slow down. It felt as if her ribs were crushing her lungs, and when she filled them to accost Mr. Drake, pain stabbed into her side. Eva paused to get her wind, and when she did, Drake suddenly turned a corner and vanished. Now Eva was confused. There were no houses in the direction Drake was headed, only stables, workshops and warehouses.

She looked back at the Chase house with its brightly lit windows and heard the orchestra playing a polka. Then she went to the corner and peered after Mr. Drake. The man was skulking in the shadows like a burglar. What was so important that he'd left a cabinet member's ball and risked offending so many important government officials? Whatever business he had, it couldn't be legitimate. Honorable affairs were conducted in daylight, or at least in gaslight.

The pompous, severe and honorable Mr. Ryder Drake was on his way to something clandestine. Eva's gaze drifted to the Chase house once more, then back to Drake as he sidled between a blacksmith's shop and a barrel maker's.

Her curiosity blossomed. Eva left her corner perch and scurried after Mr. Drake. This was still a safe neighborhood, and the worst she risked was getting the hem of her gown muddy. It would be worth it, to catch the upright Mr. Drake in some nefarious deed. Eva briefly allowed herself to wonder what would happen if Drake caught her spying on him, then discarded the thought. She had no intention of getting caught.

Shortly after Eva left the ball, a black-lacquered carriage with its shades drawn moved slowly away from Secretary Chase's house. The man inside wore immaculate evening dress. His shirt was fastened with pearl studs, his cloak lined with black velvet. On his hands were kid gloves, and one of them rested on the embossed silver handle of a walking stick. He had pulled his elegant top hat down so that it shielded his eyes, which were closed. His driver knew how to negotiate the streets of the capital in a circuitous route that made sure they weren't followed.

In privacy and repose the face of the man known as Iago was curiously blank. Perhaps the lack of expression came from having had to protect himself from his father, whose irrational and unpredictable rages had so terrorized the family. Revealing any weakness—indeed, anything at all about himself— had brought cruel taunts aimed at destroying his self-respect and his will. All that had been long ago, of course. It had been many years since his father had dared torment him.

The last time had been when he was sixteen. He returned home from church to find that his father had gotten drunk and was entertaining himself by using his son's beloved dog for target practice. The monster had tied the animal to a tree and sat on the veranda drinking whiskey and taking shots at the gentle mastiff. When Iago reached the animal it could hardly move. Lifting the dog in his arms, he whispered to it gently and kissed it. His father had roared for him to get out of the way because he wasn't finished yet. Looking at his pet, Iago's soul had transformed, inculcating years of abuse into a furnace of outrage and determination. He'd endured his father's physical torment and emotional battering without having ever rebelled, but what he wouldn't do for himself, he would do for this gentle, loving creature. Iago had laid the animal down and stalked to his father, keeping himself between the shooter and his pet.

He reached his father, tore the rifle from his hands and returned to the mastiff. Turning the animal's head away so that he couldn't see, Iago killed the only creature to whom he'd ever given his complete love. Next he gripped the rifle by its barrel and bashed it against the tree. Dropping the remnants on the ground beside his dog, Iago retraced his steps while his father bellowed in rage at the destruction of his gun.

Reaching the drunken man, Iago ripped the whiskey bottle from his father's hand, broke it against one of the veranda columns and slashed the man's face open with the jagged edge of the bottleneck. His father howled, but Iago slashed again, ripping a deep gouge across the other side of the man's face. He proceeded to methodically beat the man almost to death. He stopped only because he could no longer summon the strength to punch. Then he went into the house, where he told his cowering mother and the slaves to leave his father where he was. Iago took two field hands and, carrying the mastiff himself, had a grave dug beneath the old hawthorn tree outside the window of his bedroom.

His father never fully recovered from that beating. He never touched Iago or his wife again, and Iago made it his business to keep the man in fear for his life until the day he died. And he did it without lifting a finger again. It was amazing how a few words could invoke sniveling, pants-wetting fear in a bully.

The carriage stopped, tearing Iago from his memories. He got out at banker W. W. Corcoran's new art gallery and walked north, then east down H Street, keeping to the shadows. He slipped past his destination to stand in the darkness of the portico of St. John's Church. He peered around a column to watch the house across the street. It was rather plain, although large, with steps up to the first floor from the street. When he was satisfied that no one was watching the house, Iago strolled across the street, and at the last moment vaulted over the wooden fence. He entered the house through the back door, went through a mudroom, past a kitchen, to the front. Mrs. Rose Greenhow was waiting for him in her parlor. She was seated beside a lamp, engaged in her embroidery. A wealthy widow, Mrs. Greenhow's charm and dark good looks had assured her a prominent place in Washington Society.

"Ah," she said when she saw him. "You're here.

I've several cipher messages for you. You're sure you weren't followed?"

"My dear Mrs. Greenhow, I wouldn't be here if I had been."

"Where would you be, sir?"

Iago bent and turned down the lamp. "Why, disposing of the body of whoever followed me, of course. Now may I see the ciphers, madame?"

He translated three messages and handed them back to Mrs. Greenhow. The widow immediately threw the papers in the fireplace, and together they watched them burn. As he studied the flames, Iago spoke casually.

"Tell me, Mrs. Greenhow, did you read those messages?"

"Of course not, sir. I know better."

Iago stared at the woman, his eyes expressionless. He decided she was telling the truth. He wouldn't kill her. Besides, her death would create a stir he couldn't afford at the moment. Not if he wanted to be able to slip out of the country unnoticed.

"I understand you have a packet for me," Iago said.

Mrs. Greenhow went to a Federal-style cabinet by a curtained window. Opening one of the drawers, she pressed something inside, and a door swung open in the side of the cabinet. From it she retrieved a polished mahogany cigar box fitted with a shining brass lock. Iago took a small key from his vest pocket, opened the box and lifted the lid half an inch. Mrs. Greenhow didn't bother to look, and busied herself pouring two glasses of sherry. Iago satisfied himself with the contents of the box, locked it and took the sherry glass the widow offered.

Ten minutes later Iago was walking back to his carriage with the box under his arm. It didn't take him long to sight the carriage, but as he headed toward it he heard a bawdy tune being sung, and a well-dressed man lurched around a corner and bumped into him. The box nearly slipped out of his grip.

"Whoa, there, young man."

A cloud of bourbon wafted up Iago's nostrils as the man grabbed him by both shoulders and hung on. He wore a monocle and his hat sat on the back of his head, revealing bushy white side-whiskers. It was old Hannibal Dow, the biggest gossip in Washington Society. Iago's stomach roiled as it always did when faced with drunkenness, another legacy from his father.

"By God, it's you," Hannibal slurred. "Haven' seen you in ages. Where you goin', my boy? Never mind." He wobbled a bit, then stood erect. "What've you got there? Cigars? Didn't think you smoked. An' at this time o' night too. Gimme one, my boy, and do me a good turn and take me home. 'S too far to walk with eight glasses of Queenie O'Brady's finest in my gut."

"I'm afraid I can't."

"Oh, come on, my boy. Be a sporting fella and help me out. Where've you been? The streets are all shut up hereabouts."

Iago made a decision and slipped his hand under the older man's arm. "Oh, just out for a stroll. Let me help you into the carriage." He couldn't have old Dow waking the neighborhood. It was bad luck they'd met so near Mrs. Greenhow's house.

They got in the carriage with some effort, and

Iago rapped on the roof with his cane. The vehicle lurched into motion, and they headed out of town. His companion didn't notice because the shades were still drawn, and by the time he realized it was taking an awfully long time to get to his house, Iago was ready.

"Say," Hannibal said, sticking his face close to Iago's. "Your driver must be lost."

Iago toyed with the silver head of his cane. "Not at all, I'm afraid."

"Huh?"

The silver grip twisted. There was a click, and the sound of metal slipping against metal. Iago grabbed Dow's arm and pulled him close as he slipped the stiletto between the man's ribs, aiming up and straight into the heart. Hannibal grunted; his mouth worked and saliva spilled between his lips. Iago waited for the telltale gurgling gasp before withdrawing the stiletto and wiping it on the dead man's shirt. When the blade was clean, he slipped it back into the cane. Rapping on the roof of the carriage again, he called to his driver.

"I've a desire to see the Potomac by moonlight."

"We're almost there, sir."

Iago set his cane aside and began to empty the drunk's pockets, taking anything that might make the body easy to identify. It would be necessary to see to it that Dow's body wasn't discovered for some time, which meant weighting it and sinking it in the river. A nuisance, but something that could be done successfully given the number of disguised Southern merchant vessels plying the Potomac. Iago collected Hannibal's papers, pocket watch, money and jewelry. These would be sunk in the river as well, but in a different place than the body. The more confusion upon discovery of the corpse the better.

Iago yawned. It was late, and by the time he got back home it would be almost dawn. He would wait to sleep, however. He had much to arrange before he sailed for England.

# CHAPTER SIX

❧❧

THE WIND PICKED up, blowing last fall's dead leaves past Ryder's feet. In the dark sky, silver clouds sailed across the moon, making him squint to see down the alley he'd entered only moments before. Disgruntled at having to leave the ball before he'd cornered the lovely Lady Eva again, he walked carefully over the dusty ground and stopped at the corner of a building. It was so dark, he was having trouble distinguishing structures from one another. He looked at the sky and decided to wait. A few moments later the glowing clouds dimmed and floated majestically out of the path of the moon's light. Ryder's eyes adjusted, and he could see to his right a narrow street at the end of which was a building with a rough, hand-painted sign over its door that read "Beamish and Quick, Purveyors of Fine Conveyances." He happened to know both Beamish and Quick well enough to appreciate the irony of the sign. Both men liked their liquor and were late risers. Right now they were most likely in a saloon drinking themselves into a stupor, which was why he'd chosen their premises as a meeting place. In addition, there were plenty of laborers in this part of the city, and his agents wouldn't attract too much attention should they be seen.

Throughout the walk to Beamish and Quick his thoughts had returned to his failed quest and that annoying, cantankerous little peahen Lady Eva Sparrow. Ignorant and conceited, that's what she was. She'd refused his simple request, locked him in the room, and trotted off to dance with Hamilton, all because he hadn't courted her with pretty compliments and gallantries. Wouldn't listen to him, wouldn't budge from her refusals.

Ryder paused by the door to Beamish and Quick and muttered under his breath, "Confounded, contrary, sour-mouthed woman. No conception of the gravity of things. I wish I could pick her up and drop her down a muddy well."

Reaching over his head, Ryder took a brass key from its hiding place on top of the Beamish and Quick sign and opened the door. He slipped inside and was swallowed in blackness. Blinking, he waited until his vision cleared, aided by high, dirty windows that let in moonlight. He was inside a warehouse that took up almost half a block and was inhabited by decrepit vehicles of all kinds. In front of him sat an ancient landau, a four-wheeled carriage with facing seats and a roof that divided in half and folded down. One seat was missing and the leather roof had holes in it.

Ryder went around the landau and passed several freight wagons with cracked spokes and missing brake handles. He found his way blocked by a stagecoach riddled with bullet holes. From his daylight visits he knew that its doors bore the legend "Butterfield Overland Stage." Rufus Quick had bought the coach cheap in St. Louis and driven it back east thinking he could fix it up and make a profit. Quick had more imagination than sense.

Gazing past an ancient two-wheeled curricle that had lost most of its paint, he saw two wagons and an omnibus. Once he was beyond these Ryder perceived a faint glow coming from behind a brougham cab in the corner. He pursed his lips and whistled softly. Another whistle answered, and Ryder approached the cab. He stepped over the tongue and nodded at the man waiting for him.

Josiah stepped from the shadows into the light cast by a small lamp and stuck his thumbs in his waistband. " 'Bout time. I been signaling for days and days."

"How was I to expect you so quickly? What happened? Did Eastman catch you spying?"

"Naw, I found out something real important and came on."

Ryder sighed. "I'm sure you think so, Josiah, but there's hardly been time for the South to arm herself, much less plan a big campaign."

"Ain't nothing about no campaign, nor no weapons. You just hush up and listen to what I got to say, Mr. Ryder."

Josiah squatted beside the lamp and Ryder did the same.

"At first I tried listening when Mr. Eastman had gentlemen over to talk about the war, but all I ever heard was how they was going to whip the Yankees in a week or two and come home. That and a whole lot of talk about how to pay for guns and such. After a while I was beginning to think old Eastman was going to be a disappointment, but one time I heard him talking to that newspaper fellow, and they was whispering real low. I was bringing coffee for them, and I stopped outside the door. It was open a crack, but I couldn't hear nothing. Then they stopped whispering, like they was through talking secret. That's when Mr. Eastman told the newspaper fellow that the next meeting was Sunday night at old Mr. Erasmus Vickery's place."

"So you went to the Vickery plantation that night?"

"I did. I got real good at sneaking past the overseer's house. I wore dark clothes like you said, and I kept to them oleander bushes. Anyway, I had to wait a powerful long time, way past midnight, but finally they come. Not all at once, but in a trickle, never more 'n two at a time."

"Who was there?"

Josiah shifted his weight so that he was sitting cross-legged and leaned toward Ryder. "Well, there was Mr. Eastman and the newspaper fellow, Mr. Ward. And o' course Mr. Ambrose Vickery was there, but not his pa, who is ailing. Some of them I never seen before. Oh, and there was Mr. Sullivan Cole."

"Go on," Ryder said.

"Well, sir, there was a whole lot of talk about factories and guns and powder and cannons and such. And they was powerful worried about something called production—lemme see, what was it called— production...capacity. Production capacity, and how the South didn't have enough. Nor did it have enough men. But they said they could fix all that if the British would come over and lend a hand."

"Really."

"Yessir, they said they was gonna fix it so the

British would want to help them. One of the gentle-men, one I didn't know, said he knew of only one fella that could to do the fixing."

Ryder drew nearer the lamp and said carefully, "Josiah, what did they mean, fix it so that the British would want to help the South?"

"See? I knew you was going to want to hear about this."

"Please, Josiah!"

"All right. This is how it goes. They reckoned as how they could kill a real important British fella and blame it on abolitionists. Then the British would be so riled up they'd take the South's side and whip the Yankees for them."

"This is very important, Josiah. Who were they planning on killing?"

"Don't know."

"What do you mean, you don't know? You just said—"

"Nobody ever said a name. Not out loud. Once they got to talking about who they was going to kill, they quieted down something fierce, like they was afraid the pictures on the walls was listening."

Standing, Ryder paced in front of Josiah, running his fingers through his hair and cursing.

Josiah watched him anxiously. "The only thing I heard when they was whispering was something about furniture."

"Furniture?"

"Yeah, a cabinet."

Ryder went still. "A cabinet. The cabinet? Dear God, they're going to assassinate a member of the British cabinet!"

"What's that?"

"The cabinet is made up of gentlemen chosen to help the prime minister rule the country."

"Well, they said it wouldn't be too hard to stir up some of those abolitionists that have gone over there to England to tell folks how awful the South is. Said the abolitionists are always spewing hellfire and talking crazy anyway, and they're all fired up about Britain being so partial to the South that it should be easy to fix it so it looks like one of 'em got so crazy mad he shot somebody."

"Oh, dear God." Ryder sank to his heels and pressed his palms against his face. He looked up suddenly. "Tell me you know when, Josiah, please."

"Oh, yeah. I forgot. Mr. Vickery said he'd worked it out that the killing should take place around the third week of June."

"But that's less than two months from now."

Josiah nodded rapidly. "That's why I came ahead. I found me a wonderful lady who—"

"You're sure you didn't hear who it was they plan to kill?" Ryder asked.

"I would have remembered that." Josiah looked insulted.

"Of course you would. Sorry. I'm just worried. If we don't know who the victim is . . ." Ryder paused and lifted his head. He'd heard something, a small sound that didn't belong in the warehouse. Signaling for Josiah to remain calm, he said, "Tell me the whole thing again from the beginning."

While Josiah talked, Ryder slipped into the shadows between a couple of buckboards and circled the old cab where the ex-slave remained. His quarry was lurking behind a wagon, and from the bell-shaped skirt and diminutive size, he could guess who it was. What in hell was she doing here? She'd probably heard everything, damn it. Ryder crept up behind Lady Eva Sparrow. Relishing his advantage, he slipped a hand over her mouth while snaking an arm around her waist and lifting her.

As he'd expected, she screamed into his hand and began to writhe in his arms. Abruptly he realized his mistake. Eva's hips ground against him, and even through the thickness of the gown and petticoat he felt the firmness of her flesh. Ryder gasped and gritted his teeth to prevent himself from getting into a state no woman could mistake. He failed. Without warning his captive twisted in his arms, glimpsed him and stopped struggling. Her body settled against his, and she looked up at him with relief that rapidly turned to outrage. Her eyes snapped with anger, and to his embarrassment, her wrath whetted his already aroused state.

"Damn."

Lady Eva uttered a wordless hiss in response.

Not daring to look into her eyes again, Ryder lifted Eva over his hip and carried her to where Josiah waited. The ex-slave was large-eyed and incredulous. Ryder was furious with himself and determined not to reveal his humiliating lack of control. Irrationally, he blamed the lady for his state and dumped her on the floor. She landed in a mountain of petticoats and skirts, gasping. Lady Eva blew several auburn curls out of her face and glowered at him.

"This is beyond everything, Mr. Drake. How dare you lay hands upon me?"

Perhaps she hadn't noticed his physical response. Ryder folded his arms and glared at her. "How dare you spy on me?"

"I was not spying. It appears that you are the spy." When he didn't reply, she blushed and continued.

"I—I was trying to speak with you, and you left before I could. So I followed you. How was I to know you were going to some clandestine meeting?"

"Miss Eva?"

Lady Eva glanced up as Josiah approached and smiled ruefully. "Hello, Josiah."

"Let me help you, Miss Eva." Josiah offered the lady his hand and helped her get to her feet.

Ryder looked from one to the other. "You two have met?"

"Yessir," Josiah said with a beatific smile. "This here is the lady I tried to tell you about. She helped me get out of Natchez and come to Washington. She bought me, and then she freed me. She went to a powerful lot of trouble to fool Miz Eastman. Miss Eva is a saint sent by the Lord to help us."

Studying the intruder in astonishment, Ryder said, "A saint, is she?" He shook his head. "Well, I must compliment you, Saint Eva, on your ingenious disguise. I never would have suspected you to be a servant of the Almighty."

"This is hardly the time for levity, Mr. Drake."

"No," Ryder snapped. "I should arrest you and have you deported before you can blather what you heard tonight to your friends."

Lady Eva sighed in an irritated manner as she tucked stray curls into place and dusted her skirts. "Don't be absurd. It's not astonishing that we both know the Eastmans, given how small Southern High Society is. So you're going to sit here with me and listen to Josiah, and then I am going to help you figure out what to do."

"Is that so?"

"Yes, it is. And then I shall go home and introduce you to my uncle Adolphus."

Ryder was having a hard time keeping up with the changing situation, but at least this demented conversation was taking his mind off Lady Eva's body. He watched her tug at her gloves and settle the mantle she wore straight on her shoulders. He opened his mouth, but she interrupted him.

"I was going to tell you I'd changed my mind about helping, Mr. Drake, so there's no point in blustering just because I overheard you. You would have had to tell me about this dreadful plot anyway."

Desire vanished, and one of the muscles in Ryder's jaw began to twitch. This was just what he'd feared once he approached Lady Eva—interference. But if he objected to letting her stay now, she might change her mind again about introducing him to her uncle. He couldn't afford to ruin his chances because of a woman's fit of pique. Confound her, she knew all this and was enjoying his predicament. He could tell by that little smirk that curled her lips into a china doll smile.

Gritting his teeth, he cleared his throat. "I'm most grateful that you've changed your mind, Lady Eva, but you needn't bother with these details. It's chilly, and this is no place for a lady. Please allow me to escort you back to the ball. Josiah can come with us, if you like."

"Indeed not, sir. I'm not the least chilly, and Josiah should remain as inconspicuous as possible." Lady Eva found an old box, upended it and sat down. "Continue, please, Josiah."

Josiah looked from Lady Eva to Ryder. Drake glared at her, then gave in since he had little choice. He nodded at the young man. Soon both of them were huddled near Lady Eva, and Josiah's soft voice continued its tale in the dark warehouse, among the skeletons of landaus, phaetons and stagecoaches.

There was no London when Caesar invaded the British isles in 55 B.C. The river Thames flowed its sinuous way through southeast England's verdant lands until its estuary emptied into the North Sea. By 60 B.C., however, the Romans had established Londinium, a place of fortified camps protecting a bridge across the river, where before there had been only isolated homesteads. Under Roman rule Londinium grew into a port and commercial center, the capital of the province of Britannia. From this small town perched on the north bank of the Thames grew the mighty heart of the British empire.

Ryder Drake arrived in a very different place than the bucolic, forested riverbanks of Roman times. The city that greeted him belched Newcastle coal. It had expanded to well over three million inhabitants, and the rapid growth had strained the city's resources so that the masses of poor suffered consumption, dysentery, smallpox, typhus and dropsy. London might sport the world's busiest port and an ancient seat of government in a sprawling empire, but it also contained the likes of Spitalfields, Clerkenwell and Whitechapel. Ridden with polluted tenements, these districts made Washington's muddy, cow-trodden streets seem a paradise.

At the moment Ryder was far from the slums of the East End. He was sitting in the drawing room of Tennyson Place, one of the few houses in London that still boasted its own grounds. Situated near Hyde and Green Parks, Tennyson Place was close to Grosvenor Square. The house was a neoclassical stone marvel including Corinthian columns and exquisite plasterwork by Robert Adam. Ryder was in the garden drawing room, two walls of which consisted of twelve-foot glass doors set in recesses with rounded-arch tops. These looked out on gardens filled with beds of roses, ancient oaks and gravel paths lined with Roman and Greek statuary.

Leaning back in his white and gold chair upholstered in royal blue velvet, Ryder reflected on the whirl of activity that had brought him here. After he'd talked to Josiah and Eva that night at Beamish and Quick's, he'd checked his other sources and conferred with Alan Pinkerton. Whispers of the plot to involve Britain in the war had reached the agent too, but unlike Ryder he had nothing definite. They informed the president, who agreed that Ryder should go to London. Lady Eva left ahead of Ryder. The plan was for her to tell her uncle that she'd invited an Anglo-American gentleman to be a houseguest for a few weeks. Since Drake's family was originally English, her friendship with him wouldn't seem so out of the ordinary to her relatives. Ryder took several of Pinkerton's men with him and set sail for England. He docked on the morning of May 7, frustrated at the slowness of ship passage and anxious to begin tracking his quarry, whoever that might be.

Upon his arrival at Tennyson House, Drake had been met by a fish-eyed butler with the improbable name of Mr. Tilt, who had escorted him to the garden drawing room. It hadn't been long since Ryder had settled into his gilt and velvet chair, but he was already agitated. Every moment wasted was a moment the enemy had free to plan his attack.

He hadn't been back to London, except for brief trips, in years, even though he'd inherited the Drake barony from his father. He rarely thought about the fact that he was Lord Drake. After his father's death he had visited the estate, a half-ruined Elizabethan house in Sussex surrounded by farmland. The estate was entailed, and there was nothing he could do but maintain it as best he could. Ryder had sold the personal property Simon Drake had left and applied the funds to help free the family slaves in Virginia. These actions he kept from his mother, for she would have objected stridently. Once the business was done, he had informed his mother. Hysterics of monumental proportions had ensued, but when Ryder pointed out that he'd established a trust that would keep her in style, Felicita had quieted.

Since then he'd seen little of his mother. One of the advantages of living in Texas was its distance from Felicita. He could go for months without thinking about her. That is, if she didn't write to him. When she did, he had a habit of leaving the letters unopened for weeks. If he was lucky, the missives got lost while he was on a trail ride or riding fence lines. When he did read her letters it was always a shock to find her the same as she'd always been. Somehow, part of him expected her character to improve over time, expected her to mature. Instead he read about how difficult it was to go about Charleston in a small carriage and how kind people were to take her in their larger vehicles.

Ryder growled and thrust himself out of his chair. He shouldn't have begun to think about his mother. He only grew angry and miserable, and he needed his composure for the coming meeting with Lord Adolphus Tennyson. He wished he could dispense with these formalities, but the English didn't take to American plain speaking. Cutting right to the point would only startle Lord Adolphus and make him skeptical. Ryder had to control his impatience. He'd be better off thinking of Lady Eva. After finding her spying on him, he'd calmed his anger enough to realize how generous it was of her to overcome her feelings and retract her refusal to help him. The lady had more sense than he had given her credit for. She was sympathetic to the cause of abolition as well. Ryder would never forget his consternation upon hearing that it was she who had helped Josiah get away from Natchez.

He doubted Lady Eva realized the consequences of her generosity. Had she been caught, she would have been arrested and possibly brought to trial. Her rank and connections might have saved her eventually, but Ryder wasn't certain, given the rabid hostility of some Southern politicians. Josiah would have suffered the most, of course. Ryder also doubted that Lady Eva understood the true seriousness of the situation in the U.S. Still, she had been willing to help, and that was most important. Given the shortness of time, she was going to approach her uncle about Ryder's mission this evening. Before that, Ryder wanted to thank her once again, for her role in this affair would end tonight. Even Lady Eva would have to withdraw once he and her uncle began to discuss so grave a matter as political assassination. He'd still be able to see her, and he found he looked forward to that with more excitement than he'd felt about a woman in a long time.

Ryder wandered over to look at the garden through one of the glass doors and turned when he heard another door open. A tiny terrier with an unruly mop of fur shot into the room, saw Ryder and skidded to a stop on the marble floor. It immediately pointed its nose at the ceiling and barked as a woman entered the room. The dog's cries echoed noisily off the walls while its owner shushed it to no avail. The lady must have been in her seventies at least, for her face and hands were a web of wrinkles. Dark brown hair did little to alter this impression, and Ryder assumed that the corkscrew curls that framed her face were part of a wig. The lady was as thin as a lamppost and wore a gown that had been fashionable over twenty years ago. Her skirt stood out from her body due to at least half a dozen heavy petticoats, while her gown sported enormous puffed sleeves with frilled epaulettes.

The lady was staring at him through a pair of wire-framed spectacles that she held on her nose. The dog scampered around its mistress and barked even louder from behind her skirts. Ryder winced as he bowed to the lady.

"I don't know you, young man. Who are you?"

"I am Ryder Drake, a guest of Lady Eva's, ma'am."

"Don't just stand there," the lady said. "Open the door for Juliette."

Ryder frowned. "Juliette?"

"The dog, young man. She wants to go into the garden. Where are your wits?"

Feeling as if he'd missed half of a conversation, Ryder opened one of the glass doors to let the dog scramble outside. He shut the door and found the elderly lady at his elbow.

"I am Lady Eva's great-aunt, Lettice Tennyson Biddulph, widow of Sir Wilbur Knatchbull Biddulph. Perhaps you've heard of him?"

"I'm sorry, no."

"Well, you should have." The lady didn't elaborate. She looked him up and down, then extended her hand to be kissed. "You may call me Lady Biddulph, young man, and I shall call you Bartholomew."

Ryder blinked and hesitated. "If you wish, my lady, but my name is Ryder."

"Oh, is it? Then why did you tell me it was Bartholomew?"

Speechless, Ryder stared at Lady Biddulph, who stared back at him.

"You're quite handsome, young man. Is my little Eva going to marry you?"

Ryder opened his mouth as Eva herself came into the drawing room with an older man. He felt his pulse quicken at the sight of her. Her hair and eyes gleamed in the sunlight, and she walked with the quick, sure step that reminded him of a dancer. To his surprise, his mouth was dry, and he had no idea what to say to her. By God, he couldn't be tongue-tied! Luckily Lady Eva saved him from having to speak.

"Oh, Aunt, I didn't know you'd come down."

"Eva, did you know there's a young man here? He's almost as handsome as Sir Wilbur was, but he's rather dim-witted. I wouldn't marry him if I were you. Your children would be slow."

Ryder stared at Lady Eva in alarm, but she appeared to consider what Lady Biddulph said and made a grave reply.

"You're right, of course, Aunt. I shan't marry him."

"Good. If you need me I shall be in the garden with Juliette."

Ryder hastened to open the glass door for Lady Biddulph, who paused to inspect him again before she left.

"Perhaps I know of a girl more suited to you,

Bartholomew. I shall give the matter my consideration."

Ryder found his tongue. "You're very kind, my lady."

When the old lady was gone Eva introduced him to Lord Adolphus Tennyson. The older man offered his hand, and Ryder shook it, noting his firm grip and bright gaze.

"I must give you my thanks, Mr. Drake, for being so considerate of my aunt. She was born ten years before the turn of the century and sometimes is a bit hazy of mind."

"I understand, my lord."

Adolphus Tennyson had a beneficent expression in his eyes. Of modest height and scarce hair, he had a round face and slight potbelly expertly disguised by a Bond Street tailor. What little hair he had marched around his skull in a half circle in wisps of auburn and gray. Whenever his glance fell on Eva he would smile fondly. It was evident to Ryder that Lady Eva returned her uncle's affection. He took it as further proof of her good-hearted nature.

Mr. Tilt entered with tea and coffee, and Lady Eva proceeded to guide the conversation along neutral paths. Ryder was asked about his ranch in Texas and about his family. Lord Adolphus talked of his experiences in the Crimean War and promised to introduce Ryder to several gentlemen at his club. Thus his initial meeting with Lord Adolphus was conducted in a typically stately English manner.

"So you're here to take care of the business of your estate," Lord Adolphus said to Ryder.

Ryder glanced at Eva, who nodded her encouragement. "Yes, my lord. My manager has been writing for several months that my presence is needed. I will meet him here in London at my solicitor's."

"I see," his host said with a confused look.

Eva hastened to add, "As an American, Mr. Drake doesn't use his title, Uncle."

"Ah." Lord Adolphus rose, as did Ryder. "I hope the press of business isn't so great that it will keep you from allowing me to introduce you about town, Mr. Drake."

"I would be honored."

"Good." Lord Adolphus went to a glass door through which Lady Biddulph could be seen trying to lift Juliette in her arms. "If you will excuse me, I must help my aunt." He went outside, leaving the door open. "Oh, and perhaps after dinner this evening you and my niece will tell my why you're really here, Mr. Drake."

# CHAPTER SEVEN

❧

EVA SAT IN Uncle Adolphus' study and divided her attention between her uncle, Mr. Drake and the terrier Juliette. Mr. Drake was talking gravely with Lord Adolphus, his dark, brooding features giving drama to his words. Eva tried to give him her full attention, but Juliette needed watching, as she tended to attack pillows and cushions if she became bored. Mr. Drake was sitting near Juliette. His hand slipped down to fondle the terrier's short, flipped-over ears, and Juliette rubbed her face against his fingers. Eva was surprised, for the dog didn't take to strange men easily. She was even more surprised that the stern Mr. Drake seemed not to realize how revealing of his character his attentions to Juliette were. Eva watched his long fingers tangle in the dog's fur. A sudden image flashed into her mind—of those strong fingers gripping her waist in the dark in Beamish and Quick's, of their bodies pressed tightly together. She could feel her face grow hot and quickly forced herself to attend to the conversation.

"I quite understand your concern, Mr. Drake," Lord Adolphus was saying. He turned in his leather wingback chair and eyed the end of his cigar. "Lord Palmerston definitely leans toward the Southern states in his sympathies. Simple economics, young man. Our mills need cotton, and the South supplies it. Still, the prime minister is unlikely to enter into the fray, you know. He's impulsive, but he won't take Britain to war over cotton."

Eva rose and went over to her uncle. "I agree, but you don't know the whole story, Uncle. Tell him, Mr. Drake."

Ryder Drake described the events at Beamish and Quick's in detail. As he talked, Adolphus Tennyson's brows drew together. When his guest described the assassination plot, Lord Adolphus leaned forward, his expression blank with shock. After Drake finished there was silence, except for the crackle of the fire and little snorts from Juliette, who had fallen asleep.

"I don't understand the reasoning behind this plot," Adolphus said at last. "These Southerners hope to blame this assassination on abolitionists? But I've never thought of these people as violent."

"Then you haven't heard of the incident involving Mr. John Brown," Drake replied.

Adolphus leaned back, recognition plain in his face. "Dear God."

"The reasoning is somewhat convoluted, but it works," Drake said. "A Southern agent will carry out the assassination, but he will see to it that all the evidence of the crime points to an abolitionist. There are many of them here in London working for the North, trying to stir sympathy among those in power. The plot is intended to make it seem that the abolitionists greatly fear that the cabinet favors the South. A lot of people already think their fanaticism smacks of lunacy anyway, so it wouldn't be hard to make it seem that one or two of them went mad and killed a minister who was siding with the very people they believe are so evil. Britain will blame the mad Northern abolitionists and do what the plot is designed to make them do—declare war on the United States."

Eva put her hand on her uncle's sleeve. "I've been to the South. I know how dedicated her people are. Not just the rich planters, Uncle, but the merchants, the farmers, the blacksmiths, all of them. They're determined to be free of the Union, and once the North invades their states, they will fight to the last man and woman."

"And they know they're outnumbered and lack munitions," Drake added. "These men from Natchez are prepared to even the odds, although most Southerners think they'll beat the North in one or two battles simply because their cause is just and they're better fighters."

Adolphus nodded. "I understand, Mr. Drake, but there's a problem. I can hardly go to the prime minister with this wild tale, based on the word of one slave."

"Oh, Uncle." Eva pressed his arm. "I can vouch for Josiah, and so can Mr. Drake. You may depend upon Josiah's account. And he's not a slave anymore. He's a free man who works as an agent of the United States government, just as Mr. Drake does." She could see skepticism in her uncle's eyes.

"In any case, Mr. Drake, you don't even know who the intended victim is or the identity of the assassin."

Drake moved to the chair opposite Tennyson. "I

believe that the agent who goes by the code name Iago is the only man employed by the Confederates who is experienced enough to carry out such a plot, my lord. I've heard rumors that Iago is headed for England. He might already be here."

"And who is this Iago?"

Drake shook his head. "No one knows that."

"Then it's as I said. You don't know who is the target, or who is the assassin."

Eva folded her arms across her chest and stared at Lord Tennyson. "Now, Uncle, are you saying you won't help? Are you going to ignore Mr. Drake's pleas and wait for these people to strike? What will you say then? 'Oh, I say, you were right after all, old man. So sorry, Mr. Dead Cabinet Member, do forgive me, won't you?' Really, Uncle."

Tennyson held up his hands in protest. "No, no, of course not, my dear. But you must admit the whole tale is fantastical."

"If you'd been to any of the Southern states you wouldn't find it fantastical at all. Shall I repeat some of the stories I told you about slavery?"

"Absolutely not, my dear." Adolphus glanced at Drake. "My niece has been altogether too vivid in her descriptions of the suffering of slaves, sir."

Drake gave Eva a bow and then let his gaze linger on her. "Indeed, my lord. Lady Eva has a gentle heart and fierce courage. I am in her debt."

Eva stared at Drake in disbelief.

Sighing, Adolphus rose, took Eva's hand and patted it. "You've convinced me, my dear." He began to guide Eva out of the study. "Mr. Drake and I will discuss what's to be done. Thank you for your efforts."

Eva hung back, realizing that Uncle Adolphus was dismissing her. "Wait. There's much more to do."

"Yes, my dear. We'll see to it."

Drake smiled at her in gratitude. "Good night, Lady Eva. I won't forget your kindness."

Eva dragged her hand free and sidled around her uncle. She planted herself in his wingback chair before either man could object.

"You're not getting rid of me, Uncle. You're going to need my help."

"Now, Eva, this is a serious matter and it's not your place to interfere."

Eva glowered at him. "I've already interfered. If I hadn't interfered you wouldn't know anything about this cursed plot. Without me, Josiah would still be in Natchez trying to get to Mr. Drake with his information. Without me, nothing would have gotten done in time, and time is what we have the least of. Remember, gentlemen, how close the third week of June is, and that's the assassin's deadline."

"My lady," Drake said. "I am most conscious of your efforts on behalf of my country, but your part is over now. Action and risk are the duties of gentlemen. Neither I nor Lord Tennyson would see you exposed to any peril."

Eva set her jaw. "Let me point out a few things you brave gentlemen seem to have forgotten." She began to count on her fingers. "One, you have no reason to assume Iago is a man. Two, most of the Southerners who have been sent to London have brought their wives and go about in Society so as to pursue their aims. Thus I am in a position to invite many of your suspects to this house for you to inspect. And three, I refuse to be relegated to knitting and making calls, so you might as well accept my help. I think both of you know the strength of my determination. Think about it a moment and save me the trouble of demonstrating my resolve yet again."

Adolphus rolled his eyes and turned to Drake. "Unfortunately, she's right, Drake."

"But, sir, it's not fitting, and she's capable of getting herself into a great deal of trouble. Why, back in Washington—"

"I know, young man. I could tell you tales of her escapades in Egypt that would turn your liver white. Believe me, she's not going to go away, so you'd better accept her help with good grace. Otherwise she'll make us both damned uncomfortable."

Eva watched Drake wrestle with his desire to get rid of her. His eyes glittered in the firelight, and he turned them on her so that she felt bathed in angry green flames. He was furious. Well, he would just have to overcome his anger. She had no intention of allowing him to intimidate her with his dark fury and menacing stares.

Lifting her chin, she locked gazes with him. She felt a tingling jolt, for something passed between them that had nothing to do with their current argument. She had never felt anything like it—her body seemed beset with crazy sensations. Prickling, tingling breathlessness and heat assaulted her, and she felt an almost irresistible urge to go to Drake and touch him. Drake's eyes widened as if in alarm, and he broke the link between them by looking away. Eva swallowed hard and tried to dismiss the moment. It had been so brief. She'd imagined that something had passed between them. Ryder Drake possessed a charm and an almost magical appeal of which he seemed unaware. It was all her imagination, and it was best she forget about it.

Drake turned to Lord Adolphus. "Very well, my

lord. But I must state my objections to allowing a lady to become involved in such serious business. Granted, Lady Eva has great spirit, but I am trying to protect my country from destruction. She has no experience in government affairs, and she could endanger herself and anyone with her."

"I will not!" All right, Ryder Drake had beautiful green eyes and the body of Michelangelo's David, but he was still a bully.

Lord Adolphus waved a hand. "I see your point, my boy, but Eva will be involved mostly in social aspects, inviting people to dinners and balls. The family has wanted her to go about in Society for years, and that's what she'll be doing. Besides, if she doesn't do this, you won't be able to attend our functions. The ladies, dear boy, control the guest lists. Your Southern spy is going to have to move about more in Society to do what he wants, and to move about in Society, one must have a sponsor. Lady Eva is your sponsor, Drake. There's no one else."

Eva couldn't help smiling at Drake, who glared back at her in impotent vexation. She would help prevent an assassination, but she would also receive the added benefit of causing discomfort to Mr. Ryder Drake.

Far from Tennyson House, in the shadow of St. Paul's Cathedral, lay the insalubrious poor districts of London. These included places like Spitalfields, a damp district of broken drains, decayed foundations and rotting houses. Near the Spitalfields workhouse festered a nightman's yard that held a pile of dung and other garbage the size of a large house. Close by the nightman's yard lay tenements interspersed with narrow, filthy streets and broken sewers littered with the bodies of dead cats and dogs. People slept twenty, thirty to a room in the rookeries, in beds made of dirty rags. In the stinking outhouses, broken pipes and sluggish streams lurked typhoid, dysentery and cholera.

In the St. Giles district an unlucky soul who wandered into the area quickly found himself surrounded by pale, scowling denizens with brutal eyes and filth-infested rags for garments. If he was allowed to live, he might find a hole in a wall of rotting timbers into which he might step. Climbing down a rickety flight of stairs would bring him into a cellar inhabited by various pickpockets, burglars and forgers. It was in one of these choice London districts that Iago had chosen his headquarters, for there among the dregs of the English classes he could work without fear of being discovered.

Iago had been in London for over a week, time enough to rent his rooms from a scrawny woman named Mrs. Growler. She was always clad in musty black and rejoiced in being the rent collector for a section of a rookery called Pomary Church. Her hair was iron gray, her skin sallow and her teeth stained brown. She wore a dirty white house cap and a ring of rusting keys that jingled from a chain on her belt. The clank of those keys preceded her wherever she went. Woe betided anyone who was late with the rent, for Mrs. Growler had unpleasant ways by which to encourage punctuality.

Now Iago walked down an alley, stepping carefully over the body of an old man who lay snoring on the ground with his face resting in a puddle of filthy rainwater. Overhead, a bridge constructed of scrap wood led from Pomary Church to another tenement block. Mrs. Growler kept order in Pomary Church by hiring a numerous brood of cutthroat sons, nephews and grandsons, who guarded either end of the tenement. The two on the bridge watched Iago with murder-hardened eyes but let him pass unmolested, which was fortunate for them.

Iago entered Pomary Church but didn't stop to bid Mrs. Growler good day even though she was sitting in a decrepit rocker counting rent money.

"Luvely day, innit, Mr. Peach." Mrs. Growler addressed him by the name Iago had taken when he went to the East End. Iago ignored her, and she continued to count her coins.

He climbed down to the cellar to reach a hole under the stairs. From this hole he wound through a maze of passages, runways, traps and bolt-holes that led him to another stair and then to his apartment on the third floor. Here the holes in the floor and walls had been patched. All the windows had been blocked.

But Iago had been busy making his lair comfortable. Crimson velvet hangings covered ancient gray walls. A Turkish carpet muffled his footsteps. A few pieces of mahogany furniture of ornate design graced the rooms, and the dark crimson upholstery matched the curtains. There was a chaise longue and a highback chair set before a small table on which rested an onyx writing set. Against the wall was a bookcase, while beyond the first room lay one in which stood a four-poster bed with a well-stuffed mattress.

In a wardrobe, which was fitted with a lock, resided Iago's professional tool kit—revolvers, a couple of specially made rifles, various knives and stilettos, wire used for garroting and an apothecary's box containing obscure poisons and other drugs. Also locked in the wardrobe were a case of theater cosmetics and a box containing wigs, beards and mustaches as well as hair dye. Iago had sailed from America with almost everything he would need to accomplish his task. Perhaps the most important item in the wardrobe, to Iago, was the box of cigars. These were custom made for him in South Carolina—a blend of ingredients that only he and his cigar maker knew.

Keeping all this opulence in such a place would ordinarily guarantee its disappearance, but Pomary Church had an evil reputation even among the most vile of London's criminal set. Those who caused trouble there ended up floating facedown in the Thames. Iago employed several of Mrs. Growler's young thugs to keep watch over his rooms. There had been four guards, but one had tried to steal from Iago. He was now at home nursing the bloody hole where his ear used to be. Mrs. Growler was furious with him for getting caught.

Iago took off his coat, stoked a fire and lit a lamp. Sitting down at the writing table, he pulled from his frock coat pocket several engraved invitations and spread them on the polished wood. He produced an appointment book, in which he began to enter his engagements. Stopping to pour a snifter of brandy, he savored the smoky flavor.

Setting the brandy aside, Iago pressed one of the acanthus leaves carved into the side of the table. A hidden compartment clicked open, and he withdrew a letter in cipher he had received from an associate in Washington. The letter had been an unpleasant surprise, for it named Ryder Drake as one of Lincoln's intelligence agents. It foretold the arrival of Drake in

London, and Iago had gone to the docks to observe his enemy disembarking. That Drake was an agent was disappointing as well as surprising, and Iago didn't like surprises. Who would have thought the Unionists would have got wind of his plans so soon? Certainly none of his colleagues back in Richmond or Natchez would have suspected Lincoln's men of being so efficient. Yet Drake was here scurrying about London with his men, asking inconvenient questions, searching ships' passenger lists, seeking out rabid abolitionist groups.

Iago stared through the brandy snifter at the fire, watching amber flames dance. Surprise and anger had faded, and now he was amused. Drake had chosen his own fate, regrettable as it was. In this fight, scruples about hurting admirable men had to be set aside. In any event, Drake was a worthy opponent. This mission was going to be far more entertaining than Iago had thought. It would be a test of skill— Southern gentleman against turncoat Unionist, professional against amateur. There was no doubt of the outcome. The most intelligent one, the most ruthless and the one with the most courage to do what had to be done without regard to morals would win. It would relieve the tedium to design a few false leads and distractions to keep Drake off balance and send him haring off in the wrong direction after supposed victims. By the time he was finished with Drake, he would be so misled Iago would be free to pursue his real quarry at his leisure.

Humming to himself, Iago returned to his invitations. Once his business in London was finished, he would have to arrange a small accident. It wouldn't do to allow Drake to return to America to meddle further in the affairs of the Confederacy. No, far better that his adversary end up stabbed to death in a brawl in some Whitechapel gin shop over the favors of a sailor's tart.

He would see to it as soon as his primary business was concluded. To bring his opponent to an untimely end before that might attract undue attention, and Iago didn't want to make Lord Adolphus Tennyson any more suspicious than he already was. In any case, it would be amusing to watch Drake's antics in the next weeks, futile as they would prove to be.

# CHAPTER EIGHT

RYDER DRAKE GUIDED his horse around a carriage drawn by matched grays. Hyde Park was crowded this morning with fancy carriages, riders like himself and the Tennysons, who rode on either side of him, and countless pedestrians. Fashionable London was on parade. Drake didn't know how he was going to tolerate much more of it.

He'd been in London for three days, three days in meetings Lord Adolphus had arranged with the prime minister and Lord John Russell, the foreign minister, and other members of the British cabinet. Convincing those gentlemen of the threat posed by Iago had proved to be harder than he'd imagined. In the end Lord Palmerston had acquiesced to Drake's plan of protection only as a favor to Tennyson, and then only through the end of June. Drake didn't care how he got permission to set guards around the ministers, so long as they complied. Scotland Yard was brought in to supply the men, who were ordered to be as unobtrusive as possible in order to avoid public exposure. If the press were to discover Drake's mission there would be a political scandal, and relations between the United States and Britain would suffer even more than they already had. The South would accuse Lincoln of some fantastical plot to discredit the Confederacy, and Britain might believe such claims.

The risk of exposure meant that while his men roamed the docks of London inspecting passenger lists for likely Southern spies, Drake was stuck in the midst of Society, trying to discover the identity of the assassin Iago.

This was because of the intricate nature of the Southern plot. Ordinarily a killer could simply approach a minister leaving a building, pull a pistol and shoot, but Iago didn't want to be seen or traced to the murder. He wanted to frame someone else for it. This more complicated approach required a tightly controlled plan in which the real assassin remained unknown. It also demanded detailed knowledge of the victim's habits and routine, which could best be gained by moving in the circles frequented by the queen's ministers.

In no time at all fashionable London had sucked Ryder into its vortex. Because of Lady Eva's efforts on his behalf his life seemed to consist of paying endless calls, making certain he was seen at the proper places, like here on Rotten Row in Hyde Park, at the correct time and attending interminable dinners and balls. So far he'd met half a dozen social paragons, including Lord and Lady Palmerston, two dukes and their duchesses, several earls and their countesses and no end of lords and their ladies. All these introductions meant that he would be included in invitations to all the best gatherings along with Lady Eva and her uncle. Since Iago was an American, Drake would have to sort through those of his fellow countrymen considered socially acceptable by the British. Hopefully this group would be small.

Once, he'd thought hell would resemble a life led in High Society in the South. Now he realized no torture could compare with an afternoon spent making calls in London. One drove in a smartly fitted carriage to the residence of Lord and Lady Trumpet, presented oneself to a butler, who conducted one to a drawing room, where one sat on uncomfortable furniture. One passed precisely fifteen minutes in sparkling conversation on acceptable topics—the weather, hunting or shooting, the latest speech in Parliament, the lovely qualities of the Honorable Miss Do-Nothing or the undoubtedly fine character of the Earl of Insomnia. After a sip of tea one took one's leave and drove on to the next town house to repeat the whole process over again. By the end of an afternoon like this Drake longed for a hard day in the saddle on the Texas range—rattlesnakes, bull nettle and festering heat notwithstanding.

On a call yesterday just when Drake thought he would scream from boredom he had glanced at Lady Eva. She had been listening to her uncle's conversation with Lady Palmerston, and as he had gazed at her, he had realized she wasn't listening at all. Her eyes had grown unfocused, and she appeared to be daydreaming. Suddenly she had lifted her teacup to her lips, and Drake had watched her hide a yawn as big as the one he'd just stifled. She had blinked hard several times, and Drake had been certain she was trying not to fall asleep.

Just then she had met Drake's gaze, flushed red and looked away like a guilty child. For the first time

Drake had really understood that Eva Sparrow might dislike the social whirl as much as he did. He supposed he would have known that if he'd thought about it. After all, she had spent a great deal of time away from home in strange places like Egypt and Constantinople. Hardly the occupation of a lady enamored of Society. It was clear that Lady Eva wasn't as much like these other fashionable ladies as he'd assumed.

Drake glanced at his hostess. She was riding beside him on her favorite Arabian, a shapely young gelding named Xenophon. Adolphus Tennyson had moved his horse beside his niece. Her severely tailored riding habit set off her weathered-copper hair and her figure. He found it hard to believe she was a widowed woman. She looked more of an age with the young ladies who swept through the balls and musicales of London in their first Season.

He was beginning to realize that Eva Sparrow was a tiny bundle of contradictions. She had the figure of a delicate china doll and the smooth skin to match, yet she had no fear of allowing herself to gain a few muscles from exercise or a little color to her complexion from exposure to the elements. Most women would avoid both in order to appear as delicate as possible. That was the problem: Eva looked the epitome of English gentility, but she acted like an American cavalry officer. She was unpredictable when he needed her to be consistent and stubborn when he desperately wanted her to follow his orders. He dreamed of her eyes crinkled at the corners from a smile when he shouldn't be dreaming about her at all. Damn, damn, damn.

Drake's horse tossed its head, drawing his attention to his surroundings. He pulled on his reins when Lady Eva stopped to greet two ladies in a carriage. As he and Lord Adolphus tipped their hats, two men rode up calling Ryder's name.

"There, Locke, I told you he was in town." Lucian Bedford Forrest and Hamilton Locke joined them. Drake gaped at them, then recovered and introduced his cousin and Forrest to Lord Adolphus.

"What are you two doing here?" he demanded.

Locke was grinning at him. "I, dear cousin, have been appointed by Secretary Seward to represent the antislavery cause to the British. I'm making speeches all over—Lancastershire, Devonshire, Yorkshire, here in London. You must come hear me."

"Why didn't you tell me you were coming to England?" Drake asked.

"The secretary asked me at the last moment, and when I tried to find you to tell you, you'd gone off somewhere without telling anyone. How was I to know you'd be here?"

"True, Drake," said Lucian. "You didn't tell anyone where you were going. Whereas I told everyone my plans."

"I'm afraid your friend's neglect is my fault, gentlemen." Lord Adolphus tipped his hat. "I've kept Mr. Drake too busy to write letters to his friends, even if he'd known you were here."

"Oh, Drake never tells anyone anything," Lucian said with a smile. "For example, he hasn't told us why he's come to England."

"Business," Drake snapped. "My father's estates."

"And you came over here now, with all that's going on at home?" Locke asked, eyeing him. "I thought you'd be joining the army or at least helping with the war effort."

"That's just it," Ryder said. "With war coming, I

must make sure my affairs are in order over here, legal arrangements and such."

"Still, you could have told us," Lucian said with a flick of his whip. "But we're all here now. I suppose we'll see you about."

"Of course. I have the honor of being Lord Adolphus' guest at Tennyson House. Lady Eva, you remember my cousin Hamilton and Lucian Bedford Forrest."

Forrest and Locke exchanged greetings with Lady Eva and obtained invitations to the ball she was giving a week hence. All the while Drake chafed under the delay. He needed to circulate so that he could meet suspects, and so far he hadn't met one.

Seething with impatience, he turned to Lady Eva. "We're not making any progress. There are too many people here. I told you this was a waste of time."

"Don't be hasty, sir." Eva glanced at him with raised eyebrows. "If you'll look ahead there, you'll see something of interest."

Looking in the direction she indicated, Drake saw that Lucian had stopped beside a grand open landau in which the prime minister was riding. A liveried driver and footman dressed in forest green and gold sat behind four matched bays. Henry John Temple, Viscount Palmerston, had been born in 1784, the son of an Irish peer. Experienced in foreign affairs, he had already had a distinguished political career and had been prime minister previously in 1855. Palmerston was tall, with an imposing mass of white hair, a high forehead and a distinguished, straight nose. His step was lively, his manner urbanely careless and joking.

"Well?" Lady Eva said. "Don't just gawk, follow me."

She rode over to the prime minister's carriage, and

Drake trotted after her. Lord Adolphus went in another direction, to speak to some friends who were calling to him. Palmerston hailed them as Lucian rode away.

"What a pleasure to see you, Lady Eva, Mr. Drake." Palmerston's eyes sparkled with mischief. "I've escaped from government business to take some air. Reading all those blasted bills and documents gives me an astonishing headache. Lady Eva, have you met Mr. and Mrs. Cornelius Bird? No? May I present them, then. Mr. Bird is a Texan too, Mr. Drake. East Texas, I believe. Cotton plantations and the like."

Drake glanced at Eva, who gave the Americans a gracious smile and offered her hand to Mr. Bird. Cornelius Bird was aptly named, for his features were definitely avian. Unfortunately for him, the bird he most resembled was a Texas turkey vulture, with his hunched shoulders and his hairless head, which jutted forth from his scrawny neck. Cornelius wore a sour expression as he surveyed Ryder.

"Drake. Heard the name, sir. Aren't you the rancher who supports the damned abolitionists?"

"I am, sir."

"Humph. For a young fella you're damned certain of your opinions. Why is it that you don't support your state?"

"Now, Bird," Lord Palmerston said. "You're going to upset the ladies, and me too. No political discussions on this lovely day when I've come out to enjoy the air."

"Of course," Cornelius replied, his cloudy expression clearing. "My apologies, Lady Eva, Mrs. Bird."

"Oh, don't apologize to me, sir," said Eva. "I like

political discussion. So much more interesting than talking about the weather."

Mrs. Josepha Bird spoke up for the first time. "Speak for yourself, Lady Eva, my dear. I much prefer the weather to political talk. Such discussions nowadays always seem to degenerate into terrible quarrels about slaves and states' rights. I simply don't understand why the North won't leave us alone. Our servants are none of their affair, and if they'd realize that, we'd all get along beautifully."

Drake had heard this sort of talk from other Southern planters' wives, but he could tell that Lady Eva wasn't used to it. She was staring at Josepha as if the woman were mad. Josepha was much younger than her husband, a black-haired beauty with enormous brown eyes, lush red lips and a perfect creamy complexion. She was in a smart day dress of scarlet plaid tartan festooned with yards and yards of French lace. She twirled a parasol in her hands and flashed a smile at Drake, a smile that told him the lady was well aware of her appeal. Drake glanced at Eva, who wore an almost derisive look while all the men smiled at Josepha.

Lord Palmerston said something gallant to Mrs. Bird, and Ryder realized that the prime minister's headache had been a convenient excuse to spend some time with Josepha. Palmerston's reputation as a rake was well known. One of the reasons Queen Victoria and Prince Albert disliked him was his loose moral attitude. The prime minister had the looks, charm and graceful elegance of a Regency gentleman, which sat ill with the morally rigid prince consort. Palmerston had once tried to seduce one of the queen's ladies-in-waiting under the sovereign's roof at Windsor. The prince and Victoria, ever the dutiful wife, had been horrified. Yet most women found the prime minister irresistible. Drake suspected that Josepha Bird was one of these.

After a few more minutes of conversation the prime minister and his guests drove on. Ryder watched the landau make its stately progress down Rotten Row.

"How long has Cornelius Bird been a guest of the prime minister?"

"I don't know."

"Dang it, Lord Palmerston didn't say anything about him when we first talked to him about the assassination."

"He probably doesn't think Mr. Bird is a threat."

Drake frowned. "You heard him. Cornelius is a die-hard states' rights slave owner, and he might be the Rebel assassin. I'm going to have a watch set on him."

"Good, then we're making progress."

"Not really."

"Why not?" Lady Eva exclaimed.

"Because even though I can't ignore the possibility that Cornelius is Iago, I have a feeling our spy is too clever to espouse Southern sympathies so openly."

"But the point isn't to keep Southerners' sentiments concealed. After all, Iago doesn't know you're after him."

"True," Drake muttered.

"If Iago is as accomplished as you think, he might hide behind a character as transparent as Mr. Bird appears." Eva gave him a sidelong glance. "Isn't that so?"

"Damn. Pardon me, my lady." Drake glared at

the back of the prime minister's landau. "You're right, of course."

Lady Eva nodded. "Come along, Mr. Drake. It's growing late, and we have to attend Lord Russell's dinner tonight."

"I received a letter from Mr. Pinkerton," Ryder said as they rode toward Lord Adolphus. "It contained a bit more information on Iago. He's rumored to be a rich Southern gentleman with a penchant for luxury. In February he was in Alabama while the Southern states organized the Confederacy. Then he hijacked a gold train on its way to Washington, D.C., and took the shipment to Canada. It seems he thought it would be amusing to finance his operations with Union money. In March he sabotaged three warships being outfitted for the Union navy at Annapolis and killed several men, including the captain of a frigate. Pinkerton says he's only now beginning to discover a few of Iago's accomplishments. And what's worse, no one who has seen Iago ever lives to tell what he looks like. Pinkerton got a tip that he was staying at Willard's Hotel in Washington and that he frequented a barbershop down the street from the hotel. When Pinkerton and his men showed up, they found that the barber had been killed by tripping in front of a stampeding freight wagon."

He looked at Eva and saw her shiver.

"He killed the poor man?"

"And vanished. We think the barber got suspicious, possibly because Iago had dyed his hair. That's consistent with the descriptions from the hotel employees, which seem to indicate that Iago was in disguise. It bothers me that he was staying at Willard's. The president stayed there on his first night in Washington, and Willard's is the premier meeting place for influential Unionists."

"What do you mean?" Lady Eva asked.

"I mean that one can meet powerful congressmen and senators in its sitting rooms and bars, along with financiers and military officers, not to mention lobbyists and contractors. A lot of delicate government business gets discussed at Willard's. I don't know what Iago was doing there, but it was important enough for him to kill someone to avoid discovery."

Drake stopped his horse and turned to Lady Eva. "Perhaps now you'll understand why I was so reluctant to involve you. Iago won't hesitate to kill you if he suspects you're out to expose him."

Smiling at him, Lady Eva nodded. "Thank you for your concern, Mr. Drake. But I have no intention of sitting idle while this madman threatens my country. My mind is made up, sir."

Lady Eva kicked her horse into a trot and rode ahead, preventing Drake from pursuing the argument. When they reached Tennyson House, Eva went into the drawing room with the cook to plan menus before Drake could talk to her. He dragged his gaze from her petite figure as his chief assistant, Noah Frye, came out of the library with a report on the American arrivals in London for the past month. So far they had found nineteen people of Southern sympathies. One of these was an elderly man who had since died. Three were children of a merchant from Georgia, Charles Hunter Sheridan, and his wife, Clara. The Sheridans were Quakers and could be ruled out as suspects. Lucian and Hamilton were on the list and could be crossed off as well. That left eleven people.

Frye reported that at least three men in this remaining group had been sent by Jefferson Davis, the president of the Confederacy, to lobby the British government on behalf of the South. These and four other wealthy men in the group were moving in influential and powerful circles, ostensibly on private business. Another couple was visiting relatives in the city, as were the last two individuals. Of these the first was a man named Zachariah Gordon, who had made his fortune selling slaves then settled down to the life of a gentleman planter with cotton plantations in Georgia and tobacco farms in Virginia. The second was a West Point graduate, formerly a captain in the United States Army, who was now a Confederate colonel. His name was Nathan Longstreet, and no one could locate him in London.

It took hours to cull the list of suspects and confer with Scotland Yard about setting a watch on the rest. The man in charge of the Yard's part in this manhunt, Inspector Oliver Palgrave, had already let Drake know he considered his mission a waste of time. For some reason known only to Palgrave, he thought it impossible that an American would dare kill an officer of the British government. As Palgrave said, "It simply isn't done, sir."

After engaging in a battle of wills with Palgrave, Drake returned to Tennyson House to change for the dinner at Lord John Russell's. He waited for Lord Adolphus and Lady Eva in a small sitting room at the front of the house and huddled by the fireplace. May in London wasn't nearly as warm as it was in San Antonio or Washington, and he wasn't used to the chilly evenings. He was gazing out a window that looked onto the front courtyard. A storm was coming, and the wind whipped through the trees, causing their branches to scrape the glass and cast wild shadows on the floor.

Drake watched leaves and twigs skitter across the gravel drive and the gaslights on the stone wall that surrounded the grounds flicker. He glanced back at the fire, but as he did so, something caught his eye, a shadow that moved with purpose. He went to the window and moved the heavy damask curtain aside. The coachman was driving the carriage from the stable, but that wasn't what he'd seen. Drake's gaze swept the grounds, moving through the ancient towering hawthorns and chestnuts, stopping at the fountain with its shell tiers and sparkling water. He saw nothing unusual. Perhaps he'd seen a servant, a footman on some errand.

Returning to the fireplace, he heard the door open and turned to see Lady Eva. Drake caught himself staring at her and covered his gaffe with a slight bow and a murmured greeting. She was wearing a gown of forest-green barege. The color was so dark it almost looked black, but in the light the rich green shimmered. In her hair, which she wore low on the back of her neck, were intertwined green ivy and dark russet flowers. At her neck Lady Eva wore a collar of diamonds and emeralds, and the same stones hung from her earrings. Drake was used to seeing women in dinner dresses, but usually they wore five or six flounces to their skirts, dozens of bows, puffs and pleats, beads and lace, lace, lace. Lady Eva simply wore a green gown. Not a flounce or bead to be seen, and her crinoline was much reduced. The result was that he looked at the woman who wore the dress. He was acutely aware of flawless skin, curved shoulders and shining copper hair.

Lady Eva hesitated in the doorway. "Perhaps I should see what's keeping Uncle."

Shaking himself from his daze, Ryder hurried to her and closed the door before she could leave.

"We're both early, Lady Eva, and I wish to speak with you privately."

"I can see from that mulish expression on your face that you're determined to harangue me again." She passed by him, leaving him breathing in the scent of roses, and perched herself carefully on the edge of a sofa. Folding her gloved hands, she nodded. "You may begin, sir."

Her tone made him snap, "Why in Sam Hill are you so all-fired upset when all I'm trying to do is look out for you? You don't seem to understand the danger you're headed for, and this time you're going to listen to me."

"Very well," Lady Eva replied. She cleared her throat and settled farther into the sofa. "I'm listening, sir."

Eyeing her distrustfully, Drake rubbed the backs of his arms and returned to the warmth of the fireplace. "I've just finished going over more than a dozen names, and there are a few very dangerous men who could be the one we're after. Take just one, Zachariah Gordon. He used to be a slave dealer. In fact, he used to hunt runaways. Do you know what that means? It means—"

"That he hunted men with a pack of dogs, guns and no doubt a whip," Lady Eva said.

"Well, yes." He'd forgotten she'd been in the South. How was he going to impress this woman with the peril of the situation? He smiled. "He used to sell slaves at city hall and put the runaways he'd captured in the city jail until he bought land and built his own auction house. Have you ever seen an auction house, Lady Eva, or the kind of men who run them?"

"Indeed, yes."

"You're joking."

"No, Mr. Drake, I'm not." She sighed and rested against the arm of the sofa. "Despite my failures elsewhere, I attempted to purchase slaves in Virginia. There was an auction house in a market town called Fern Springs on the way to Washington. It had cells that resembled stables, only horses are better housed. There was no water, no facilities for privacy. The inmates were forced to live in their own filth, with stinking rags for clothing. I won't describe the smell or the infestations of lice to you."

Drake caught himself gaping at her. "*You* went to the Fern Springs auction house?"

"I wasn't there long. There was a big sale going on, but the moment I appeared havoc broke out. It seems that ladies don't go to slave auctions. Such shouting and waving of walking sticks and cigars. The owner of the auction house escorted me off his property." She grinned at him. "I thought he'd succumb to apoplexy."

By now Drake was scowling. "I hope you learned your lesson. An auction house is no place for a lady."

"It's no place for any Christian person. Such places shouldn't exist."

"What do you think we're fighting about in America? Oh, don't answer. I can't believe you did that. It only proves that I'm right. You shouldn't be involved in this hunt for the assassin. God only knows what trouble you'll get into. Your presence is a distraction."

Standing, Lady Eva faced him. "I'm not a distraction. I'm of great help to you, but you're so set against women, you don't want to admit it. Gracious, Mr. Drake. However did you become such a hater of women?"

"I do not hate women," Drake said with careful enunciation and a patience he didn't feel.

"You certainly have a low opinion of them."

Drake looked away from Lady Eva. "Only some."

"I know. Only Society ladies like me."

Grudgingly Ryder said, "Not like you. I was hasty in my estimation of you, as I've already admitted." He stiffened when she walked over to stand beside him at the fireplace.

"I'm not dangerous, Mr. Drake. No need to pull up like a knight facing a dragon."

"I'm not afraid of you." Ryder met her frankly curious gaze. "I was thinking of someone else, someone quite different from you." He watched her irritation vanish, but when her eyes softened he realized she had an uncanny ability to detect the hurt he concealed from the world.

Lady Eva spoke quietly. "Who was this someone who earned your mistrust?"

"My mother." Ryder looked away from Lady Eva's startled gaze and smiled bitterly to himself. "Mama is a Southern Society lady. She lives in a world of pleasure and social frittering. Her days are taken up with calls and parties, much like our current occupations, only this is the way she has spent her entire life. Our conversations begin and end with her interests and needs. No matter what happens to me, she sees my life as an adjunct of hers. I'm the overture; she is the ballet."

"But surely she has some redeeming qualities," Lady Eva said. "To have raised a son like you."

Startled at the compliment coupled with the naive sentiment, Ryder bowed slightly. "You're gracious, Lady Eva, but you don't understand."

"I would like to," she replied. As she spoke she touched his coat sleeve with her fingertips.

Ryder caught her hand before she could withdraw it. His lips brushed those small, pink-tipped fingers. He lifted his gaze to her face. She was smiling at him like a Madonna. He found himself transfixed, until she looked down at their joined hands and dropped hers.

"You were going to help me understand," she said.

He hadn't intended that at all, but under her attentive gaze, his natural reticence seemed to dissolve. "How can I explain Mother?" He thought for a moment. "When I was eight my best friend drowned before my eyes. We'd gone to a swimming hole on the plantation. He dove in and hit his head on a rock. I tried to save him, but I couldn't. It was too late by the time I dragged him out of the water. I went into shock, couldn't speak, could only cry. That night Mother left me in the care of servants while she went to a ball. She said she couldn't stay home when everyone was expecting her. They would all be too disappointed."

Ryder stared into the flames of the fire. "So you can see why I abhorred the idea of approaching you in Washington. And I still don't want you playing a part in this most perilous game."

"I don't understand your reasoning at all, sir," she said gently.

He lifted his gaze to find her soft lips trembling

and her eyes glistening. What had possessed him to make such a confession? He looked away, not wanting to see her sympathy. He turned abruptly and put some distance between them that would serve as barrier.

With a slight smile he turned back to her. "My reasoning is quite logical. To find a lady of such inquisitive intelligence and courage has been a great pleasure. Having found such a paragon, my lady, you can hardly expect me to relish exposing her to danger."

Lady Eva blinked rapidly and turned pink.

"Why, Mr. Drake, you're kind indeed, but I'm capable of navigating the tempestuous waters of the Season without protection. The greatest danger I face is falling asleep at the table and drowning in my consommé."

"Damn it!"

Lady Eva jumped.

"Damn it." Drake threw up his hands. "Stubborn, bullheaded woman."

She drew herself up. "I'll not stand for that kind of language, sir."

Striding to her, he looked down from his superior height, breathing hard in his agitation. "All right. Have it your way. I'm blamed if I can stop you. It's beyond me why I find you so—" He stopped as she glared up at him.

"So what, Mr. Drake?"

"Never mind, blast it. You're going to drive me mad!"

Lord Adolphus burst into the room before he could say anything else.

"Ah, there you are. Sorry I'm late. Shall we go?"

Drake whirled away from Lady Eva, gripped the

marble fireplace mantel and glared at the flames. Eva swept out of the room ahead of her uncle, and Ryder trailed them. What idiocy had almost escaped his mouth? He was under greater stress than he'd thought. That was it. He was tense and worried, and the strain was getting to him. It was the not knowing who his enemy was or where he was or when he might strike. He wasn't thinking clearly, and his emotions had run rampant.

It wouldn't happen again.

# CHAPTER NINE

❧

AFTER A FORMAL dinner the ladies always left the gentlemen at the table so that the men could enjoy cigars, brandy and talk about serious subjects unsuitable for women. Lord Russell's dinner followed this tradition, except that one of the gentlemen refused to stay in the dining room once the cigars came out. This was why Eva was having a most revealing conversation with Lucian Bedford Forrest about Mr. Ryder Drake. She contemplated Lucian's fair, refined features while she listened to the story of Drake's life.

"So you can see, dear Lady Eva, why old Ryder is so severe. Having the Drakes for parents would drain anyone of enjoyment and humor. Hamilton and I call him the Black Cloud. Annoys him, but if we don't chide him about it, he goes around raining on us and depressing our spirits." Lucian turned his head, covered his mouth and coughed. "I beg your pardon, my lady. I caught a whiff of smoke before I retreated from the dining room."

"I understand completely, sir. I do hope you have the name of a good doctor in Harley Street. Just in case your lung trouble reoccurs."

"Indeed, I do. You're kind to ask."

"Mr. Drake is fortunate in his friends, sir."

"Thank you. We're the lucky ones. Did you know that when Hamilton freed his slaves he made no provision for his own welfare? Ryder is the one who furnished Ham with the money to rebuild his fortune. If he knew I'd told you, he'd take a horse whip to me, so I pray you don't let him know I've exposed his good deeds."

"Of course."

Eva was going to ask more about Felicita Drake, but the drawing room doors opened and in strode the gentlemen, including the subject of their conversation. Drake was talking to a new acquaintance, Zachariah Gordon. Eva could tell by the burning glow in Drake's eyes that Gordon had annoyed him. In London, as in other capitals, Rebels and Unionists were thrown together at social events, where they were forced into a peaceful truce by their hosts. Ordinarily Drake maintained his air of grave formality and politeness, but Mr. Gordon seemed to have blasted it away almost entirely. He and Drake moved nearer to Eva and were joined by Hamilton Locke and another gentleman.

Eva studied the man who had so obviously irritated Ryder. Gordon was a tall, thickset man with a rolling gait from years spent in the saddle. He had curly black hair, long bushy sideburns and a luxurious beard. His narrow blue eyes were as hard and cold as arctic ice, even when he was in a good humor, as he was now. Though she'd only met the man this evening, Eva had already deduced that Gordon liked being the center of attention. Eva had disliked him immediately. He made her nervous for reasons she found hard to put into words. It wasn't just his former occupation that she abhorred. There was a cheap craftiness about Gordon despite his expensive clothes and good manners.

"I almost envy you, Drake, for having gotten rid of your slaves." Gordon toyed with his watch fob. "I was happy to give up the slave trade and pursue farming."

Hamilton Locke opened his mouth, but Ryder gave him a black look. Locke turned on his heel and left the group. Lucian stifled a wordless expression of disgust and glanced at Eva, who gave him a pained smile.

"What most Yankees don't understand about slavery is that the Negro is a creature who needs guidance and direction. I'm sure you agree, Drake." Gordon went on without giving Ryder a chance to reply. "They're a lazy, shiftless race of heathens. When they're told to do a job, they mostly only do it halfway, or they do it ten times more slowly than a white man would. You have to watch them constantly or they lie about or steal or run away. Why, I know of a lady in Florida who raised an orphan Negro child, trained him up to be a house servant, gave him nice clothes and good food. Then about fifteen years later her husband died, and on that very day that Negro boy knocked her in the head, stole her jewelry and money and absconded."

"Was the lady killed?" asked one of the listeners.

"Thank the Lord, no. I got wind of the case and set about finding the boy. Trailed him all the way to Kentucky before I caught up to him in a ditch beside the road to Louisville. I told him to give up, but he came at me with a knife. Had to give him a powerful beating before he stopped fighting, but I got him back."

"What happened to him afterward?" Ryder asked.

"He died on the way back to Florida. I must have knocked him in the head by accident. But I recovered the jewels and most of the money. The owner was most grateful. Anyway, you can see why the Negro must be governed. He has no business running around free. How would he live? As a savage, I tell you. It's up to white folks to see to it that the Negro lives a productive and civilized life."

Eva waited in the shocked silence that followed Zachariah Gordon's discourse, her gaze fixed on Ryder. She was relieved when he tore his eyes from Gordon and abruptly changed the subject. She could see the way his hands had balled into fists, the knuckles white, and she'd expected an outburst that would have been just as rude as Gordon's callousness. The group of men moved away from Eva and Lucian as a servant passed out cups of coffee.

Lucian shook his head. "I do apologize for my fellow American, Lady Eva. I trust you know we're not all ignorant barbarians."

"Of course I do, Mr. Forrest."

Glancing over his shoulder, Lucian said, "Oh, dear. I'd better go to Hamilton. He's seething like an unwatched kettle, and if I can't calm him down we'll be subjected to a burst of outrage. Please excuse me, my lady."

When Lucian left, Drake slipped away from Gordon's group and took his place. He brushed a lock of hair off his forehead and hissed at her.

"Say something to me, anything."

"What's wrong, sir?"

"Don't be absurd. If you don't distract me, I'm going to punch Zachariah Gordon in his thick face. Help me, please."

Eva picked up her evening shawl, holding it out to Ryder. "Mr. Drake, I do believe it's quite close in this room. Might I prevail upon you to take me onto the terrace?"

Getting up quickly, Drake took the shawl, tossed it over Eva's shoulders and offered his arm. Eva had to slow him down or they would have rushed outside, causing those in the room to comment. Once they reached the terrace she turned and looked up at Drake.

"Calm down, sir."

"You heard that bast—idiot." Drake paced back and forth in front of Eva. Then he threw up his hands. "Why is it obvious to no one but me that if you treat people like animals and deny them the fruits of their labor they have no reason to work well for you? I could name dozens of clever, hardworking Negroes of my acquaintance. And why wouldn't that boy take the first chance he got to run away? Any man with gumption would do the same, and I for one think he showed great judgment in taking a knife to Zachariah Gordon."

Eva shook her head sadly. "This is a blindness on the part of many. No wonder the slavery question has come to violence."

Drake's pacing grew less frenzied. He rubbed the back of his neck, then paused beside Eva and gave her a rueful look.

"Thank you. I was about to do something rash in there. You have great presence of mind for a . . ."

"Woman?" Eva said with irritation.

"Well . . ."

"Mr. Drake, someday you're going to have to learn that not every woman is like your mother."

Drake's head jerked around. "I know that."

"Then why do you persist in making such ridiculous remarks?"

"Lucian's been talking about me, hasn't he? That blasted bookworm."

Eva regarded Drake's seething form calmly. "You should be grateful to him, sir. I have a much higher tolerance of your foibles now that I know more about you."

"I, my lady, do not have foibles." Drake drew himself up to his full height and glared down at her.

Eva didn't flinch. "Perhaps not. Perhaps you have grave faults of character, but it helps me tolerate them if I think of them as foibles."

"Don't be so all-fired prissy, Eva Sparrow." Drake brought his face closer to hers. "I'm not the only one with faults of character."

Raising her eyebrows, Eva said, "Indeed? No, don't continue. This isn't the place. You shouldn't allow your foibles to distract you from your task, sir. Were you able to speak with Lord Russell?"

"No," Drake snapped. "Too many people. I need to make him see how great the threat is to him. He's a popular figure because of his efforts to extend parliamentary representation to the common man. His death would create havoc, just what Iago wants. And Russell keeps dismissing the Scotland Yard detectives assigned to protect him."

"Don't worry. You'll get the chance to speak with him. I've arranged to meet him tomorrow morning. You see, I happen to know that Lord Russell is an antiquarian, so I arranged for a private tour of some new acquisitions at the British Museum."

"Excellent work."

Eva smirked. "Yes, for a woman."

"Are you going to bring that up again?"

"Often."

Drake walked toward the doors to the house. "Then I'm leaving."

"Just like a man," Eva called after him. "Retreating in the face of defeat."

Jerking open the door, Drake muttered, "Confound it!" He shut the door and marched back to her. Folding his arms across his chest, he loomed over Eva. With his height and stark good looks, he produced a menacing atmosphere with little effort.

"Damn it, woman, it's not enough that I'm trying to prevent a murder. I have to put up with you and your insults too."

Something else flickered in Drake's eyes. Eva met his gaze, but he looked away.

"Why, Mr. Drake, I do believe you're secretly afraid of me."

Drake looked at her again, his mouth open in consternation. "What are you talking about?" His eyes narrowed when Eva chuckled.

"I can see it in your eyes, sir. You're afraid."

There was a short pause, during which Eva heard Drake catch his breath. He was several paces away, but he moved closer while he shook his head as if in wonder, which made Eva a bit nervous. What had she said?

Drake murmured softly, "Well, well. You don't know as much about men as I thought you did. Certainly not as much as you think you do."

Something had changed. She could hear it in his voice, a low, rough quality filled with a new kind of tension. Eva shivered and tried to see his expression, but his back was to the light coming through the glass doors. Shadows had turned his eyes into pools of black liquid and moonlight silver. His movements had become even smoother than usual, as if he were approaching a startled deer in the forest. As he advanced, Eva backed away and came up against the stone balustrade of the terrace.

"What are you doing?"

"You should know."

Before Eva could respond, Drake's arms went around her.

"Mr. Drake!"

"Hush now," he whispered. "I forgot how sheltered little English girls are."

"But—" Eva lost her voice when his lips grazed her neck.

Drake brushed his lips over her ear. "Someone has neglected your education, my little English peony."

Eva was lost in the overpowering sensation caused by his breath in her ear and barely heard him. His body was trembling as much as hers, and she felt the length of him pressed against her, straining. He murmured something about autumn-leaf hair. Then his lips descended to hers, and she felt his tongue inside her mouth. Eva started, but Ryder held her firmly and taught her mouth to respond to his. The night receded around Eva as sensation burst inside her. His tongue seemed connected to nerves inside her that had never been touched. Then his lips were gone.

"What in blazes am I doing?"

The warmth of his body receded. Eva opened her

eyes to find herself bent backward over the balustrade in an awkward and revealing position. All she could see of Ryder was his back as he went inside the house.

Eva quickly straightened, patted her hair and touched her lips with her handkerchief. Then she scurried after Drake, hoping her cheeks weren't as flushed as they felt.

The next morning Eva had no desire to face Ryder Drake. She'd spent the remainder of the evening avoiding him. He'd kissed her to prove a point, and he'd succeeded. She had been dazed and made to appear foolish. She'd wilted in his arms like some heroine in a melodrama. The trip home in the carriage had been conducted in silence. Eva got little sleep last night, and when she did drift off, she dreamed of much more than that kiss. She woke disturbed and shocked at herself. So embarrassed was she that she deserted the house early and went shopping, leaving word that she would meet Drake at the museum.

She arrived in the courtyard of the British Museum only two minutes before they were to meet Lord Russell. Drake was waiting under the loggia formed by tall Corinthian columns. To Eva's relief, Lord Russell's carriage pulled up as she was being handed down from hers. Thus she was able to face Drake on the minister's arm. She needn't have worried, however. Drake's expression was cool and polite, as if nothing had happened.

This in itself was disconcerting. Had that kiss left him unmoved? Was he so jaded that he felt nothing? His cousin had remarked enviously on the attraction Drake exerted upon women. No doubt Ryder Drake had been with so many ladies that Eva Sparrow impressed him not at all. This was hardly surprising. She was a widow, not a young beauty. Besides, she had already made up her mind about what her life was going to be like. It would be absurd to allow a kiss to change her ideas.

A pity, though, for that kiss had provoked a night of dreams and tantalizing feelings, ones she'd never had for her husband. When had she given up hope of love? It had been some time after marrying. The endless days of predictability, of rectitude and polite distance on the part of her husband had eventually worn down her spirits. The world had seemed gray on the sunniest day. She'd thought she'd never be happy because she'd always wanted something more. Her family hadn't understood how she could be unhappy, and at first she dreamed that some wonderful gentleman would rescue her, like in a children's fairy tale. Her fantasies included a secret desire to fall in love with a man whose imagination and sense of adventure matched her own. Of course, that rescuer had never shown up.

Then one day she'd gone below the stairs to the kitchen in the enormous country house she'd shared with John Charles. She'd gotten no more than halfway down when the noise and bustle in the great warren of rooms hit her. She stopped and watched Cook marshal three assistants, two scullery maids and two footmen and snap out orders. The family butler was nowhere in sight, but the place was orderly and everyone obeyed Cook instantly. Square-jawed and thin-lipped, Cook had been with John Charles for over twenty years. She produced good plain meals or the most intricate formal dinners one could imagine, always on time, with never a squashed soufflé or dry morsel of veal.

In those few moments the contrast between herself and Cook dawned upon Eva. A self-assured widow, Cook managed her own life and her work and that of her underlings with confidence. With her superior advantages in life, Eva Sparrow ought to be able to do the same. That was when she began to suspect that fairy-tale rescues were unnecessary. If she wanted rescuing, she should and could do it herself.

Eva had thought her widowhood, which meant new freedom, was the rescue she craved. And it had been for quite a while. But for some time she'd been aware that a life without purpose was not only shallow but also deadly boring. In addition, her old girlish dreams of love had resurfaced, and it was all on account of Ryder Drake's forward behavior. It was a thousand pities that her heart had chosen to awaken to the touch of such an annoying man.

A curator met them inside the museum and led them into the Egyptian wing. The Honorable Wilfred Snape was a slight, pale man with smudged spectacles and a wispy mustache. He spoke in a whispery voice, as if he were afraid the artifacts could hear him.

Long lines of granite and limestone statues greeted them, stiff, staring over their heads, looking at them from a distance of three thousand years. An irrelevant thought flashed through Eva's head—a museum was one of the few places where the human body was displayed so frankly. In these statues she saw more of the male form than she'd ever seen during her marriage. John Charles' idea of a satisfactory marital encounter meant a hurried fumbling in pitch dark, during which he never removed his nightshirt.

Her husband certainly hadn't resembled the wide-shouldered, lean-hipped pharaohs she saw here. Mr. Drake did, but then he was exceptional. At this thought Eva sternly turned her attention fully to the museum.

There were few visitors this early, but the galleries seemed crowded anyway with all the sculpted figures that had been stuffed into them over the last hundred years. They passed the image of Ramses II wearing a kilt and the double crowns of Upper and Lower Egypt. Tall columns carved in the shape of lotus buds and papyrus stalks framed archways that led to glass cases protecting mummies.

The mummy room was deliberately left in shadow to preserve the delicate remains. A few cases lay in the soft yellow glow of gaslights. Eva stared into the eyes of a death mask of some princess who had lived fifteen centuries before the birth of Christ. It was made of sheet gold, and the lifelike glass eyes seemed frozen with dread of the afterlife. A shadow flitted over the mask. Eva looked over her shoulder, but the others were gathered around the coffin of a pharaoh.

Deciding the shadow must have been caused by an irregularity in the gas supply to the lights, Eva strolled around the room. Some of the bodies lay in painted rectangular boxes; some were in coffins shaped like the mummified human form. Inside most of these lay rigid bodies wrapped in hundreds of yards of linen bandages. Eva clutched her shawl about her shoulders, wondering at Lord Russell's avid interest in such a morbid display. Perhaps it was the minister's own ill health that caused him to dabble in the funereal remains of an ancient civilization.

Mr. Drake wandered over to stand beside her and

nodded at a mummy. "The search for immortality, it has gone on for longer than one can imagine."

Eva regarded him gravely, wondering how he could manage to think about such impenetrable questions at the same time that he was enduring incredible strain. "Providence has provided the answer to that question for us. Don't you agree?"

"Ah, yes," Drake said, smiling faintly. "Providence. I wish, however, that the Lord would invest a bit more attention to this troubled mortality. What kind of world would it be, do you think, if men could look into one another's hearts as Christ could?"

Eva cocked her head to the side and looked up at Drake's strained features. "Then, sir, men wouldn't be men; they would be divine."

"My country could use a bit of divinity right now."

"Come," Eva said quietly. She marveled that after last night she could forget herself and join Mr. Drake in such conversation. "Mr. Snape and Lord Russell are leaving."

The curator took them through a small room in which the glint of gold predominated along with precious stones—armbands, necklaces, broad collars and seal rings. Eva glimpsed turquoise, lapis lazuli, red jasper and carnelian. Finally Mr. Snape took them down several flights of stairs. The landings were crowded with statuary and boxes of artifacts, which made walking difficult. At the bottom of the stairs they entered a darkened corridor.

"We keep the new things down here while they are being accessioned and curated," Snape whispered. "Then we bring them up to the galleries."

"Heavens," Lord Russell said as he regarded the endless line of figures that crowded a vast room behind the stairs. "How many mummies does the museum have?"

"Oh, hundreds," Snape replied. "There are too many, so we've tossed some into the rubbish bins. Ah! Here we are."

Snape produced a key and unlocked a thick door, swinging the heavy portal back to reveal a vaultlike room filled with shelves and cabinets. A small table sat in the middle. They followed him inside, and Snape opened a locked cabinet drawer. He carefully withdrew a velvet-lined tray that was covered with a linen cloth and set it on the table. With a flourish he removed the cloth to reveal an exquisite broad collar made up of thousands of tiny barrel-shaped and cylindrical beads, all of gold. Drake whistled, and Lord Russell bent over the object to peer at it intently. Eva joined them, and had to put her hands behind her back to resist touching the collar. Snape nodded and smiled at them.

"I just finished restoring this, my lord," Snape whispered. "Do you see this counterpoise? It's inscribed with the royal cartouche of the pharaoh Seti the First. I was in Cairo at an antiquities dealer I have known for twenty years. He offered the collar to me because we're such old friends. A most amazing find, I'm sure you agree."

"Absolutely," Lord Russell said. "Seti I, you say? I'm not surprised. He had one of the largest tombs in the Valley of the Kings."

Snape and Russell continued to discuss Egyptian history, but Drake wandered over to Eva. "When are we going to get him alone? I can't talk to him with old Wilfred hovering over us."

"Patience, sir. Unseemly haste puts off an English gentleman. Once they finish talking I'll suggest tea."

"After that, I need to talk to you about last night on the terrace," Drake murmured.

Eva swallowed hard, her earlier ease gone. She made her tone light. "Whatever for?"

"Not now."

Lord Russell had finished his discussion with the curator, and Eva was thankful when they left the vault room.

"Oh, dear," Snape said as he walked into darkness. "The lights have failed again. I'll light a lamp. I declare, this is always happening, and no one seems to be able to fix it. I blame the gas company."

Snape led the way down the corridor, holding his lamp. As they approached the stairway, more and more crates lined the walls. The boxes were stacked on top of one another, so that the hall looked more like a tunnel. Eva followed Snape while Drake came next and Lord Russell was last. Their steps sounded loudly in the deserted hallway.

Eva found herself looking right and left to see between the slates of some of the open crates. Inside, fantastical figures stared back at her—gods with human bodies and animal heads. Her gaze slid from a jackal's head to a lion's and then to a creature with the head of a hawk. They were so lifelike she felt as if they could reach out to her. Snape stepped into the stairwell, and Eva did as well. She glanced back to find that Lord Russell had stopped some distance behind her.

"Did you hear something?" he asked.

Everyone hesitated, and a moment later there came a loud whining noise. Eva frowned.

"What is that?" Drake asked. He was a few steps behind Russell.

Out of the corner of her eye Eva glimpsed movement.

One of the tall wooden crates stacked on top of a large box was leaning. It tilted at a precarious angle, and Eva suddenly realized it was going to fall.

"Look out!"

Lord Russell turned to stare at Eva, who was pointing at the crate behind and above him. Ryder sprang at him as the heavy box started to fall. Snatching Russell's arm, Ryder yanked him out of the way as the crate crashed to the floor. The wood split, and the life-size statue of a god with the head of a ram shattered in three pieces.

"Aw, hell," Drake said. "Stay here." He released Lord Russell, and raced back down the corridor.

Eva dropped her shawl and ran past the minister. "Mr. Drake, stop!"

Ryder vanished around a corner without answering, and Eva hurried after him. As she rounded the corner she heard another crash and a cry. Drake lay facedown on the floor next to a shattered alabaster jar. Eva hesitated for a fraction of a second, not even breathing until she saw Ryder move. Weak with relief, she raced to Drake. Eva heard a door slam as she reached him. He groaned and turned over. Kneeling beside him, she held him as he tried to sit up.

"Mr. Drake, Ryder, can you hear me?" Her voice was shaking.

Silence. Eva felt him collapse against her and heard another groan. Blood was seeping from a cut on the back of his head, and a knot was growing rapidly around it. Alarmed, Eva pulled her handkerchief from her pocket and pressed it against the wound. Drake yelped and sat up, but she held the handkerchief in place with one trembling hand.

"Ryder, can you hear me?"

"Mm."

"Answer me, Ryder. Can you hear me?"

"Yes, damn it. Ouch!"

Eva gave a relieved sigh. "Be still. You've got a big knot on your head, and you're dizzy."

"I know I'm dizzy, woman. You're lucky I haven't vomited on you."

Eva grinned. She could tell he was angry with himself and not with her.

"Someone was here," he said. "He tried to kill Russell."

"I know, and he almost succeeded in killing you."

"I have to find him." Ryder tried to get up but collapsed again. "Damn!"

"It's too dangerous," Eva said as she helped him sit. Her arm barely reached around his shoulders, and she resisted the urge to crush him to her. "You're in no condition to chase anyone. You wouldn't get ten yards."

"I should have brought one of my men." Ryder groaned, and Eva winced in sympathy.

"This will teach you to rush after murderers all by yourself. You should have waited for me."

"Absolutely not. I won't risk your getting hurt."

Eva gritted her teeth. "We'll talk about it later."

At that moment Lord Russell and Wilfred Snape came around the corner.

"Good Lord," Russell said. "What happened to you, Mr. Drake?"

"He managed to jostle that alabaster jar, and it fell on his head," Eva said.

"Oh, dear!" Snape was kneeling before the shattered vessel. "Oh, dear." It was clear that the demise of the alabaster jar was of more concern than Drake.

"Will he be all right?" Lord Russell asked.

" 'M fine," Drake muttered, lifting his head.

Eva held his shoulders as he tried to sit up again. "We shall have to watch him for a few hours. If he remains alert, he should be fine. I'll take him home and summon Dr. Parkhurst."

"I'll help you, my dear." Russell assisted Drake in standing.

"Thank you, my lord."

Drake pulled free of Eva's grip and began to sway. Eva grabbed his arm and steadied him. "Ryder, you're going to have to hold on to us, or you won't make it upstairs."

Mr. Snape had gathered the pieces of the jar in his hands. "There's another stairway just down this corridor. It's closer than the way we came, and less cluttered."

They helped Drake upstairs and into Eva's carriage. Lord Russell followed them in his. Drake sat with his head against the squabs and his eyes closed. Eva watched him anxiously.

"Ryder, can you hear me?"

"Why do you keep asking me that?"

"I hit my head once, and the doctor kept asking me questions to test my alertness."

"Well, I can hear you just fine."

She was sitting opposite him. Leaning forward, she said, "Open your eyes, Ryder. Can you see me?"

He growled and did nothing.

"Ryder Drake, you open your eyes at once."

"Oh, all right!" He sat up and looked at her. "There."

"How many fingers am I holding up?"

"Thirty-seven."

Eva gave him a stern stare, and he sighed.

"Three. You're holding up three fingers, and yes, I do see you clearly, from that autumn-leaf hair to those little bitty shoes. If you'll lift your skirt just a smidge, I'll tell you if I can see your ankles too."

Eva blinked at him. "I can see you're getting better already."

He grinned, then grimaced. "Ow. It hurts to smile. Tell you what, why don't you come over here and let me rest my head on your shoulder again."

"Oh, are you in pain?" She moved to sit beside him and touched his shoulder.

Ryder sighed and leaned against her. "No, but you're a mighty soft resting place, Eva Sparrow."

Eva stiffened, turned bright red and shoved him off her shoulder. "Get off me, sir. You are not yourself. The blow to your head has robbed you of your manners and made you act drunk."

"Naw," he said with a chuckle. "Ouch! It does sting a powerful lot."

Moving back to the other seat, Eva snapped, "Then it's most rude of you to make fun of me when all I was trying to do was help you."

"Sorry."

"Next time I shall let you suffer."

"Now, Eva, don't get in a snit. Not when we were getting along so well."

"I'm not in a—a snit, as you call it."

"Good, 'cause we're almost home, and I wanted to ask you if you saw anything."

"No, by the time I got to you, whoever it was had fled."

"Damn."

Eva steadied Ryder as the carriage pulled up in front of Tennyson House. "At least some good will come of this."

"What's that?"

"Now no one can accuse you of exaggeration."

She allowed the footman to help her down and watched him hold on to Ryder as he left the carriage. "You can point to that gash on your head if they want proof." She turned and preceded him into the house. "All in all, perhaps your nearly getting killed was good luck."

"You're a cold woman, Eva Sparrow. A danged cold woman."

# CHAPTER TEN

❧

RYDER SAT OPPOSITE Lord Russell in the drawing room at Tennyson House and ignored Lady Eva. He was having a hard time doing this because she was sitting nearby on a sofa with her silk skirts billowing around her, looking every inch a model of feminine disapproval. She had a way of regarding him as if she expected him to justify her low opinion of his good sense. He hadn't wanted to admit it, but he was in a fix: The woman maddened him and fascinated him, and he was afraid that sooner or later he wouldn't be able to keep his hands off her. She, in the meantime, was waiting for him to collapse because he'd refused to see a doctor, but he couldn't afford to wait any longer to tackle Lord Russell.

"You could have been killed, my lord. I hope you realize that."

"My dear sir, there's no reason to suspect this morning's events had anything to do with this Rebel plot of yours. We might have disturbed a thief.

After all, there's a great deal of gold in the museum vaults."

Pressing his lips together, Ryder controlled his impatience. "It's too much of a coincidence, don't you think? The existence of an assassination plot and this attempt on your life?" He sat forward and caught the minister's eye. "Are you willing to risk your life when the simple measures I advocate could save it?"

"Hmm."

Eva spoke up. "Our information is accurate. I've seen the young man who is its source, Lord Russell. He's not given to wild tales and fits of fancy. Let me tell you about Josiah and the other slaves I encountered on my visit to the Southern states."

Ryder studied the foreign minister as Eva continued. Lord Russell was the third son of the sixth duke of Bedford. Perhaps it was his delicate health that gave him his generous sympathy for the British poor, for which he was famous. He was small and rickety, with a habit of nervous fidgeting. Even his voice was weak, but his heart was great. As an adolescent he had remarked that it was a pity that a man who stole a penny loaf of bread was hung, while one who stole thousands in public money was acquitted. Russell had served in Parliament since the age of twenty, and after much perserverance he succeeded in passing a reform bill in 1837 that extended representation to the common man. Some said that this single act might have saved Britain from revolution. Those who heard him speak knew that they had listened to a man of great vision. The sponsor of much enlightened legislation, Lord Russell was the nation's most ardent advocate for the poor and had served as prime minister in 1846, with Lord Palmerston as his foreign secretary. Now the men's roles were reversed, and

Russell was foreign minister to Palmerston. It was rumored that he would be raised to the peerage in the summer, to become Earl Russell.

To Ryder the foreign minister's zeal for his fellow countrymen was admirable. However, it led Russell to favor supporting the Confederacy in order to protect the livelihood of mill laborers who depended upon Southern cotton imports. Eva's descriptions of the plight of slaves were softening him, but the man still had trouble imagining that anyone would try to kill him. He was listening to Eva with an expression of disbelieving horror on his face. Perhaps the lady was making headway at last.

"So you mustn't believe those who say that the Negro is savage and backward. It's against the law in some states to educate them, after all. And if they were indeed lazy and indolent, how would all that cotton get picked?"

Russell held up his hand. "Cease, Lady Eva. I beg you. You've given me much to contemplate."

"Then you'll accept the protection of Scotland Yard?" Ryder asked, rising as the minister stood.

"I will. If for no other reason than to placate this most determined lady." Russell rose, took Eva's hand and bowed. "My thanks for a most exciting excursion, my dear. You have my word that I shan't dismiss my bodyguards again. It's the least I can do, considering the trouble to which I've put Mr. Drake. As for the rest, we shall see." He turned to Ryder. "Good day to you, sir. You have my deepest gratitude for your assistance to me at the museum."

When Russell was gone, Eva cornered Ryder and made him sit on the sofa. Summoning Mr. Tilt, she ordered more tea and threw a cashmere blanket over Ryder.

"I don't need this," he said, shoving the cover off his legs.

Eva grabbed it and threw it back over him. "You will once you stop moving around."

He kicked the blanket back off his legs again, and when she reached for it, he held her off with one arm and threw his legs over the blanket. She backed up and regarded him with that disapproving look. He was beginning to resent that look. She was treating him like a naughty child.

"Stop messing," he growled. "I'm fine, and you're driving me to distraction. Ow! See what you made me do? I'm getting a headache."

Eva threw up her hands and retreated to an armchair. "You gave yourself pains in the head by refusing to see a doctor and not sitting still. Ah, Mr. Tilt."

The butler entered with fresh pot of tea and a plate of hot scones. He set them on the small serving cart between the sofa and Eva's chair and produced packets of mail, which he handed to each of them. Eva set hers aside and poured tea while Ryder opened his. There were three letters from Pinkerton giving the situation in America and reports on Southern clandestine operations. Ryder arranged these by date and read the earliest one first.

He glanced at Eva and found her watching him eagerly. He couldn't help smiling at her. "Would you like to hear the news from Washington?"

"Please."

"The war has brought us to desperation already. Mr. Lincoln has suspended the writ of habeas corpus, and the military can now make summary arrests of people who are suspected of aiding the Confederacy and hold them without trial indefinitely. Unconstitutional, of course, but we're riddled with Southern sympathizers who spy on us constantly. Maryland and Kentucky are wavering, and we may lose them to the South. Kentucky is tied to the Confederacy by blood and trade, but Henry Clay was also from that state, so we shall try to hold her as well."

"Why?"

"Kentucky controls the south bank of the Ohio River, which is vital for military and trade purposes. Mr. Lincoln is trying to keep her neutral." Ryder folded the first letter and sighed, rubbing his forehead. "Fighting has broken out in Missouri, which is a border slave state. The governor is pro-secession, but Nathaniel Lyon controls St. Louis, and his faction is for the Union. I fear the state is split. Lincoln is trying to hold the border states while building up for war at the same time. Dear God, the fate of the nation is in his hands. I don't know how he bears it."

"Indeed. Mr. Lincoln has inherited a terrible responsibility, but he seems a most thoughtful and caring man. Rather like our Lord Russell."

Ryder met Eva's eyes, saw them crinkle with humor and smiled at her again. He seemed to be doing that more and more. "You're most perceptive, my lady."

They looked at each other without speaking. Eva grew solemn and met his gaze frankly. This was a woman to whom he could talk, he realized. He suspected he could tell her almost anything and receive sympathy and good judgment, without censure. How rare. She was turning pink, by God. He looked away and opened the second dispatch. By the time he finished and went on to the third, she had regained her composure. Ryder glanced at the top sheet of Pinkerton's report, saw a name and folded the pages. He was slipping them back into their envelope when Eva spoke.

"What's wrong?"

"Nothing. Just tedious military statistics."

Eva leaned back in her chair and drummed her fingers on its arm while she contemplated him. After a few moments she asked, "Who is Mrs. Gabrielle St. Cloud?"

"You can read upside down? However did you acquire such a skill?"

"It came in handy when my parents received letters from their—their intimate friends."

"Intimate friends," Ryder repeated. He eyed Eva, then said softly, "It seems you and I have had similar experiences in the past. My father wasn't the most faithful of husbands."

Eva managed a bright smile. "Among the nobility in England such things are to be expected."

"I know, but that doesn't make them right, or any easier for children to understand."

"I—I felt sorry for my mother," Eva said. She was tempted to go further, but at the same time the years of silence seemed an insurmountable barrier to speech. "They . . ." She tried again. "Th-they sent me away to a French boarding school, and at the time I thought it was— Oh, I don't know. I suppose every child feels abandoned when sent off to school without warning."

"Why did they send you away without warning?" Ryder asked, his expression softening.

Eva flushed. She couldn't speak of it. After all these years, hearing the words was a frightening prospect, for saying them aloud might release all the terrible pain she had experienced at the time. She searched for a distraction.

"That's not important. You haven't told me who Mrs. Gabrielle St. Cloud is."

Lowering his gaze, Ryder tightened his grip on the dispatches. "Alan Pinkerton says that she's suspected of being a Southern spy."

"Why?"

"She's from Louisiana, part French, and has become quite a popular hostess in Washington. Her family are spread from New Orleans to Nacogdoches in Texas, quite wealthy. Rice, sugar and cotton, I believe. Anyway, Mrs. St. Cloud has been entertaining high governmental officials from the Department of War as well as influential members of the Senate Appropriations Committee, and Pinkerton thinks she's sending information to the Confederates. Mrs. St. Cloud is a widow."

"Like me."

"Uh, yes."

"Is Mr. Pinkerton going to arrest her?"

Ryder frowned and turned his gaze to a window. "No. He hasn't any proof of her guilt. In any case, she left Washington suddenly, and she's here in London. Should have arrived yesterday."

"Good. I'll invite her to my ball. That way we can keep an eye on her."

"No!"

Eva stared at him.

"I mean, she isn't Iago, so there's no need."

"She might be Iago. I keep telling you it's dangerous to assume the assassin is a man."

"If you knew Mrs. St. Cloud, you wouldn't suspect her."

"So, you know her."

"A little."

Eva set her teacup down and rose. "Good, then you can introduce us."

"Wait!"

"I'm going to send a note to Dr. Parkhurst. You're looking pale, and I'm not going to listen to any more arguments, Ryder Drake."

Before he could stop her Eva was gone. Ryder thrust himself off the sofa, and pain immediately spiked through his head. Cursing, he subsided on top of the cashmere blanket.

"Aw, hell. Just what I need, Gabrielle St. Cloud."

How long had it been since he'd seen her? It had been almost ten years since he first met Gabrielle, because he'd been no more than twenty-three when he returned from Europe to take up his responsibilities at home. Once back in Virginia after so long an absence, he had been unable to tolerate the South's "peculiar institution;" he argued constantly with his father about slavery. Youthful intolerance made no allowance for what Simon Drake had known for a long time—his debts were such that any loss of income from Felicita's lands would mean a substantial reduction in the couple's position in Society. That in turn would mean the end of his marriage. Ryder had had no patience with such selfish motives; he still did not.

A year had passed, during which he and his father fought constantly. Finally, to distract his volatile son, Simon sent him to Louisiana to settle large debts he owed to several good friends. To Ryder's ire his father had sold two paintings from one of the country houses in England to finance the repayment. However, debts were matters of honor.

He had stayed with Jean Louis Racine and his wife, Marie, Creole friends of the family who lived in New Orleans, and it was there that he was introduced to one of the most beautiful ladies in the city, a young widow. Gabrielle St. Cloud was half French, half Creole, and a descendent of the founder of New Orleans, Jean Baptiste le Moyne, sieur de Bienville. The first time he saw her was in the interior court-yard of the Racine town house. He looked down at the fountain surrounded by bougainvillea and shaded by an ancient magnolia tree and glimpsed a young woman. Her lush figure, golden blond hair and violet eyes jolted him out of his habitual angry fugue. He hastened downstairs to be introduced.

"*Bonjour,* Monsieur Drake."

Three words and he was in love. She didn't say his name, she breathed it in a French accent—Drahhhk.

"It is so *charmant* to meet a man of culture, and you've recently returned from France, I understand. I would be most grateful if you could spare me a few moments of conversation about my second home."

All he could do was nod and allow her to take his arm for a stroll about the courtyard. He barely heard her comments at first, for he was sinking under the spell of an older woman for the first time in his life. Unlike the younger belles of the South, this woman had nothing of the nymph about her, no shy blushes, no callow innocence. Gabrielle gave him frankly ad-miring glances suffused with a natural sensuality. She communicated with fiery eyes, full lips and generous curves. Yet her sensuality contained a charming sweetness that wrapped its tendrils around his heart as it excited his body. Somehow, as they talked of Paris and Martinique, Versailles and Lyon, she gave him the impression of one of those Renaissance paintings of a nude woman on a gilded couch sur-rounded by cupids and overflowing cornucopias. All this combined with a very French sangfroid to make

Ryder feel as if he'd met the most fascinating woman in existence. And Gabrielle St. Cloud knew how he felt from the beginning.

Before she left that afternoon she contemplated him from behind lowered lashes as she slowly waved a black lace fan. "Monsieur Drake, you must come to visit me with your friends. A poor widow does not attend balls and parties, and I am so lonely in my empty house. Sometimes my only company is Mama Gris-gris, who raised me. Come when Monsieur *et* Madame Racine visit me."

He stuttered his acceptance and suffered torments of impatience waiting for the day when Jean Louis and Marie would call upon Madame St. Cloud. The lady lived in a sun-drenched town house filled with Louis XIV furniture and built around a courtyard filled with palm trees, orchids and a giant magnolia. The first time he visited with the Racines a tall, stately Negro woman met them at the door. She wore a red turban, a black bombazine gown and dozens of clicking bracelets on her arms.

"Welcome, gentlefolk," she said in low, full tones that reminded Ryder of the voice of a cardinal he'd heard in Rome.

Without warning the woman fastened a direct and searing gaze on him, something Ryder wasn't accustomed to from a servant. She wrapped a big, strong hand around his arm, pulled him closer and stared deep into his eyes.

"Mama Gris-gris sees your soul, boy. You be warned. Papa Ghede is coming for you."

Jean Louis burst into laughter, as did Ryder, but Mama Gris-gris scowled at them and went to find her mistress. There followed days of tantalizingly formal calls during which he could do nothing more than drink in the sight of Gabrielle St. Cloud, and these were followed by nights of excruciating arousal. He was helplessly infatuated with a woman five years older than he was. Jean Louis noticed, of course, and warned him he didn't know what he was doing. Ryder paid no attention. He would have called upon Gabrielle every day, but such forwardness would have been unacceptable to Society. So he began to go on long rides out of town, skirting the marshes and swamps, driving himself to exhaustion in an effort to rid himself of his passion and get a peaceful night's sleep. He had been doing this for a couple of weeks when one day he took his customary path through a grove of moss-covered oaks. Something appeared ahead of him, and he blinked. Gabrielle rode toward him through shimmering sunbeams.

"Monsieur Drake, what a surprise. Are you a— what is it called—an *adorateur du soleil*? A worshiper of the sun, like me?"

Both of them knew her presence was no accident. Ryder's heart soared as they walked their horses side by side. Blood pounded in his temples while thunderclouds advanced upon them, bringing violent winds and rain. Had she also known there would be a storm? They took shelter in a shack in a field of sugarcane, and he rushed about making a suitable cushion out of old potato sacks and hay. His teeth were chattering, for the storm had brought a cold wind. Finally she caught his arm and made him drop the armful of hay he was carrying. Her fingers loosened his collar. He dared not move, for fear of breaking this spell of intimacy. Outside, the cold wind battered the old shack, and inside, Gabrielle tasted the hot furnace of his mouth. She took his face in her hands.

"Ah, *cher enfant,* you are so beautiful. I must

confess that Mama Gris-gris told me you would be here. Do you forgive me?"

"Of—of course, but how did Mama Gris-gris know where I'd be?"

"Ah, Mama Gris-gris knows many things. She is my second mother, and she has great power." Gabrielle touched a fingertip to his lips. "Perhaps, *mon ami*, it was she who brought us together with her magic."

"You are magic," he blurted out.

Gabrielle looked into his eyes and shook her head slightly. "*Dieu*, you are so innocent. They should have warned you about me. To my credit, I tried to leave you in peace. Now it is too late, and you must save yourself. Go now, for I will not give you this chance again."

Of course he didn't go, as she had known he would not. Hours later he left that shack as much a slave as a white man could be. Weeks passed by like seconds, during which he lived only for their brief and secret meetings. Often Gabrielle would send word to him by Mama Gris-gris, who would appear suddenly at night in unexpected places, catching him alone. At Gabrielle's direction he rented an apartment in Jackson Square. When she could get away safely and undetected, she came to him there. She became the tutor and he the student in such arts as he had never suspected a well-born lady could acquire. Letters from his parents arrived and went unopened. Jean Louis called at Simon Drake's bidding, but Ryder told him to go away.

He attended social functions only if Gabrielle was going to be there. He stayed only as long as she did and cast furtive glances her way when he thought himself unobserved, feeding the hunger and savage lust she awakened in him. He was only happy in her presence, and out of it, he thought only of her. Gabrielle had but to express a wish and he tried to make it come true. He showered gifts upon her—jewelry, costly fabrics for gowns, an Arabian mare. Had he bothered to reflect, he would have seen his father in himself, but Ryder wasn't thinking.

Six months passed in hot, obsessive thrall, and on the twelfth day of the seventh month—it was December—Gabrielle failed to come to him at the appointed hour. He waited all night for her, growing more and more frantic, until he finally went to her house. It was one o'clock in the morning, and the house was dark. He climbed an aged pecan tree to her balcony and found the lady asleep. Waking her, he demanded an explanation.

"Did you not get my message?" she asked sleepily.

"What message?"

Gabrielle yawned prettily. "Oh, dear. You must pardon me, *mon cher*. I forgot to write the note. Unexpected company. Friends from Paris arrived, and I couldn't leave. You understand. Now, don't pout, dear boy. It doesn't become you, and I simply cannot tolerate it."

Then Mama Gris-gris appeared out of nowhere, grabbed his arm and whispered, "Foolish boy. Mama Gris-gris done warned you. Now Papa Ghede has you in his power."

Gabrielle, in the midst of silk sheets, her hair tousled, smiled at them.

Ryder stared from one to the other. "What are you ranting about, woman?"

Mama Gris-gris released him and cackled. "Papa Ghede be the ruler of death and sex. He wear a black undertaker's coat and a black top hat, and he dance like you never saw no decent man dance." Mama Gris-gris began to hum and sway, then she twirled around him. "Papa Ghede dance like this."

Ryder gaped at the woman as she performed an erotic dance. She drew close, grabbed his hips and imitated the act of copulation until he shoved her away. At his look of horror, Gabrielle's musical laughter poured over him.

Mama Gris-gris danced close to him again and stopped abruptly. She hit him on the shoulder and placed her hands on her hips. "Too late for you, boy. Papa Ghede got into your soul, and he give you to Kalfu. Kalfu be black magic and most dangerous. Now death sit on your shoulder, boy."

Backing away from this bizarre woman, he heard Gabrielle's voice. "Go away now, *cher* Ryder. Indeed, you're becoming altogether too tedious."

That was the beginning. A few days later Gabrielle told him not to call on her, for fear of exciting talk. When he objected she grew furious and threatened not to see him at all. He capitulated and stayed away for a week. But his resolve broke, and he maneuvered an invitation to join Jean Louis and Marie in attending a party Gabrielle hadn't told him she was giving. It was there, maintaining a discreet distance, that he saw her giving another man the same sexual appraisal she had once given him. It was all he could do not to explode into a rage. He quickly left and got drunk. He skulked back in the middle of the night to confront Gabrielle once again. This time she was cold and distant, listening to him rant with a raised eyebrow and tapping foot.

She banished him from her presence, until he groveled at her feet, begging forgiveness. To his relief she did forgive him, and their relationship seemed to return to normal. Then a week or so later Gabrielle suddenly accepted an invitation to visit friends on their plantation on the Mississippi. She was gone.

Ryder prowled New Orleans like a trapped leopard. He haunted Gabrielle's house on the chance that she might come back unexpectedly. The days crawled by in misery, until he learned one afternoon from an acquaintance that Madame St. Cloud had returned. She'd been back for several days and hadn't sent for him.

He rushed to her house, heedless of appearances. Charging past her butler, he burst into the drawing room. She was with the man she had been with at the party, the Spaniard named Villafranca. Their backs were to him, and he was on one knee with his lips pressed to her palm. Ryder stopped to gawk at them, speechless. But the young man saw him and had plenty of words. Their tempers blazed, and then without warning Villafranca slapped him with a glove and challenged him to a duel. Gabrielle was furious, but neither man paid her any heed.

That was how Ryder ended up at the edge of a mist-ridden swamp the next night with his back to a young man barely twenty, with a dueling pistol in his hand. He'd refused the entreaties of all his friends, his rage and desire feeding off his jealousy. He thought of nothing but Gabrielle, certain that he could prove his greater worthiness and win her back.

So he stood on mushy ground shivering and batting away mosquitoes. The air was so thick with moisture it was like breathing water. Ryder's second was pleading with him, but he shook his head, his mind filled with the sight of Gabrielle with Villafranca, her new lover. Before he knew it, the count began.

They turned, and Ryder heard a shot. Something whizzed by, stinging his cheek as he fired his pistol. His adversary spun around and dropped into the fog. At that moment Ryder's obsession shattered like dropped pier glass. Stumbling numbly over the soggy field, he knelt beside Villafranca. His rival stared up at him in pain and surprise.

"It hurts," he said in a boy's voice. "It hurts." He swallowed. Blood appeared at the corner of his mouth and trickled down his neck.

Hands pushed Ryder aside. A surgeon and a priest busied themselves over Villafranca. Ryder got to his feet and watched, but the surgeon shook his head and mumbled something to the priest, who began the last rites.

Villafranca looked up at the priest in horror. "No! Please, I don't want to die."

Ryder turned away, and to his shock saw a shadowy movement. Moonlit mist parted to reveal the tall, cloaked form of Mama Gris-gris. The woman said nothing but raised her arm and pointed at him, her bracelets setting up a ghostly clatter as she laughed softly. As suddenly as she had appeared, she vanished, leaving swirling mist behind.

All these years later Villafranca's dying words haunted Ryder. And the shame, and the guilt. The blood on his hands. He would never forgive himself or Gabrielle. Sitting on the sofa in Tennyson House, Ryder dropped his head into his hands and groaned as the memories tormented him. Enslavement drove a man to great sin.

# CHAPTER ELEVEN

೧೨

EVA WAS EXHAUSTED but determined to remain alert. She was making polite conversation with Mr. and Mrs. Bird while they waited for all the guests to arrive at the house of Lord and Lady Radwinter for a dinner party. Having given her own ball last week, Eva had yet to recover from the strain.

Three hundred and fifty guests. Her hand still ached from writing the invitations. Giving a ball was akin to being in charge of military maneuvers. There was the orchestra to engage; the ballroom floor had to be polished with beeswax. Refreshments had to be provided, and cloak rooms and card rooms for the older guests arranged. A supper with an elaborate menu was mandatory. Besides the menus Eva had to supervise the decorations—thousands of lilies and roses and gold tissue, ferns and shrubbery to hide the orchestra.

On the fateful night she stood for an hour receiving guests as they came in the front door. Then the ritual of opening the ball came, in which she danced with the guest of highest rank, who was a duke. All this effort so that Ryder could slither among the American guests and worm his way into their acquaintance. The only American he hadn't wanted there was Mrs. St. Cloud. Ever since he had found out the woman was in town he'd been acting strangely. He refused to talk about her, and any mention of her name made him close up like a bank vault. He would discuss other Southern operatives, but not Mrs. St. Cloud. Eva wanted to know why.

Ryder's men had already secretly investigated the houses and rooms of several suspects—the Birds, Zachariah Gordon and others. So far they'd found no evidence that any of them was the assassin. The ball allowed Ryder to wangle invitations to call on Cornelius and Mrs. Bird, as well as Mr. Gordon. Most important, Eva had invited the Honorable Henry Spencer-Howling and his houseguest, the elusive Colonel Nathan Longstreet. Longstreet turned out to be the epitome of the dashing cavalry officer. Resplendent in a new gray uniform with gold braid, he impressed the English ladies with his gallantry.

Eva found herself swept up in Longstreet's charm as well. Clean-shaven, dark-haired and lean, he teased her about her lack of height and her copper hair, but he did it so sweetly that he had Eva laughing at herself. In the midst of their exchange Ryder drew Longstreet away to engage him in talk about West Point and the growing Confederate army. Eva could have told him such a ploy would be useless. Longstreet was no fool. Later Ryder sent Noah Frye to follow the officer for a few days and report back on his movements.

With the ball over, Eva had an entire day just to recover from sore feet and fraught nerves. Now she was back at the social grind at yet another large dinner party, and the only reason she felt able to endure it was that Mrs. St. Cloud was to attend. Lady Radwinter had sought Eva's help with her guest list and seating plan, for the order of precedence was a tricky, complicated affair. Many a dinner had been ruined by a hostess' blunder in failing to comprehend the Byzantine rules of rank and title.

The early minutes of a dinner party were perhaps the easiest. Guests were greeted by a pigeon-breasted butler and proceeded upstairs to the first-floor drawing room to converse boringly until everyone had arrived. Once everyone was together, the host and hostess circulated to discreetly pair off the ladies and gentlemen according to rank. To figure out the order of the procession into dinner, the hostess had to consult *DeBrett's Peerage*. This publication listed each member of the aristocracy according to lineage and assigned a number value to every peer, his wife and his children. Eva watched with sympathy as Lady Radwinter hesitantly marshaled her guests. She glanced behind her to see that Ryder had been paired with a last-minute arrival.

Eva's eyes widened as she took in the burnished gold locks corkscrewing at the back of the lady's head. The newcomer had enormous eyes of a unique violet shade that caught one's attention and held it. Looking at this smiling beauty made Eva feel even shorter and more ordinary-looking than usual. Ryder had been struck by the lady's appearance too, for he stood beside her stiffly, looking straight ahead as if he was afraid he would stare at his partner.

Eva's escort, Lord Montague, began to move, and she dragged her gaze away from the startling lady. That, she thought, had to be Gabrielle St. Cloud. She knew this because Lady Radwinter had asked her advice on pairing off the Americans, and Eva had suggested that Mrs. St. Cloud could be placed safely with Mr. Drake without fear of insult. If Mr. Drake wouldn't talk about the lady, Eva would have to see what happened when they encountered each other.

Eva's eyes narrowed with thoughts about Ryder and Gabrielle St. Cloud. The moment she'd seen Ryder's reaction to Mrs. St. Cloud's name in that dispatch from Mr. Pinkerton she'd known there had been something between them. She'd been excruciatingly curious ever since. It was intrusive and rude, but she couldn't seem to help herself. She hated the idea that Mrs. St. Cloud might be important to Ryder. If Ryder shared a past with her, he might not be as careful around her as he should, even though he knew she was a suspected Confederate agent.

What if Mrs. St. Cloud had been sent to harm him? This, along with the incident at the British Museum, was why Eva had put a small derringer in the pocket of her gown this evening. She was determined to carry it as long as Ryder was in danger. Wincing at the thought, Eva reflected that his welfare had somehow become terribly important to her. Having the derringer in hand had forced her to admit this to herself, but she wasn't prepared to examine the extent of her attachment to this glowering, handsome American.

Once they were downstairs and seated in the dining room, Eva glimpsed the pair once again by peering around an enormous, heavy silver epergne squatting in the middle of the table. She continued to watch the pair, for Ryder's sake, of course. Mrs. St. Cloud was looking at Ryder from beneath thick lashes with a shy smile, but Ryder was still staring ahead. The man seemed frozen, almost as if he was frightened. Worried, Eva studied Ryder until a raucous laugh distracted her. She looked farther down the table to see Zachariah Gordon wiping tears of amusement from his eyes.

As the dinner began everyone followed the rule of conversing with the person on his left, which left Eva talking to sleepy old Sir Horace "Bug Eyes" Fotheringay from the soup through a turbot and sauces, the pâtés, the veal, sweetbreads and cutlets with peas. She kept glancing at Ryder and Mrs. St. Cloud, but both were studiously conversing with other people.

After the venison and salads the conversation circle was reversed to continue during the next course of goose and asparagus, plovers' eggs in aspic, candied fruits, jellies and creams, beets, more salad, along with sardines and cheeses. Now Ryder and Mrs. St. Cloud were talking. The lady was whispering to him, and her gaze seemed fixed on his hands. Ryder stiffened and turned pale. He barely nodded, but this seemed to satisfy his partner, for she smiled in a gratified way and popped a candied apricot into her mouth. Five kinds of cake followed in the next course, accompanied by ices and fruit. The ladies stood to retire to the drawing room, and Eva realized this was her chance to meet Mrs. St. Cloud.

Eva hurried past several ladies, a countess and an honorable and caught up with Lady Radwinter. As the lady of superior rank it was for Eva to request an introduction.

"Dearest Louise, what a splendid dinner," Eva said as she intercepted her hostess.

"Oh, do you think so?" Lady Radwinter whispered as they entered the drawing room, where coffee and tea awaited them. "Lord Radwinter was so anxious that this party succeed. As the assistant to the chancellor of the exchequer he's most eager to demonstrate his suitability for a higher post."

Eva tapped Louise Radwinter with her fan. "An absolute success, my dear. And such a lovely mix of people. All the right ministers and just enough foreigners to make things interesting. Oh, by the way, I simply must meet that lovely lady with the golden hair, if only to ask her where she buys her gowns."

"Yes, of course. She's Mrs. St. Cloud."

"Oh, so that's the lady you were concerned about in the seating arrangements."

"Yes, and you were right. Mr. Drake's fascination for the ladies proved most helpful. I do believe she's enjoying herself." Lady Radwinter took Eva to a group of chairs by the fireplace and introduced her to Mrs. Gabrielle St. Cloud before leaving them alone.

"May I compliment you on your gown, Mrs. St. Cloud?"

"Why, *merci,* Lady Sparrow. Monsieur Worth is a genius, is he not?"

Mrs. St. Cloud wore a coral gown with a silver diagonal embroidered sunburst. The rays for the sunburst started at the lower right of the skirt and swept across the gown to the lady's waist, an unusual design in an age of flounces and lace.

"I understand we have a mutual acquaintance. Mr. Drake," Eva said, watching the American closely.

"Oh?" Mrs. St. Cloud's flawless brow furrowed, then cleared. "Ah, yes, dear Ryder mentioned he was staying with Lord Tennyson and his niece, Lady Sparrow." She gave Eva a speculative glance. "I must say I expected an older lady, but that was only because you were described as a widow. I of all people should not make such a mistake. *Oui?* But tell me, how long have you known dear Ryder?"

"Not long."

Mrs. St. Cloud dropped her gaze to stare into the fire pensively. "Ryder and I have been friends for many years. He is a . . . He is a special friend, *un ami intime,* if you will."

"Your pardon, Mrs. St. Cloud, but I happened to glance your way during dinner, and Mr. Drake appeared uncomfortable. I hope there was no unpleasantness."

The American uttered a low, gruff chuckle that made Eva's skin crawl. *"Mais non."* Mrs. St. Cloud leaned closer to Eva and began to whisper. "I feel that you are a lady one can trust with confidences, so I will confess something. You see, years ago in New Orleans Ryder fell in love with me. He was such a beautiful young man, but I was a new widow, and my heart was frozen. I fear Ryder still suffers from *la grande passion.*"

"Indeed," Eva said coolly. Before she could think of a retort, more ladies joined them and the conversation shifted back to Mrs. St. Cloud's stylish gown.

Monstrous woman, Eva thought. How presumptuous. She probably thinks every man she meets falls in love with her forever. Eva stalked over to a servant and accepted a cup of tea.

"She's probably right too. What a disgusting thought."

"My lady?" the servant said.

"Oh, nothing. Thank you."

At that moment the gentlemen rejoined the ladies, and the room filled with laughing, talking groups of guests. There was to be a performance by a famous opera tenor as the after-dinner entertainment. Eva tried to speak with Ryder, but he was engaged in an earnest conversation with Lord Russell.

Thwarted several times from cornering him, she decided to retreat to the necessary facilities reserved for the ladies down the hall. The whole time she was growing more and more apprehensive about Mrs. St. Cloud. What if Ryder was still in love with her? The idea repulsed her. Just imagining him groveling before that odious woman sickened her.

More worried than she cared to admit, Eva was adjusting her gown in front of a mirror when she heard something in the hallway. All thoughts of Mrs. St. Cloud vanished as she listened to a pair of voices. The first was Zachariah Gordon's, the second Cornelius Bird's.

"Got to go at once. Make my excuses to Lord and Lady Radwinter."

"You should do that yourself," Bird said. "What's wrong?"

"Urgent business, vital, in fact. Must go at once, man. No time for leave-taking."

Footsteps hurried away, and Eva poked her head out the door in time to see Cornelius Bird headed toward the drawing room while Gordon rushed the other way. What urgent business could an ex slave-dealer have in London? No legitimate business, she was sure. Considering Zachariah Gordon's character, the business had to be as evil as the man.

Eva moved rapidly after Gordon, who was already into his coat and stepping outside. She watched him leave, realizing that there was no time to do anything but follow him if she wanted to know where he was going and what was so important as to make him depart so precipitously. A servant brought her cloak and reticule, and she rushed outside to see

Gordon's carriage driving down the road, going east toward Parliament.

Heedless of the butler's offer to summon her carriage, Eva hailed a passing hansom cab and ordered the driver to follow Gordon's carriage. As the journey continued east toward the slums, Eva began to wish she'd had time to find Ryder. Her hand clutched the derringer in her pocket and stayed there. Finally the cab slowed.

" 'E's got out, m'lady," the driver said. He opened the cab door and handed Eva down. "You sure you want to be roamin' around 'ere? This ain't no place for you, m'lady."

"Thank you, driver. Please wait for me." She handed the man several pounds and promised more for his time if he was there when she returned.

"Right, m'lady. But don't go too far. This 'ere's Whitechapel, and it ain't fit for no lady even in daylight."

Gathering her skirts in one hand and her derringer in the other, Eva set off after Zachariah Gordon, leaving the hansom cab behind. The streets were shrouded in a dense, yellow fog so thick she couldn't see past the length of her arm. The pavement was broken, the drains noxious, but the weight of the gun in her hand reassured Eva. She could brave a few dark streets after surviving the American frontier.

Eva followed Zachariah Gordon deeper into Whitechapel, down streets crowded with gin shops, prostitutes and drunks. An inebriated costermonger stumbled into her path from a tavern.

"Well, well. If it in't a lady all pretty and proper. Give us a little smack."

Eva raised the derringer and aimed it at the man's stomach. "I think not."

The costermonger hiccuped and stumbled away. Zachariah Gordon was ahead of her, and he turned into a back street that grew narrower and less crowded. He quickened his pace, and Eva tried to match her steps with his for fear he'd hear her. The fog ebbed a bit, leaving her in dirty, dripping blackness relieved only by the faint glow of a sputtering gaslight.

Eva slipped around a corner following her quarry and found herself in a narrow, covered passage called Threadneedle Alley that ran between two lanes. A gutter ran down the middle of the passage, and it stank. What was worse, she couldn't see or hear Gordon anymore. She could hear the muffled raucous noise of gin shops, distant street fights and the calls of vendors hawking meat pies and pastries. But Gordon seemed to have vanished, and Eva began to get a feeling that she was being watched. She tightened her grip on the derringer and walked as quietly and slowly down the passage as she could.

Even the *drip, drip, drip* of condensation off rooftops seemed loud in this isolated and stinking warren. Eva reached the end of the alley and halted, certain that someone was waiting for her beyond the cover of the passage. She jumped as the distant Big Ben tolled twelve o'clock. More frightened than if she were facing a band of Comanches, Eva held her breath and strained to hear anything. At last she detected the sound of breathing—harsh, labored, wet. She retreated a few steps, but an enormous black bulk suddenly appeared in the alley and loomed out of the shadows. She cried out and aimed her derringer, but the figure made a peculiar gagging sound.

Eva froze as she glimpsed Zachariah Gordon's white face and the blood dribbling from the corner of his mouth. His hands were wrapped around a knife protruding from his stomach. Eva screamed and retreated as Gordon tumbled forward and hit the ground. When she stopped screaming she heard a welcome sound. Ryder Drake was calling to her from several streets away.

"I'm here in the alley!" Eva cried.

She stood over Gordon, clutching herself and shivering as Ryder appeared and rushed to her. Sweeping her up in his arms, he nearly crushed her.

"Are you all right?"

"Y-yes. Just shocked. He's—he's dead." Eva buried her face in Ryder's shoulder, and he squeezed her even tighter.

"God, when I heard you scream I nearly died from fright," he said. "Be quiet for a moment." Eva lifted her head and saw that he was checking the passage for danger and studying Gordon's body. Suddenly his grip tightened, and he looked down at her. "Dear God, you could have been killed."

She knew he was going to kiss her, and she suddenly wanted him to; it was what she desired, and it would make the fear go away. She stood on tiptoe. At the same time he squeezed her hard, and she gasped.

Ryder loosened his hold but kept her within the circle of his arms. His hand touched her chin and lifted her face, and he kissed her hard. Then he released her abruptly, and his mood shifted.

Glaring down at her, he almost shouted, "Don't ever run off by yourself like that again. Do you understand me?"

Eva merely blinked at him. This man's kiss could enrapture Medusa.

"Did you hear me?" he growled.

"Oh, yes."

"Good. I was looking for you and questioned the butler, who said you'd rushed off after Gordon."

"Not now, Ryder." Eva stepped away from him. She was still shaking, even more so now because of the kiss. She wished she could ask him what the kiss meant, but ladies didn't ask such things. Pointing to Gordon's body with a shaking finger, she said, "Someone stabbed him."

Ryder glanced at the body, then walked carefully up and down the alley. He kicked open the door to a shed, but it was deserted, and he returned to Eva.

"Whoever did it is gone now." He bent over the corpse and searched it. "Nothing of interest. He has no money on him either. Must have been robbed."

Fighting nausea, Eva steadied her breathing and walked in the direction from which Gordon had come. Just past the covered passage, she drew near the door Ryder had kicked open. The shed leaned against a larger building.

"Ryder," Eva whispered. "When I was following Gordon, he seemed to vanish. I think he might have gone in here."

Ryder went ahead of her. The door to the larger building opened onto a small room. Its furnishings were discarded vegetable boxes and burlap sacks. There was one half-spent candle stuck in a tin cup. Ryder lit the candle. Calmer now, Eva noticed a sheet of paper sticking out from beneath one of the boxes. She pulled it loose and saw that it was an antislavery pamphlet published by the Sons of Freedom, a group known for its secrecy and the anonymity of its members. They raided plantations in border states, setting fires and freeing slaves. There had been several instances during which gunfire resulted in the deaths of overseers or plantation owners.

There was nothing in the pamphlet to indicate who had printed it or who its author was. Beneath another of the boxes, on which rested a pile of sacks, Ryder discovered a piece of chalk and more pamphlets. Tossing the paper and sacks aside, he revealed a crude map drawn on the top of the box. It was of London's fashionable Mayfair district, with the location of Lord Palmerston's town house clearly marked.

Ryder looked up from the map, his features severe. "There's only one reason Gordon would know about this place."

"You think he was creating evidence to be used to implicate the Sons of Freedom in the assassination," Eva said.

"He certainly wasn't an abolitionist himself."

Eva frowned. "Then what happened to him?"

Ryder went outside and came back with something clutched in his hand. He opened it to reveal a wad of money and coins.

"Like I said, robbery," he said. "You must have interrupted the thief and he dropped this."

"Heavens."

Sighing, Ryder leaned against the door frame. "I never would have guessed. To hide behind a guise so utterly fanatical, it's so unlike what I've learned of Iago. What luck that he fell victim to an ordinary robbery in the slums."

"You think Mr. Gordon was Iago?" Eva cast about the shed uncertainly.

"Hiding in plain sight, I suppose."

Ryder stuffed Gordon's money in his pocket and began to gather up the pamphlets. Eva watched him for a moment, then picked up a sack and rubbed the chalk map off the box lid.

As she scrubbed, she thought about Zachariah Gordon. "Ryder, I'm not convinced that Mr. Gordon was Iago. He was violent enough to be an assassin, but I don't think he was clever enough to do the things Iago has done."

Ryder struck a match and touched it to the pile of pamphlets. "That's just it. Iago is clever enough not to appear clever when he's on a mission. The guise of Zachariah Gordon would suit such a purpose. I never would have suspected him."

"But—"

"There's one thing we haven't considered." Ryder dropped the burning pamphlets on the floor. "We don't know whether Gordon contacted the abolitionists he was going to use as dupes. From what I've seen here, I assume he has." He cracked the door open and looked outside. "Still deserted. If he was meeting an ally, the commotion probably warned him away."

Eva shivered and said, "May we discuss this on the way home? I hate it that Mr. Gordon is lying out there. Shouldn't we summon the police?"

"No. One look at you and they'll be asking all sorts of inconvenient questions." Ryder offered his arm, and Eva took it as they left the shed. "My cab wouldn't wait. We may have to walk a long way to get another."

"My hansom is waiting for me still, I hope."

They were lucky to find the driver asleep on top of his cab. On the way home Eva still felt unsettled, and it was more than having seen a man murdered.

"Why would a Confederate agent leave so much evidence at his hideout?"

Ryder shrugged. "He didn't leave anything that would incriminate him, only evidence that would point to the presence of abolitionists. That's the point."

"And what about the robbery and murder? It's too much of a coincidence, and anyway, I thought Iago was too skilled to fall victim to a Whitechapel ruffian." Eva twisted around on the seat to confront Ryder. "Zachariah Gordon was supposed to be an ordinary planter, so who would want to harm him?"

Ryder shook his head. "You're overcomplicating things. The simplest and most logical explanation is that Gordon was killed by a robber. Anyone can be caught unaware."

"I don't like it," Eva said as she sat back in the seat. "There's more to this killing than a simple robbery gone wrong."

Ryder turned and looked at her closely. "Now see. I knew this would happen. You're allowing your imagination too much freedom. You're very pale. This bloody business is too much for you. Are you going to faint?"

"Of course not. Don't be absurd, and quit staring at me as if I were having vapors. I'm perfectly fine."

"You're shaking." He squeezed her hands and kissed her cheek.

Eva drew a deep, unsteady breath. "I'll be fine. I just don't think we should stop looking for the assassin."

"I'm not going to stop. I know there may be others involved in the plot. It would be foolish to drop my guard. The danger isn't over, but the most likely explanation for what we've seen is that Zachariah Gordon was the one for whom we've been searching."

"And I still don't believe we know the truth."

Having reached an impasse, they lapsed into silence. Ryder pulled her close to him, and Eva didn't object. If she could she would have burrowed against him and shut out the world.

Eva pulled her cloak closer about her shoulders. "Did you learn anything from Mrs. St. Cloud?"

"No."

"Surely after an absence of so many years you had much to say to each other."

Ryder turned to stare at her. "What do you know of our acquaintance?"

"Oh, Mrs. St. Cloud claims you as an admirer."

Eva watched him closely. He had one of those faces that could reveal great depths of emotion, but he knew how to maintain a neutral expression in the face of much provocation. Only moments ago he'd been as attentive as a lover. He'd been genuinely worried about her—frantic, even. Yet there was the matter of Mrs. St. Cloud.

"Perhaps I was an—an admirer many years ago," Ryder said faintly. He loosened his hold on her.

"She claims you're still in love with her."

There it was, that look of frozen pain she'd seen at dinner. It was gone in an instant, so that she almost thought she'd imagined it.

Ryder shrugged. "Mrs. St. Cloud has a lively imagination. I admired her when I was quite young, but things happen, and . . ."

"What happened?" Eva asked.

Ryder shut his eyes briefly; then his lips twisted into a smile. "It's a private matter of no consequence to the business at hand, which is Zachariah Gordon. I'll contact Scotland Yard about him. We should intensify our efforts to search out the Sons of Freedom and the other fanatical abolitionist groups."

"You can confide in me about Mrs. St. Cloud," Eva said gently.

"No."

"But—"

"I said no!"

"Don't you shout at me, Ryder Drake."

"I'm sorry."

The haunted look on his face made Eva change the subject. "I think there's more to Gordon's murder than you suspect."

"I have no intention of dropping my guard, but you know very well that Whitechapel is a dangerous place. You're lucky something terrible didn't happen to you as well."

"What if someone killed Gordon and left those clues in the shed on purpose?"

"You're letting your imagination run wild. Seeing Gordon like that has been traumatic, and you're overthinking things. Look at you. You're still trembling."

"From the cold," Eva said. She didn't want to admit just how upset she was.

The carriage arrived at Tennyson House. Wanting to demonstrate her steadiness, Eva jumped out unaided.

Ryder shook his head and followed her inside. "You're a stubborn woman, Eva Sparrow."

Adolphus Tennyson hurried out of his study. "Where have you two been? Do you know what a furor you caused? Eva, my dear, if I hadn't been there to stop it, there would have been a scandal. I made up some silly excuse, which I hope everyone believed."

"Zachariah Gordon left suddenly, and she followed him without thinking," Ryder said.

Eva sighed. "I did think, but there was no time to warn anyone that I wanted to follow him."

Tennyson clucked and patted her arm. "Really, my dear, you should have fetched Mr. Drake."

Ryder folded his arms over his chest, his eyes gleaming in satisfaction as he nodded.

Eva gritted her teeth. "I told you. There was no time." She bit her lip, then continued quietly. "Besides, I had a gun for protection."

"What!" Both men stared at her in consternation.

Eva produced the derringer, holding it nose-down.

Ryder snatched it. "I'll take that, if you please."

Eva held out her hand. "Give me the gun."

"Now, Eva," her uncle said, "Mr. Drake is right. You shouldn't carry a gun. Ladies don't carry guns."

"They do if they're hunting criminals."

"But you're not going to hunt criminals," Ryder pointed out. "No more running about Whitechapel for you, my lady."

Lowering her hand, Eva fixed both men with an irritated stare, but they remained united in masculine disapproval. Eva rolled her eyes and headed for the stairs. She ascended, but halfway up heard Ryder's swift tread across the marble floor. She turned to see him leaning on the banister, gazing up at her with a worried frown.

"Eva," he said. The lofty ceiling and abundant marble amplified his voice. "You frightened me."

It was hard to remain adamant with a man as handsome as Ryder gazing up at her. "I'm sorry you were frightened. But I won't be put in a glass box on a shelf. I want to experience life, not watch it pass me by."

"Your way of experiencing life is going to cut mine short by scaring me to death."

As appealing as he was, she had no intention of letting Ryder Drake charm her into submission. "You can't have it both ways, sir. You dislike useless, vapid women, so you must get used to those of us who aren't."

Eva left him staring at her, but as she reached the landing she heard him chuckle. "Dang. Are those my only choices?"

# CHAPTER TWELVE

❧

A DEVILISH GLOW hung over Lambeth Market in the New Cut, South London. It was the twenty-sixth of May, late afternoon, but the sky remained dark from the clouds that hung low over the city. Buildings oozed moisture, and fog penetrated the bones of that ubiquitous entrepreneur, the costermonger—from the blacking sellers, nostrum vendors, apple and flower sellers to the vendors of bootlaces, knives, chestnuts and bonnets.

In Lambeth there were hundreds of stalls and barrows from which hung gas lamps that burned with a white light, or old-fashioned grease lamps that gave off an eerie red glow. More reddish light issued from the baked-chestnut stoves, while the less fortunate made do with a candle set in a sieve. Through this sparkling light issued an endless cacophony: " 'Ot chestnuts right 'ere!" "Flahers, pretty flahers!" "Oo will buy my strawberries, ripe strawberries?"

Such a jostling and calling, hustling and pleading, all before the Lambeth shops, the butchers, the tea dealers, whose gaslights fluttered and sparkled in the breeze. The whole market teemed with artificial light, so that from a distance the New Cut looked as if it burned with a hellish fire. And yet shadows and dark places abounded—alleys and dead ends, forgotten passages and deserted warehouses clustered at the edges of the market.

The fog glowed red with the Lambeth light, making the whole place an otherworldly nimbus. Into this glow slipped the man known as Iago, the collar of his coat turned up, a soft hat low upon his head. He carried a cane with a sterling silver top in the shape of a wolf's head. He had been diligent in his work, researching and investigating, looking for just the right opportunity to carry out his task. The timing of his task was crucial, and discovering the right time demanded creativity. At the same time he had distracted his enemy, providing an opportunity for Ryder Drake to discover the perfect would-be assassin. And as Providence would have it, an additional chance to toy with Drake had appeared, which was why Iago was skulking about Lambeth Market in near-darkness.

He strode past a butcher shop, his walking stick clicking over the bricks. He turned down a passage used to reach the animal stalls, and into the next street. There the glow of Lambeth faded, although he could still hear the cries of the costermongers. He went to the door of a secondhand bookshop, opened it with a key and slipped inside. A bell over the door tinkled, but no one answered its call. His ally would be there any minute. He had seen her approaching from the other end of the market, her hooded cloak disguising that luminous gold hair and shadowing her violet eyes.

Iago leaned his cane against the book dealer's counter. Wiping his face with his gloved hands, he grimaced. The fog clung to his skin, leaving a greasy film that was most unpleasant. He sniffed, wrinkled his nose and glanced around at the myriad shelves of old books. Carts filled with bargains littered the floor, and over everything hung the odors of dust and mildew. Iago wasn't happy. In spite of her usefulness he disliked working with the lady, with anyone. If his superiors hadn't ordered it, he would have never contacted her. He was always careful never to leave behind witnesses to his doings. Now he had not just a witness, but an associate, and an unpredictable one. Possibly it would be necessary to make sure that the lady never talked about her adventures in London. The bell over the door tinkled again, and his associate entered.

Gabrielle St. Cloud pushed the hood off her hair and waved a hand in front of her face. "*Merde,* what an evening. Lambeth stinks, and so does this place."

"I hope you guard your language when you're with Drake. He doesn't care for rough women."

"Don't tell me how to behave," Gabrielle sneered. "I can deal with Monsieur Drake."

"You'd better. My plans are complete, and the next few weeks are crucial. Make sure Drake is in no condition to think clearly. Destroy his peace; shatter his reason and consume his every thought. You did it once before. You should be able to do it again. With Drake's mind wrecked, I'll have a free hand. After that, you may leave London for Washington."

Gabrielle noded and strolled around the shop, running a gloved finger over the spines of books. "And how am I to accomplish this destruction of his peace? He isn't a boy any longer, not so easily led.

I saw him at the Radwinter dinner. He's interested in me, but not like he was in New Orleans."

"So he's no longer so susceptible to your charms? If he isn't, you're of no use to me."

Stopping near Iago, Gabrielle planted her hands on her hips. "No man resists me. It's just that the experienced ones take more work. You should have warned me what he's like now. He has changed, and I may have to take—shall we say, special measures."

Iago lunged for her, grabbed her wrist and yanked her close. "Don't do anything to make him suspicious. Don't underestimate Drake, and stay away from Lady Eva Sparrow. Drake has been trying to keep her out of this, but she's got a mind of her own, and I can't afford to have an English lady snarled in this mess." He released Gabrielle, who glared at him and rubbed her wrist. Iago ignored her. "See to it that Drake is too distracted to apply his mind to his work, or at least impede his ability to think logically. That's all that's necessary. He has already fallen for my last ruse."

"You mean Zachariah Gordon. That was clever."

"I'm glad you approve," Iago said without sincerity. "I'd much rather have killed Drake, but his death would alert the British." Picking up his cane, he offered his arm to Gabrielle. "Come, I've something to show you. It's the reason I chose this place for our meeting."

They went through a back room littered with boxes, straw and old store records and out a door that opened onto a narrow passage. They walked to an intersection with a large street, where Iago paused beside a rusted, filthy grate set in the road. He tapped the grille with his cane to indicate the putrid mass in the drain below the grate. A foul odor drifted up in the yellow mist that issued from the drain. Gabrielle gagged and covered her nose with a silk handkerchief. She would have moved away, but Iago's grip on her arm prevented her.

"Behold the infamous London drains, madame. What you smell is a gourmet concoction—discharge from gasworks and tanneries, dead dogs and cats, offal from the slaughterhouses and cesspools, street refuse, dung from stables and pigsties and of course the odd corpse of some victim of foul play."

Mrs. St. Cloud glared at Iago over her handkerchief. "I know what sewers contain."

"Ah, but let me draw your attention to a peculiarly English refinement." Iago leaned closer to the drain. "There, can you hear that tapping and sloshing? That's a tosher, a sewer hunter. They climb into the drains from the ancient openings at the riverbanks and search the sewage by hand. Did you know that the sewers in some of the best areas are in the worst shape? Under the great houses of Mayfair, Grosvenor Square, in Belgravia the sewers are so badly blocked they almost clog the house drains. This lovely world is but a few feet beneath the fashionable houses where you eat and sleep while the toshers scavenge for valuables. If they're not careful, they can drown in the filth at high tide."

Freeing herself with a jerk, Gabrielle coughed and gagged again as she stepped back from the drain. "What are you trying to tell me?"

"I thought it obvious." Iago tapped the grille with his cane. "I'm most displeased that my associate disclosed my identity to you. However, I have overcome my anger and allowed you to be of service. But if you fail me, my dear, you will find yourself sharing the fate of those cats and dogs. I shall put you in a sack weighted with stones and toss you into the sewage. Drowning is a terrible fate, but drowning in a London drain is far more hellish. I trust I make myself clear."

Gabrielle dodged away when Iago offered his arm. "I don't have to put up with your threats."

Iago merely smiled. Mrs. St. Cloud backed away from him until she was ten yards distant. Then she turned and hurried down the street, disappearing around a corner. Iago watched her leave. Humming to himself, he walked in another direction, one that would take him through the roughest sections of the docks. He walked with a leisurely pace, his cane tapping, secure in the knowledge that, even in this perilous area of the city, he was far more dangerous than anything he would encounter that night.

Eva held a lantern in one hand and her skirts in the other as she went up the stairs to the fourth floor in Tennyson House. It was the evening after Zachariah Gordon was killed, the twenty-seventh of May, and the time left before the assassination was growing much too short. She hadn't been able to find Ryder to make him return her derringer. So she was going to replace it before the Cornelius Birds, Hamilton Locke and Lucian Bedford Forrest came to dinner.

The stair turned and gave onto a landing. Eva drew a key from the pocket of her day dress and opened a narrow door that led to a storage room in a turret at the front of the house. No gaslight here, just dust and stacks of crates filled with the treasured possessions of generations past.

Going directly to a cabinet set against a wall, Eva

produced another, smaller key and slipped it into the lock in one of the drawers. Inside, on velvet lining, rested an array of handguns, spillover from Uncle Adolphus' collection. The derringer Ryder had was really Uncle's small twenty-year-old pepperbox revolver. Eva's hand passed over a Queen Anne flintlock and an ancient wheel-lock pistol and stopped at a new Remington double-barreled over-and-under derringer with a mother-of-pearl grip. She remembered when Uncle Adolphus had come home with this import. He'd used it at his gun club for a few months and then grown tired of it. She pocketed the derringer and a case of cartridges.

She was locking the drawer when she heard the hollow *clip-clop* of horses' hooves. Going to the narrow, cloudy window, she peered out at the front courtyard. A groom was helping Ryder mount a roan gelding; then Drake rode away at a fast trot and vanished through the high wrought-iron gate.

Where was he going at this hour? It was after six o'clock, and the American dinner guests would arrive in a little over two hours. Ryder knew she'd invited Cornelius Bird so that he could observe him more closely. Her irritation growing, Eva went downstairs with the derringer in her pocket weighing down her skirt. Aunt Lettice was in her sitting room having tea when Eva passed by, and she went to greet her.

"How are you, Aunt?"

"Tired, my dear. That awful Prussian doctor prescribed a noxious powder to steady my heart, and it makes me sleepy." Lettice straightened her lace house-cap while Eva poured more tea into her china cup. "Thank you, dear Eva." Lettice fed a morsel of scone to Juliette, who was curled up in a cushioned basket next to the fire.

"Aunt, did Mr. Drake pass by a few moments ago?"

"You mean Bartholomew? Yes. Such a nice boy, and he's so fond of Juliette. Did you know that every time he appears Juliette tries to jump in his lap?"

"I'm sure Mr. Drake is aware of the honor, Aunt. Did he say where he was going?"

"No, but earlier I happened to overhear him talking to that assistant of his, that Frye person. Juliette does not like Frye."

"Yes, but what did they say?"

"Something about the weather."

"Oh."

"Clouds, my dear."

Eva furrowed her brow. "Do you think they were speaking of Mrs. St. Cloud?"

Lettice tossed another bit of scone to Juliette. "Oh, was that what they were talking about? I thought they were talking about this dreadful weather. Something about keeping an eye on the clouds. We hardly saw the sun at all today." Lettice yawned. "That Frye person was quite upset about Bartholomew going to see the clouds. Didn't want him to, although I don't see what's so perilous about cloud-watching. Will you ring for the maid, my dear? I'm going to bed early this evening."

Eva summoned the maid and went to her own room to get ready for dinner. As she bathed she speculated on what Ryder was up to. It was obvious he'd gone to call on Mrs. St. Cloud. She was certain that something important lay between him and his fellow American. And from the pain she'd seen in his face when she'd pressed him about the woman, Eva knew that he still cared deeply about her. Eva dried herself and began to dress with a growing feeling of foreboding. If Ryder had once been in love with Mrs. St.

Cloud, was he now falling for her again? He denied it, but that meant nothing in affairs of the heart. What if Gabrielle St. Cloud was the love of Ryder's life? She went cold and clammy just thinking about him and that woman.

Eva stepped into a skirt of ivory silk and allowed her maid to draw it over her petticoat and fasten the waist. A feeling of dread was growing. She had to admit now that she'd detested Mrs. St. Cloud from her first sight of the woman. Eva sensed that beneath all that beauty lay an utterly selfish ruthlessness and an insatiable appetite for adoration. Unfortunately Mrs. St. Cloud concealed those qualities behind an almost magical personal appeal that depended more on her charm than her considerable beauty. Eva knew Ryder was an independent and intelligent man, but she suspected he was, at heart, something of a romantic. And for some reason, he was particularly vulnerable to Gabrielle St. Cloud. The question was, could the woman make him betray the Union's cause and his mission here in London?

Waving her maid out of the room, Eva sat down, her fingers intertwining and unwinding over and over. Ryder and Gabrielle, Gabrielle and Ryder. What about Eva? She couldn't have been mistaken about Ryder's affection for her and his fear for her safety. What if he simply liked her and held no great passion— No, surely she wasn't exaggerating the strength of his feelings. She wasn't the gushing, extravagant sort of female.

Eva's thoughts skittered from certainty to fearfulness to confusion until she felt as if her mind was filled with panic. She didn't have enough experience of men to understand Ryder Drake. His American heritage made him unpredictable, unlike the gentlemen among whom she'd spent her life. It was hard to make sense of a man who could abandon a comfortable life to pursue a one of hardship on the Texas frontier. Eva disentangled her fingers and sighed.

After much worrying, having finished dressing, Eva went downstairs to welcome her dinner guests. The evening passed slowly, with no sign of Ryder Drake. Eva spent half her time furious at his desertion and the other half in fear that he was succumbing to Mrs. St. Cloud's allure.

She could hardly pay attention to Cornelius and Josepha Bird, which was the whole point of the dinner in the first place. She had heard from Lord Palmerston that Cornelius was given to sudden long absences, which he failed to explain satisfactorily. If Cornelius Bird was Iago, he would have to get away from the prime minister's eye to carry out his espionage. Eva discreetly probed Mrs. Bird about her husband, but Josepha seemed oblivious to hints upon the subject. Defeated, Eva returned to worrying about Ryder. Finally giving way to anxiety, she sought out Hamilton Locke after dinner.

"Gabby St. Cloud? Yes, I know her. Wonderful lady. I can't imagine why she never remarried. She had enough offers. Old Ryder even asked her a long time ago, but she thought he was too young." Hamilton blushed. "I would have asked for her hand, but I knew I wasn't worthy."

"Oh, Mr. Locke, any lady would be honored to receive your offer of marriage."

Hamilton turned an even darker shade of red. "You're just being kind."

"I'm not, sir." Eva felt her body grow cold. "You say Mr. Drake made Mrs. St. Cloud an offer of marriage?"

202 · *Suzanne Robinson*

"Yes, but he never talks about it. It was a long time ago, in Louisiana. He went there on business and met her through mutual friends. The family heard talk about them, but when Ryder came home he was awful strange. All closed up and even more of a dark cloud than usual. Never even spoke her name. Nobody knows what happened for sure, but he was never the same after that trip to Louisiana. It was like a thundercloud swallowed him."

"How mysterious."

"That's old Ryder. As closemouthed as they come."

Eva thanked Hamilton and began to circulate among her guests while she thought. Ryder had once proposed to Mrs. St. Cloud. She was his great love, and now she had suddenly reappeared in his life while he was on a government mission of paramount importance. The coincidence was not to be believed. Eva's hands trembled as she realized the gravity of the threat this woman represented both to their effort to foil the assasination plot and to her relationship with Ryder. She would speak to him about Mrs. St. Cloud this very night. And she'd hide her personal feelings no matter what happened.

Her guests left at midnight, and Uncle Adolphus retired soon after. Eva sent the servants to bed and curled up in a chair beside the fire in the library, which was off the entrance hall. She tried reading, but she was too upset, so she paced in front of the fireplace. Long minutes passed while she stared into the flames, and then suddenly she heard the front bell and hurried to let Ryder in.

He stepped inside with a look of surprise. "Eva? Where's the groom?"

"I sent the servants to bed. We have to talk, sir."

" 'Sir.' I thought we were beyond 'sir.' "

"In the library, if you please."

"Has something happened? Is the prime minister all right?"

"Nothing like that has happened," Eva said. She couldn't seem to get rid of this stiff manner and cold formality, but the alternative was screaming at him with jealous fury. Sitting down beside the fire again, she indicated another chair, and Ryder joined her.

"What's wrong?"

"Where were you tonight?"

Ryder's eyes took on a glint, like sun-drenched malachite. "Now, look here. You've got no right to ask me that."

"I beg your pardon, sir, but I do," Eva snapped. "You were expected here at dinner this evening to receive the Cornelius Birds and your cousin and Mr. Bedford Forrest."

"Oh. I forgot. Sorry." Ryder stared into the fire.

"Instead you went to visit Mrs. St. Cloud."

Ryder jerked his head around. "How did you know that?"

"Aunt Lettice overheard you talking to Mr. Frye."

"Hmm." He rose and started for the door. "If that's all, it's late, and I need my sleep."

Eva sprang to her feet and said, "Of course that's not all. It's not like you to go off without a word."

"You were annoyed at me for taking your gun, remember?"

"You could have left a note."

Regarding her unsmilingly, Ryder said nothing for a few moments. "It wasn't that important."

"It must have been, to make you miss your dinner engagement," Eva retorted.

"You're making too much of this," Ryder said

coldly. "As it happens, my horse threw a shoe in Mayfair, and I had to find a blacksmith and get him to put a new one on before I could come home."

Eva stared at him. "And Mrs. St. Cloud?"

"I'm keeping an eye on her. Hopefully we'll be able to expose her spying and arrest her."

Screwing up her courage, Eva said, "Aren't you a little too...involved with Mrs. St. Cloud to be the one keeping an eye on her?"

Another silence. Then Eva watched understanding dawn on him.

"By God, you've been prying!"

"Shh! You'll wake everyone."

Ryder swooped close to her and hissed, "What in Sam Hill gets into you women? You pry and gossip until you've practically disemboweled a man. You listen to me, Eva Sparrow, stay out of my private affairs."

Eyes round, Eva nodded. She must have satisfied Ryder, for he turned on his heel and stalked out of the library without another word. Shaken, she leaned against a table for support. Her eyes filled with tears, but in spite of that, of one thing she was certain. She was going to break the promise she'd just made. Whatever was going on between Ryder and Mrs. St. Cloud was too dangerous to be allowed to continue.

# CHAPTER THIRTEEN

SHE APPRECIATED STYLE, so he was dressed in a Bond Street coat of charcoal gray with light gray trousers, and he'd only fastened one button of his coat, as was fashionable. His tie was loosely knotted and stuffed into a silk waistcoat. He was trussed up like a turkey awaiting a hot oven. Ryder tugged at his collar as he gazed unseeing out the window of his carriage. He was going to call on Gabrielle St. Cloud again.

Only a war could have made him reestablish his relationship with her. He winced at the thought of war. The fighting had started. It was mostly in northwest Virginia, and McClellan had routed the Confederates at Philippi. But Ryder knew better than to expect all the battles to be as successful. The Confederate Congress had authorized the recruiting of 400,000 men. Sooner or later there was going to be unimaginable bloodshed.

Ryder's chief comfort was that his network of agents had located several more Southern spies and quietly apprehended them as the appointed week of the assassination approached. If Scotland Yard heard of it, there would be hell to pay, but so far he'd been able to ship the prisoners off on clippers and freighters bound for New York. And since Zachariah Gordon's death, there had been no more attempts on the lives of the cabinet ministers or Lord Palmerston. It was entirely possible that Gordon had been Iago, and the assassination plot had already been foiled, but he couldn't count on it. The suspense was as wearing as an infestation of ticks. His relationship with Eva was just as bad.

This affair with Gabrielle had come between them, and Ryder didn't know how to mend the rift. He couldn't bring himself to speak to Eva of his past relationship with Mrs. St. Cloud. The idea of exposing his shame made him cringe. Ryder leaned against the carriage window and breathed in the crisp air of this bright June morning. June 15 was the beginning of the third week of June, the assassination deadline, and it was only eight days away. After that third week, all would be over—he hoped—and then he could repair the damage done to his relationship with Eva.

As it stood now, she hadn't believed his excuses for seeing Gabrielle. He didn't know why. It was obvious to him that he would have to keep an eye on her since Pinkerton suspected her of being a Southern spy. Eva had retorted that Noah Frye could watch her just as well. She accused him of neglecting his mission, which was untrue. It was just that in order to gain Gabrielle's trust he had to convince her he'd succumbed once again to her considerable allure. That meant spending time with her. Once close to her, he could make her reveal her clandestine role as a Southern spy. Either he would convince her he was smitten and would never betray her, or he'd find evidence of her activities in her house.

He glanced at passing shops, their bow-front windows filled with the latest Paris fashions in bonnets and shawls. An omnibus rattled by and cut off his driver, who cursed and hauled on his reins. Ryder braced himself as the carriage swerved and sped past the crowded, horse-drawn vehicle.

The trouble was that Eva sensed that something was wrong. She'd known it from his first meeting with Gabrielle.

Somehow he had become close to Eva without having intended such a thing. He could read her moods in the tilt of her head and the sparkle of her eyes; she sensed his turbulent emotions as if she could read his mind. Neither one of them had admitted this aloud, but Ryder was intensely aware of their growing attraction, especially after that perilous episode in Whitechapel. The thought of it still made him cringe. If she had been killed... Better not think about it. He needed to prepare to see Gabrielle.

He still remembered the strange feeling of displacement that had overcome him upon first seeing the woman after all these years. It was as if no time at all had passed, and he was still that enraptured fool in New Orleans. The idea of losing control over his emotions again had shaken him to his core, and he'd frozen in panic. All during that dinner he'd plunged from horror to a feeling of stunned longing when he looked at Gabrielle. All those forgotten feelings had come surging back—ravenous desire, anguished uncertainty, shame and guilt.

Ryder covered his eyes with a hand and fought a resurgence of jumbled emotions. It seemed as if that needy boy was hiding inside him and would suddenly reappear, as confused and dependent as ever. The effort to control these feelings was what made his temper short. He'd been rude to Eva several times, and the more he saw Gabrielle, the worse his moods became. He'd never had to do anything so difficult as making her think that she'd enslaved him once more. Luckily Gabrielle was only too willing to believe him.

Noah Frye said that she'd slipped away from the men sent to follow her only twice since she'd arrived. The first time had been late on a dark afternoon, and the other time had been while she'd been shopping on the Strand. That second time, all his man had had to do was circle back to where her carriage waited to pick her up again. They'd intercepted her mail as well. So far Ryder couldn't see how she was communicating with any of the Confederates in residence in London, or with anyone back home. Unlike most of the Southern sympathizers with whom they'd dealt, finding any of Mrs. St. Cloud's secrets was going to take a much more intimate approach.

All too soon he was ringing the bell at Gabrielle's residence near Belgrave Square. Mama Gris-gris opened the door, and Ryder took a step back. "*You*. I thought you'd stayed in New Orleans."

The woman grinned at him and opened the door wide. "Mama Gris-gris go where her *petite* go."

Ryder stepped reluctantly into the entry hall. Mama Gris-gris hadn't changed much over the years. She stood tall and dignified, her face almost as unlined as it had been when he first met her. Still, the hair peeking out from her black turban was white now, and her fingers showed the swollen joints of rheumatism. As she had in the past, Mama Gris-gris found him amusing and let out an evil cackle.

"Stay away from me," Ryder snapped.

Shrugging, Mama Gris-gris pointed to the velvet-draped drawing room to the right and sauntered off in search of her mistress. Ryder removed his hat and placed it on a marble-topped table along with his walking stick before he went into the drawing room. Placing one hand behind his back, he went to a window and stared out, unseeing. He felt nauseated just from setting eyes on Mama Gris-gris again. Visions of her leering at him through the mists on the dueling field tortured him. It took all his will to drag his mind away from the memory. He jumped at the sound of Gabrielle's voice.

"*Cher* Ryder, what an impetuous man you are to call on me two days in a row." Gabrielle swept into the room wearing a rose-colored day dress of some frothy fabric, her hair loosely gathered at the nape of her neck by a matching ribbon. She held a basket of white roses in one hand and a pair of garden scissors in the other.

Ryder bowed and took the basket and scissors from her, placing them on a table. He kissed Gabrielle's hand and made sure to linger over the kiss as if it were hard for him to break free of her touch.

"Madame St. Cloud, you're as lovely as the flowers you've gathered. No, more lovely."

"*Mon cher* Ryder, you are *galant, n'est ce pas?*" Gabrielle placed her hand on his arm and leaned toward him familiarly. "If you continue to shower me with compliments I shall think you are in love with me again."

Ryder turned away to hide the turmoil he was enduring. Gabrielle's pink lips curled into a secretive smile as he faced her again, and he knew she thought he was fighting a losing battle against her power over him. She went to a settee, sat down and picked up a fan that was lying on a side table. Snapping it open expertly, she began to wave it slowly. The neck of her gown was low, revealing the hollow of her throat and the creamy white skin below. Her fingers pulled at a button, loosening the neck further.

"I declare, the sun is already quite warm this morning. Come and fan me, Ryder. I'm hot."

Ryder took the fan from her and sat down. He waved it, but Gabrielle covered his hand with hers.

"Not so violently, *mon cher*. Gently. I remember how gentle your touch used to be."

Stiffening, Ryder hesitated, then resumed fanning her. "Neither of us is like we used to be."

"Indeed not."

Gabrielle regarded him through half-closed eyes. Her skin was covered with fine drops of perspiration. She dabbed at her cheeks with a lace handkerchief, but she allowed a heavy drop to trickle down her throat and disappear in the shadow between her breasts. As he was meant to, Ryder followed the drop with his gaze and shifted uncomfortably on the settee. It was time to turn the tables on Madame St. Cloud.

Ryder tossed the fan aside. "What do you want from me, Gabrielle?"

"What?" She sat up, sultry pose forgotten.

"You heard me. What do you want? You began this, and I want to know why. That's why I came today. I want you, but I'm not going to kill anyone for you again. So what is it you want?"

A fleeting look of surprise crossed Gabrielle's face, along with a brief calculating expression. "What a thing to say. You know what I want." She took his hand and kissed it.

Ryder let her touch his hand to her cheek, then

withdrew it. "You want an affair? How do you know I'll be satisfied with that? I'm not so shallow as I once was, my sweet." He suddenly moved so that he was bent over her, his lips close to hers, and spoke softly. "Light dalliance? *Que désires-tu de moi, mon coeur?* Remember, *comme on fait son lit, on se couche.*" As he whispered to her, he felt Gabrielle's breathing speed up. He slid his hand slowly up her ribs and let it rest lightly on the silk that covered her breast while he stared into her eyes. "There will be nothing between us until I see you burn as I once burned. You will have to convince me."

"I do burn, *mon cher.*"

He nuzzled his way to her ear and breathed into it. "Do you?"

Her breathing was ragged now, and she lifted her body to his. *"Oui."*

Ryder withdrew abruptly, standing and walking away. "I don't believe you."

"Ryder!" Gabrielle lay sprawled on the settee, her legs apart and her chest heaving. She bounced to her feet, pursuing him to the door. "You come back here!"

*"Bonjour, madame,"* Ryder said as he went to pick up his hat and walking stick. "It has been a pleasure."

Gabrielle charged into the hall, grabbed his arm and spun him around. "You're not leaving, damn you."

"I am leaving," he said lightly, freeing his arm. "But don't fret. I'll probably be back. Until then..." He swept her against him and plunged his tongue into her mouth while he cupped a buttock in his hand and pulled her hips against his. He kept her pinned there, rhythmically grinding his body against hers until she responded. When she tried to drive him against the wall, he released her. She gasped and reached for him, but he was at the table putting his hat on.

"Again, *bonjour*, madame. I leave you to think of ways to convince me of your ardor."

"*Le bon Dieu*, I will kill you!"

"No, you won't. Not before we've taken pleasure of each other." Ryder went out the door and shut it before Gabrielle could follow him. He was down the steps and inside his carriage before he heard her give a roar of outrage. He grinned as the carriage jumped into motion, but his grin faded as he realized his whole body was shaking. Horror, rage and desire warred with one another. Ryder cursed and gripped his walking stick with both hands. He closed his eyes, but a sharp crack made him open them again. To his surprise, he'd broken the stick in half. Dropping the pieces on the carriage floor, he collapsed against the squabs, miserable and not at all sure he could carry off the seduction of Gabrielle St. Cloud without putting more than his virtue in peril.

He left Gabrielle to her watchers for several days. That put him dangerously close to his deadline, but if he was going to manage Gabrielle, he couldn't appear too eager. Both sly and clever, she would sense his anxiety and eagerness if he gave her the least hint that he wanted to see her. So he was forced to wait when he'd rather have snatched her and deposited her on a ship bound for New York. Unfortunately, that wouldn't get him any closer to uncovering the identity of Iago or preventing the assassination.

During this enforced hiatus he reviewed reports with Noah Frye and watched the passenger lists of ships for any new and suspicious arrivals. He was running out of men now that he was shipping Confederate spies home. Each time he got rid of one he had to send a guard with him. As it was, he barely had enough agents to watch the cabinet and suspects like Cornelius Bird, Colonel Longstreet and Gabrielle. He toyed with the idea of recruiting Hamilton and Lucian but rejected it. Hamilton was such a fanatical abolitionist that his judgment might be impaired if a confrontation occurred, and the bookish Lucian suffered from debilitating asthma that could erupt at any time. He finally decided that if things got worse, he'd ask Lord Augustus for more help. The trick would be keeping Eva out of it. She had taken to giving him looks of intense apprehension as she went about the house. His continued refusal to confide in her hurt her, and he hated that.

It was June 10 before Gabrielle gave him the opportunity for which he'd been searching—a way to meet her again without seeming to have arranged it deliberately. The agents watching her told him that the next morning Mrs. St. Cloud was going to an art gallery to look at a new exhibition by a French artist. He would be there too, and would see to it that she ran into him. Knowing Gabrielle, she would be furious at being ignored and even more determined to make him pay attention to her. Ryder was surprised that she hadn't realized he was using her own maneuvers against her. He supposed no one else had ever tried it.

On the appointed morning Ryder positioned himself in the art gallery so that he could see the front door in spite of the crowd of patrons. A minor royal was expected to attend, so everyone was jittery and excited. Ladies vied with one another to be near the entrance to give their curtsey, while the gentlemen made straight for the table of refreshments at the back of the gallery. Ryder spotted Gabrielle's golden curls through a window as she stepped down from her carriage. He moved out of sight behind a pedestal bearing a huge Greek urn and watched her thread her way through the crowd. As she neared his post, Ryder walked in front of her, his gaze fixed on a painting of Chartres Cathedral hanging on the wall beside her.

"Ryder!"

"Oh, good morning, Mrs. St. Cloud," he said with a glance at her. He gave her a quick nod, moved closer to the painting and pretended to study it.

She closed in on him. "What are you doing?"

"Looking at this painting. I don't believe the artist has gotten the proportions of the spires quite right. Do you?"

Gabrielle hissed like a kettle and said, "Where have you been? I sent a note telling you to come to me, but you didn't answer."

"Oh, yes. I got the note, but I haven't had time to answer it yet. Estate business, you know. That's why I'm in London, after all."

"Business?" She said the word as if it were foreign. "You allowed business to interfere with—" Turning crimson, Gabrielle seized his wrist and snarled at him in a harsh whisper. "Don't give me that innocent look, you green-eyed incubus."

Ryder glanced down at her gloved hand on his wrist and gave her a slow, tranquil smile. Gabrielle would have growled something else at him, but someone cleared his throat. He looked up to find Lady Eva staring at him, along with her uncle and Lucian Bedford Forrest.

Lord Adolphus cleared his throat again. "Good morning, Mrs. St. Cloud, Drake. Excellent exhibition, isn't it?"

Gabrielle let go of his wrist and switched on her most engaging smile. While she chatted with Lord Adolphus and Lucian, Eva remained silent and regarded Drake with a shocked expression. When Gabrielle moved off with the two men, Ryder tried to sneak away, but Eva followed him.

"You're in love with her," she said quietly.

Glancing around to make sure they weren't overheard, Ryder hissed, "Certainly not. I'm spying, not wooing." To his consternation, she touched her eyes with her gloves. "What in blazes—are you crying?"

"Great art always makes me cry."

The idea that Eva might be jealous lightened Ryder's heart. He gave her a genuine smile, caught her hand and kissed it. "Don't worry, Eva my dearest. I'm not in love with Mrs. St. Cloud." As he spoke, he dropped her hand in case Gabrielle was watching.

Eva shook her head. "You're not yourself, Ryder. You must see that, and it's because of Mrs. St. Cloud. There is something wrong with that woman, Ryder. She's evil. I saw how she was looking at you, as if she would eat your soul. And you, you don't seem to realize how dangerous she is."

"I'm fine," he said. "I promise, there's nothing for you to worry about, but you must leave. You and your uncle and Lucian have to go so I can speak to her privately."

"But I'm so worried about you."

"Go, damn it!"

Eva stiffened and the color faded from her cheeks. "Don't you shout at me, Mr. Drake."

He lowered his voice, wishing he could touch her. "Sorry, sorry. I'm tense, that's all. She has that effect on me. Now please leave."

"You're not tense, sir, you're addled and besotted with Mrs. St. Cloud." Eva's chin was up, and her eyes glistened with anger rather than tears.

"Now, Eva—"

She held up a hand. "I'm not naive, sir. You're distracted and distant, and you won't listen to anyone. Oh, don't worry, I'm going."

"Now, hold on a minute. How was I to know you'd get jealous?" He regretted the words the moment he uttered them. Eva gasped and held up a hand, forestalling him. He watched helplessly as she concealed her feelings behind a façade of icy formality.

"You quite mistake the matter, sir. I am merely concerned for the success of our joint endeavor. After all, time grows short, and the danger still threatens. However, I've no wish for you to misapprehend my motives. Therefore I shall refrain from involving myself further. I apologize for interfering." Whirling around, Eva left him to join her uncle and Lucian.

Feeling trapped by duty, Ryder watched Eva march out the door and get into her carriage, followed by her companions. Gabrielle reappeared at his side.

"What a peculiar little person Lady Eva is," she said. "Did you know she wanders about in all sorts of foreign places? Not civilized ones. Places like Egypt and Constantinople. Étrange, oui? And that garish hair. Had I that color I would have dyed it long ago."

Ryder narrowed his eyes at her. "I find Lady Eva most enchanting."

Gabrielle lifted an eyebrow. "More enchanting than I?"

Shrugging, Ryder left her to examine another painting.

Joining him, Gabrielle whispered, "Is she a good lover?"

"How would I know?"

"Ah, but surely . . ."

"Surely not. Lady Eva is just that, a lady."

"And me?"

Ryder bent close to her ear. "Come, my sweet, we both know what you are."

Instead of being outraged, Gabrielle turned to gaze into his eyes. "Then why are you resisting me? You know what it was like between us. Come to me tonight, and let me do as you asked and prove how much I want you."

"I don't know."

"You will come tonight, or I shall not see you again. Do you hear?"

"Oh, I hear you." Ryder affected a bored expression. "Really, Gabrielle, you've become most demanding."

"Tonight," Gabrielle ground out. "Without fail."

Ryder sighed as she left and returned to his perusal of the painting. He didn't stop until he was sure she was gone. Excellent. If all went well, he was going to make a thorough search of Gabrielle's house tonight. The results would tell him whether she was involved in the assassination plot or not.

# CHAPTER FOURTEEN

❧

AFTERNOON SUNLIGHT BATHED the entry hall at Tennyson House through the eyebrow window above the double front doors. Eva and Uncle Adolphus had arrived home from the art gallery, and Ryder returned a few hours later. He'd closeted himself with Noah Frye without pausing for lunch.

Eva had been watching him as the hour for afternoon calls approached. She still suffered from humiliation and confusion after her argument with Ryder, but she was damned if she was going to allow her personal difficulties to interfere with her duty to her country. Loitering in the hall near his rooms, she saw Ryder leave dressed like an English dandy. Eva rushed through the golden shaft of light in the hall in pursuit of him. Ryder was pulling on his gloves as she caught up with him. He took his new walking stick from Mr. Tilt, and moved toward the doorway.

"Ryder Drake, you come back here!" Eva said in a loud whisper.

"Can't," he replied as he stepped over the threshold. "Got an appointment. See you this evening. Probably."

Eva stood in the doorway, glaring at him as he got into his carriage. "Our guests will call at any moment. I told you yesterday that I invited them especially for you to meet because they're the biggest gossips in Society. Don't you dare leave me to deal with them. This is our last chance to learn something useful before tomorrow!"

"We've talked about this already." He seemed to relent and smiled softly. "Your uncle is here. He'll help you. As you say, this evening is important, and I've vital business to conduct. Good afternoon, dearest Eva." Ryder tipped his hat, and the carriage burst into motion.

It took all Eva's training for her to refrain from shouting at Ryder as he drove away. Tomorrow was June 12, three days until the third week of June. Everyone was on alert, and tempers were short. Drake's men prowled London like hungry cougars keeping watch on suspicious individuals or lurking around cabinet ministers. And Ryder was still keeping her at arm's length while he pursued Mrs. St. Cloud. He was showing signs of strain. He'd lost weight, and shadows had appeared beneath his startling green eyes. He came and went at odd hours, and now Eva was afraid to ask him where he spent his evenings.

He seemed so highly strung that Eva was uncertain whether he had fallen under Mrs. St. Cloud's control or not. It was distressingly obvious that Ryder was consumed with the woman, and not just because she might be an enemy agent. This morning she had seen for herself the way his eyes fed on the sight of her. The way his body almost trembled when she came near.

She'd seen a man lose his wits over a woman before. Her husband, John Charles, had done so. She had realized what was going on when her staid and proper husband had suddenly begun wearing stylish checked trousers and plaid waistcoats. She'd noticed the way he looked at a certain dashing Miss Alexandra Reed-Smythe and later the way he quivered like a bloodhound on a scent in the presence of the risqué Lady Beatrice Fortescue. John Charles had made excuses to be with them and had had her invite them to every function they'd hosted.

Sometimes honorable, proper men, strong men, seemed to go a little mad when they encountered certain women. Men in general seemed subject to their biological nature in an almost addled and certainly foolish way. At one time Eva would have made Ryder Drake the exception to this general rule, but now she realized he was just as susceptible to it as any other man. Part of her understood, and part of her wanted to take off her shoe and hit him on the head with it.

Eva cast an angry glance at Ryder's carriage as it turned the corner, and went inside. Mr. Tilt closed the doors, bowed to her and vanished belowstairs to supervise the making of tea for the afternoon's visitors. It was her day to be at home to callers, and Eva was expecting the Honorable Harold Wimbish and his wife, Dorothea. She would compose herself and see them on her own. If there was even a hint of irregularity in the doings of London's social elite, these two would know about it and tell all.

Walking into the drawing room, Eva found Aunt Lettice already there with Juliette. The dog trotted up to her and rubbed her small body against Eva's skirts. Eva picked her up absently and received a series of the tiny licks that were Juliette's kisses.

No time left, no time left. The words kept running through her head. Someone was going to die in a few days, and she wasn't going to be able to stop it. Ryder seemed to have abandoned her as well as his primary task, and she couldn't seem to put together what pieces of this convoluted puzzle she had. Eva hugged the happily panting Juliette and buried her nose in the dog's soft fur. At that moment the bell rang, signaling the arrival of her guests.

Mr. Tilt ushered in a couple dressed in clothing that was prettier than they were. Eva had to cover a smile as the Wimbishes greeted Aunt Lettice. The Honorable Harold had slicked down his thin, dark hair with pomade, and this had the effect of making him look like a scrawny seal. He wore a red rose in his lapel, and pearl studs. Dorothea, on the other hand, was a chunky woman with skin the color of vellum who insisted upon wearing Paris fashions that overwhelmed her. Today she'd donned a gown of pale pink spotted taffeta over an enormous crinoline. Her head was shrouded in a matching pink bonnet with white flowers, lace and ribbons. The outfit would have worked well on a more delicate-looking woman but only made Dorothea seem more sallow and chunky.

Harold had never gotten over being born without a title. The second son of Lord Nigel Wimbish, he rated only an "Honorable" before his name. Both he and Dorothea resented their lack of exalted station and made up for it with a consuming interest in titles, protocol, etiquette and the affairs of Society, no matter how ridiculous or boring.

While waiting for Mr. Tilt to bring tea, Eva embarked upon her task immediately. "Dear Harold and Dorothea, it has been ages, hasn't it? I've been so anxious to have a good long visit with you. You know everyone and are invited everywhere. Do tell us about this invasion of Society by these Americans. We have one staying here, you know."

Harold smirked and said, "Indeed, Lady E. And Lord P is playing host to some Americans too. At this rate we shall be inundated with uncouth barbarians."

One of Harold's affectations was calling all his titled acquaintances by their initials. Eva listened intently while Harold nattered on about Lord Palmerston's guests and the other Americans he'd encountered.

"And I met the most extraordinary person just yesterday," Dorothea said. "It was at my jeweler's. I was buying a present for my niece's confirmation, and the earl of Lister—you know old Lister, family related to the Marlboroughs—anyway, the earl was showing a young man around the jeweler's. What was his name? Forrest, that was it. Lucian Bedford Forrest. Lister was going to show him some of our historic sites. Suppose there aren't any over in the colonies. This Forrest had the most peculiar accent. Kept calling me 'ma'am.'"

Harold leaned toward his wife and lowered his voice. "And what about that St. Cloud woman, my dear?"

"Now, Harold, Lady E doesn't want to hear about her."

Eva scooted closer to the pair. "Of course I do."

"Well . . ." Dorothea only hesitated a moment before eagerly launching into her tasty bit of news.

"Perhaps it is my duty to tell you, since Mr. Drake is a guest in your house. That French American Mrs. St. Cloud is behaving most scandalously with him. Entertains him at all hours. Our house is down the street from the one she's rented, and our footman and maids see Mr. Drake's carriage outside her house *at night.*" Dorothea leaned closer to Eva and said in a stage whisper, "And he's alone. And she has no chaperone!"

"At night," Eva said faintly.

"And he brings her gifts," Harold said as he exchanged salacious looks with his wife. "Mrs. Wimbish's maid is friends with Mrs. St. Cloud's cook, who told her Mr. Drake gave that woman pearls. Pearls!"

Eva's body went cold. Hearing someone else describe Ryder and Mrs. St. Cloud sickened her. Pressing a fist to her stomach, she swallowed hard against sudden nausea. When the feeling subsided, Eva realized that the conversation had wandered to another topic.

"Who did you say was murdered?" Aunt Lettice asked, holding her teacup halfway to her lips.

Dorothea Wimbish's eyes shone with excitement. "That nice young nephew of Lord Overhampton, Sir Richard Pembroke-Stuart. He was secretary to the queen's master of the household. No one has ever heard of such a thing, one of the queen's servants being murdered. Of course, he wasn't at the palace at the time."

"About these new Americans," Eva began, dragging the woman's attention away from Ryder and Gabrielle.

"Oh, we can hear about the Americans later,

Eva," said Aunt Lettice. "Mr. Wimbish, do tell us about the murder."

Harold was only too glad to oblige. Setting down his plate of cucumber sandwiches, he drew his chair closer. "Well, my dear ladies, I shall describe what's fit for you to hear. It seems that one of Sir Richard's duties was to deliver materials to the printer, things for the coming week, like the court calendar, royal menus, programs for court entertainment, various schedules of carriages and trains, lists of guests and their arrival and departure times. Anyway, the usual printer's press had broken last week, and Sir Richard had to find another quickly. He found one, and was on his way there when his carriage broke down. Since it was only a few blocks to the printer, he decided to walk. But he never got there. They found him in Madder Lane, my dears. Someone had slit his throat. The court tried to keep it quiet, but some reporter for *The Times* found out and printed the story today."

"There was blood all over the lane," Dorothea chimed in happily. "Poor Sir Richard dropped his case when he was attacked, and the court papers were spread all over in the grime and blood!"

"How tragic," Eva said, barely able to contain her impatience. This idea had been a bad one. The Wimbishes apparently knew nothing useful.

"Do the police know who did it?"

"No," Horace said. "They searched the area around Madder Lane. You don't know the area. It's in Whitechapel. They haven't any idea who did it, and what's terrible is that the killer only got a little over a pound. That's all the money Sir Richard had on him. Imagine being killed for such a paltry sum."

"I suppose a pound is a great sum to the poor

in Whitechapel." Eva's voice faded as several facts
jostled into place in her mind—royal servant, murder, court calendar . . . Whitechapel. "Madder Lane,
where is that exactly, Mr. Wimbish?"

"I'm not sure. The newspaper said it was between
Shoe Street and something called Sewing—no, Nee-
dle Lane? No."

"Threadneedle Alley?"

"That's it."

As Horace, Aunt Lettice and Dorothea chatted
happily, Eva thought about the coincidence of the
murder of a royal servant so near where Zachariah
Gordon had died. And the crime had taken place
only a week before the time appointed for the assassination. Was Sir Richard really killed for a pound,
or was he killed for something else he carried, the
royal documents? But who would kill for menus and
programs of royal entertainment? No one. However,
Iago might kill to get a look at something that
wouldn't ordinarily be published. Eva quickly reviewed the items the royal household printed for its
own use. She remembered most of them from the
brief times she'd served as a lady-in-waiting. Besides
the menus and programs there were invitations to
dine with the queen and the prince consort, tickets of
admission to royal functions, schedules of royal
travel, the lists of guests for each week, the court calendar of engagements.

"The calendar!" Eva exclaimed.

Aunt Lettice was petting Juliette and looked at
her. "What did you say, my dear?"

"Er, pardon me," Eva improvised quickly. "I just
realized I had no idea what the queen's engagements
are for tomorrow."

"As it happens," Dorothea said, "I spoke to

my cousin's daughter-in-law, who is in waiting this month. It seems the prince consort finally persuaded the queen to drive in the park again tomorrow. You know she has been so distraught over her mother's death in March. People said she almost went mad with grief, and she refused to go anywhere or see anyone. So the prince has had a terrible time getting her to resume her duties in time for her state visit to Ireland. But Her Majesty has finally consented to go. I think she is supposed to leave any day now."

As Mrs. Wimbish spoke, Eva's dread grew. When Josiah had reported hearing of the assassination plot, he hadn't had any idea why there was a deadline of the third week of June on the attempt. What if the reason was that the victim wasn't a cabinet member at all? What if the intended victim was the queen of England, who had been secluded in March, April and May, but would have to come out of seclusion sometime before her trip to Ireland?

The third week of June was just an educated guess—a rough guideline—on the part of the plotters, who knew that after the third week the queen would no longer be in easy reach in London. Indeed, when Her Majesty traveled to rebellious Ireland, security around her would be increased and rigid. Much better to find a way to get to the queen before she left. *That meant between now and the day she was to leave Buckingham Palace.*

Eva suffered through the rest of the visit with the Wimbishes in painful agitation. It was hard to conceal her impatience as Horace and Dorothea departed. After they left she retreated to her rooms to pace the floor while trying to think things through. The other failed assassination attempts could have been ruses designed to divert attention from the real target. The more Eva thought about the idea, the more certain she became that she was right. If a rabid abolitionist killed the beloved Queen Victoria, all of Britain would demand retribution. Reason would vanish in the face of rage, and the empire would immediately ally with the South to help defeat the Union.

The timing around the third week of June meant that the queen wasn't secluded at Osborne or Balmoral in Scotland, or at Windsor in the countryside near London. She was in London at the palace, where if she left the grounds she would be exposed to crowds of strangers. Eva stopped in the middle of her sitting room, horrified. No one was expecting an attempt on the queen. Scotland Yard was protecting the cabinet. Ryder had no idea he had been guarding the wrong people.

"She's going out tomorrow," Eva said aloud. For the first time in months the queen would drive in the park among crowds of subjects. There was no time to waste. "God have mercy!"

Eva rushed into the hall and called to a passing maid. "Has Mr. Drake returned?"

"No, my lady."

Hurrying downstairs, Eva found Uncle Adolphus writing letters in the library. "Uncle, we've been wrong all along. The Rebels aren't going to kill a cabinet member. They're going to kill the queen!"

Adolphus stared hard at her and set his pen down. "That's impossible."

"No, it makes sense." Eva explained her reasoning, stuttering in her haste and anxiety. "So you see, we have to warn Ryder and Scotland Yard, and we have to warn the queen."

Adolphus rose, knocking his chair out of the way

as he rounded his desk. "Certainly not. I'm not going to request an audience with the queen and tell her someone's plotting to kill her. She'd have me clapped in Bedlam."

"But, Uncle, she's in danger."

"See here, Eva, you're distraught, and I don't blame you. Drake has gone off after this St. Cloud woman, and you're disappointed. But you will find someone more suitable, an Englishman. Drake is too wild. Look at the great risks he takes as a government agent in this civil war. Bound to end up dead for it too."

Eva pounded her fist in the palm of her hand. "I am not upset about Mr. Drake." She met her uncle's gaze and flushed. "Very well, I am, but it makes no difference to my reasoning. You're not listening to me. I know I can't prove my theory absolutely, but it makes perfect sense that the queen is the intended victim. And if she is, we've given the court no warning at all!"

"Oh, very well. I'm seeing the prime minister tomorrow evening in Parliament. I shall mention it to him if you will calm yourself."

Eva regarded her uncle with amazement. "Mention it. Mentioning it hardly communicates the peril the queen is in. And what if the assassin strikes before then?"

"I will handle this, Eva. I can't rush about babbling of attempts to kill Her Majesty. Palmerston will think I'm mad."

"Uncle!"

Adolphus took her by the arm. "My dear, you're not yourself. You're shaking and flushed. Do you have a fever?"

"I do not have a fever," Eva ground out. She

opened her mouth to argue further, but her uncle's look of bemused concern told her the effort would be wasted.

"Oh, drat, drat, drat." Yanking her arm free, she left the library, slamming the door behind her.

Eva rushed back to her sitting room and went to her desk. She snatched up her pen, dipped it in the bronze inkwell and held it poised over a sheet of her personal stationery. Ryder thought he still had a few days before the deadline. She would send a note to him at Mrs. St. Cloud's. No, she couldn't do that. What if Mrs. St. Cloud was part of the assassination plot? Ryder seemed to think she was. How could she get word to him without arousing Mrs. St. Cloud's suspicions?

She could send a servant with word that she'd fallen ill, or better yet, that Uncle Adolphus was ill. No. Ryder was supposed to be a guest, and there would be no need to send word to a guest in such a case. Eva set her pen down and chafed her cold hands. She could go to Noah Frye or even to Lord Palmerston. Eva imagined their reaction to her story and winced. If there was one thing that American men and British men had in common, it was a low estimation of a woman's fitness for worldly affairs in spite of any evidence to the contrary. It would be hard to convince Ryder of her reasoning, but convincing some other gentleman who didn't know her well...

"What am I going to do?"

Eva rested her chin on her fist and thought hard. She could try to go to the queen herself, but one simply didn't show up at the palace and gain admittance. There would be at least half a dozen courtiers she would have to convince that her business was worthy of the queen's personal attention. Their function was to see to it that Her Majesty wasn't disturbed with trivialities. Therefore, Eva would have to persuade them that her business was grave. She imagined explaining the assassination plot to them. They wouldn't believe her. The idea would seem ludicrous to royal servants used to the awe and veneration in which Queen Victoria was held. They had no idea how far Americans had come from this reverence since the colonial rebellion.

No, her best chance was to talk to Ryder when he came home. As he left he'd said he'd be back this evening. Probably. Eva pressed her fingertips to her temples. Probably. Mrs. St. Cloud was another danger. She was obviously trying to seduce Ryder. Eva winced as she thought of how tightly wound Ryder had become. The effect of Mrs. St. Cloud had been to distract Ryder's attention from his other work. Was that the whole purpose of her presence in London? Perhaps it wasn't a coincidence that she was entertaining Ryder tonight. She might be planning to keep him with her until her fellow Confederate had killed the queen.

Eva lifted her head. She would have to risk contacting Ryder. Taking up her pen again, Eva wrote, *Mr. Drake, Please return to Tennyson House at once.* She signed the note only with her initial and slipped it into an envelope. After writing Ryder's name on the envelope, she summoned a footman and gave him instructions to deliver the note to Mr. Drake at the residence of Mrs. St. Cloud at once. He wasn't to wait for an answer. Eva didn't want the man questioned by anyone in Mrs. St. Cloud's employ.

When the footman was gone she glanced at the small porcelain clock on her desk. It was after six o'clock. Fortunately she had no dinner engagement tonight. Ryder should arrive in less than an hour. She sat down at her desk again and watched the pendulum in the little clock swing back and forth and tried to think about what she would say to convince Ryder that a fellow American was going to try to kill the queen.

# CHAPTER FIFTEEN

❧

EVA WOKE WITH a start to find that she'd fallen asleep at her desk. Sunlight streamed through the widows. She gasped and looked at the clock.

"Eight!" The queen's carriage would leave the palace grounds at ten.

Staggering to her feet, she rubbed her eyes and hurried to ring for her maid. She must have fallen asleep sometime after four in the morning waiting for Ryder, who had never returned. Earlier the footman had returned with an outlandish tale. He'd gone to Mrs. St. Cloud's residence and had been met by a tall Negro woman in black who wore a red turban and spoke with a strange accent. She called herself Mama Gris-gris, and she promised to give the note to Mr. Drake. The footman had quoted her.

"Mama Gris-gris give Master Drake your note, boy, but he ain't goin' to be goin' nowhere tonight. I tell you straight."

Mama Gris-gris had been right. By one o'clock Eva had given up and sent a second note, but no one had responded when the footman rang at Mrs. St. Cloud's darkened house. Eva had fallen asleep waiting for Ryder and planning her next course of action should he fail to appear in time to stop the queen's morning drive.

When her maid appeared Eva began to dress in riding clothes. She would wait for Ryder until the last possible moment. Then she would ride to the area between the palace gardens and Hyde Park. She would have to intercept the queen before the royal carriage left the relatively secluded path from the palace and reached Hyde Park Corner.

She was dressed before nine and sent for her horse. Before she left her room she penned a note telling Ryder where she'd gone and why. Then Eva prowled before the front windows downstairs watching for Ryder, to no avail. Finally, about half past the hour, she left the house and rode toward the palace. She reached the palace path with a few minutes to spare. Looking across a wide swath of lawn, she saw a guarded gate that opened onto the palace gardens. Ancient trees bordered the lawn, swaying in a cool breeze.

Eva surveyed the lawn and found it deserted. She could see no one in the trees, but an assassin could hide behind any of the wide old trunks with ease. The queen's carriage would drive through the gate and down the path that crossed the lawn. After searching for any suspicious-looking persons Eva stationed herself where the trees crowded close to the path on the other side of lawn. She was alone but took no comfort in the fact. She scanned the tree line fruitlessly, wondering whether she should ride toward the palace gate. Yes, she should intercept the queen as soon as possible.

As she guided her mare down the path toward the gate the guards stationed there opened it. An open landau appeared, traveling at a sedate pace. A coachman and several footmen in royal livery were at the front and back of the carriage, and inside, facing backward, sat a lady-in-waiting. Facing forward was a diminutive woman shrouded in black. Her brown hair was parted in the middle, which did nothing to flatter her plain face and sharp nose. The landau cleared the gate and started down the path, toward Eva.

Anxious to reach the queen as quickly as she could, Eva kicked her mare and began to cut across the lawn. As the horse left the curving path Eva caught a flash out of the corner of her eye. She glanced to the west and saw that the sun was glinting off metal in the trees.

"Your Majesty, look out!" A shot rang out before her words faded. A bullet splintered the lacquered black carriage door bearing the royal arms. The lady-in-waiting screamed, and the lead team of horses shied. The queen turned to stare at Eva.

"Your Majesty, get down!"

A second bullet hit the squabs beside the queen as Eva reached the landau. The royal horses bolted. Desperate, Eva launched herself into the carriage to land on top of the queen. At the same time she heard the report of another gun much closer to the landau, and a man's shout.

"Whoa there, whoa. Steady. Eva, stay down!"

Lying on top of Her Majesty, Queen Victoria, Eva was relieved to recognize Ryder's voice. She glimpsed him as he gripped the harness of the lead carriage horse and returned fire at the same time. She felt the landau wheel in a circle and pick up speed. In moments she heard the palace gate clang shut. The landau stopped, and Eva lifted her head to see Ryder steadying the lead horse while he faced the direction from which the assassin had fired. Then, beneath her, Eva heard a musical voice.

"Lady Eva Sparrow, remove your person at once."

"Oh, I'm sorry, ma'am."

Eva scrambled off the queen and offered her hand. Victoria took it and struggled back onto the seat of the landau. Her hands were shaking, but her jaw was set in displeasure. Before either of them could speak they were surrounded by the coachman and footmen, all babbling at once. Suddenly the coachman produced a ceremonial trumpet and blew a series of notes. He repeated this several times before the queen ordered him to stop, but by that time another trumpet at the palace had answered the call. Seconds later Eva saw a squad of the Royal Horse Guards galloping toward them.

Ryder appeared on his horse. He wore the same clothing in which he'd left Tennyson House the previous afternoon. Tipping his hat to the queen, he bowed from the saddle.

"Begging your pardon, Your Majesty, I need Lady Eva's help." Not waiting for the queen's consent, he leaned over, slipped his arm around Eva and lifted her onto the saddle in front of him.

"Where are you going with Lady Eva, young man?" the queen asked.

"To find an assassin, ma'am."

Ryder ignored the queen's protest, turned his horse and headed back to the gate. It opened, and he rode in the direction from which the shots had come.

Eva twisted around and glared at Ryder. "Where *were* you?"

"Not now, Eva."

Facing forward, Eva muttered, "Not now, Eva. Not now, Eva. No one listens to me!"

"We're looking for a killer, dearest. Let's do that first, shall we? You can rant at me later. Whoever it was is gone now, but we've got to look anyway. Two sets of eyes are better than one."

They neared the tree line and began riding along it, searching the shadows and underbrush as the horse walked along. Halfway to the palace gate, where the carriage path swerved closer to the trees, Eva spotted something shiny lying beneath a spray of dead leaves.

"Look, beneath that old beech tree."

They got down and hurried to the tree. Ryder scouted around, but the area was deserted. He stopped Eva from approaching too near the spot. Carefully he surveyed the ground.

"Aw, hell, no prints."

They bent over and examined the glint of metal Eva had seen through the leaves. Ryder brushed them away to reveal a rifle. Eva watched him pick up the weapon and curse violently. He gripped the stock and the barrel as if he were trying to strangle the gun.

"What's wrong?" Eva asked.

Ryder closed his eyes. "This is a Henry rifle."

"It is?"

"It's American."

"Oh."

"A .44 caliber lever-action repeating rifle. Damn good weapon. New. Accurate."

"You mean an American brought this rifle to England to use in the assassination?"

"No. I mean this is a newly manufactured weapon, expensive. A special order. See the stock?

It's polished walnut. See how the metal is engraved and gilded? Not your ordinary rifle."

Eva drew closer to Ryder and put her hand on his arm. She could feel the long sinews, rigid with tension. Ryder hefted the Henry so that the butt pointed toward her.

"Is there an engraved plate?"

Eva nodded.

"What does it say?"

Clearing her throat, Eva said, " 'Hamilton Beauregard Locke, Rosemont, Suffolk County, Virginia.' Rosemont is your cousin's home, isn't it?"

Thunder sounded in the distance. They turned to see a squadron of Horse Guards pounding toward them. Ryder sprinted for his horse with Eva close behind him.

"What are you doing?"

"I've got to find Hamilton before they do," Ryder said. He stuck the rifle under a saddle strap and held out his hand to Eva.

She looked at it. "We can't do that. We have to tell them what happened." All her misgivings about Ryder came back to her. What if Mrs. St. Cloud had somehow persuaded him to her way of thinking? He was trying to protect his cousin, but Hamilton might be an assassin.

"Look, Eva, I can't let them take my cousin. There has to be some explanation. Maybe his rifle was stolen."

"Or perhaps he panicked after he failed, and dropped it."

Ryder shook his head violently. The Horse Guards were almost on them. Eva skewered Ryder with a stare. "Very well, the rifle might have been stolen. But what about Mrs. St. Cloud?"

"Mrs. St. Cloud doesn't matter. Not now, at least."

Still unsure, Eva gave way to her most over-whelming impulse and grabbed Ryder's hand. They sprinted into the densest trees as the Horse Guard reached them. In no time they'd cleared the park and plunged into the street traffic around Hyde Park. The Horse Guards immediately got bogged down in the crowded road, giving Ryder a chance to join the throng parading up and down Rotten Row in the park. He deliberately matched his pace with the masses of riders and headed west toward Kensington Palace. They drew stares, but neither of them cared, so lost were they in their individual turmoil.

Turning down Queen's Gate, they stopped in front of a small but expensive hotel. They rushed inside and up two fights of stairs to stop in front of a pair of double doors. Ryder pounded on them.

"Ham, Hamilton Locke!"

Locke opened the door, a piece of toast in one hand and a napkin in the other. "Ryder, what's going on? Lady Eva!"

Locke gawked at Eva as she followed Ryder inside. Eva surveyed Locke's suite, noting the small table that bore china and silver and a large breakfast of eggs, bacon, toast and coffee. Ryder faced his cousin and thrust the Henry rifle into his hands. Hamilton took it, openmouthed.

"Where did you get this?"

Ryder began stalking his cousin. "Where you left it."

Hamilton backed up as Ryder came toward him. "I don't know what you're talking about. I thought it was in my trunk. Lucian and I were going hunting, but he got sick a couple of days ago." Locke stopped retreating. "Dang, Ryder, what's got into you?"

"Where have you been for the past hour?" Ryder demanded.

"Right here," Hamilton replied with a frown.

Eva joined them and said, "Look, Ryder. He's been eating breakfast. He couldn't have been outside the palace, run back here and eaten in less than an hour."

Glancing at the table, Ryder's features relaxed, and he sighed. "God, I was dead certain you'd fallen into the plot."

"What plot? Ryder, what are you carrying on about?"

Before either Ryder or Eva could answer, the door burst open, and Inspector Oliver Palgrave and several members of the Horse Guards burst into the room, weapons drawn. In moments they had Ryder and Hamilton pressed against a wall and disarmed. Palgrave snatched up the Henry rifle and sniffed the barrel.

"This is what you were looking for, Captain."

"Excellent, Inspector."

Palgrave was examining the engraved plate on the butt. "Ah. No wonder Drake was so anxious to get away with this."

Eva, who had been shoved aside in the melee, went to the policeman. "Really, Inspector, there's no need to manhandle Mr. Drake."

"On the contrary, my lady. According to the officers here, Mr. Drake fled the scene of a crime with evidence. And now we know why." Palgrave eyed Hamilton, who was being put in manacles. "His cousin is the one who tried to kill Her Majesty not an hour ago."

Ryder tried to speak, but an officer clapped him on the head.

Eva drew herself up and fixed Palgrave with an aristocratic stare. "Are you suggesting that I would aid a criminal, sir?"

"No, my lady, but—"

"Mr. Drake simply wanted to reach his cousin before the authorities so that he could demand an explanation of this rifle's presence at the scene. If he'd been trying to save his cousin, they would have left this place before you got here. They had plenty of time."

"With all due respect, my lady, you can't be sure, and you've had a terrible time this morning, what with trying to stop the assassin."

Ryder twisted around in spite of his captors. "Listen, Palgrave, Hamilton was here eating breakfast. He couldn't have fired that rifle."

"We'll see," Palgrave replied. "Meanwhile, Mr. Locke, you're under arrest."

Ryder shouted, "Wait! I told you he didn't do it. Look at the table, man."

Palgrave glanced at the remains of Locke's breakfast casually. "Evidence like that can be counterfeited, Drake. We'll do a thorough investigation, and if your cousin is innocent, it will come out."

Two of the guards had been searching Hamilton's sitting room and bedroom. One of them came in from the bedroom carrying an overcoat.

"There's something sewn into the lining, Inspector."

Palgrave produced a pocket knife and slit the lining. Out fell a sheaf of notes written in block print. Eva moved closer to read over Palgrave's shoulder. The pages spoke of the shadowy abolitionist organization called the Sons of Freedom. The notes described the group's plan to throw Britain into turmoil through the assassination of Queen Victoria. The plan, of course, was designed so that no one would be able to connect the abolitionists with the crime. The Sons of Freedom believed that the queen's death would distract the British from foreign affairs long enough for the North to defeat the South and reunite the country.

"Merciful heavens," Eva murmured. "This can't be. Mr. Locke is a gentle and honorable man."

"You've been deceived, Lady Eva. This plan is diabolical." Palgrave pocketed the notes. "Captain, take Locke away."

Locke began to struggle. "Hey, I don't know anything about those papers, and I didn't try to kill the queen!"

Eva rushed over to him.

"Mr. Locke, calm yourself," she said. "Mr. Drake and I will handle everything. I'm sure you're innocent."

"Palgrave," Ryder said from where he was being held against the wall, "you're wrong about Hamilton."

Three soldiers left with Hamilton, and Palgrave spoke to the fourth, who still guarded Ryder.

"Lieutenant, escort Lady Eva and Mr. Drake to Tennyson House and see that they remain there until I can send someone to question them." Palgrave bowed to Eva. "You're a brave woman, Lady Eva. Now, before I go, I'd like to know how you knew Locke was going to try to kill the queen."

Eva glanced apprehensively at Ryder, who glared at Palgrave. "Inspector, I didn't think Locke was the assassin. My reason for trying to intercept the queen this morning lies in something I heard from callers yesterday." Eva went through her reasoning once again, and when she finished, everyone was silent.

"Eva Sparrow," Ryder said gently, "you may be an onery little cuss, but you're also a remarkable woman."

Eva smiled at him, her spirits soaring.

The inspector nodded to Eva and followed his men and Hamilton.

"Palgrave, you ass, come back here!" Ryder shook off the lieutenant and charged after the inspector.

Eva grabbed Ryder's arm as he passed and held him.

Palgrave turned on them. "You stay where you are, Drake. Count yourself lucky I believe Lady Eva about you, for now. If I find out differently, I'm coming for you." He pointed at Ryder. "You think you're clever, coming here and telling us all about this assassination plot. But we British have a trick or two of our own. I've had a man on you from the beginning. How do you think we found you so fast?"

With this, Palgrave vanished, slamming the door. Ryder would have gone after him, but Eva kept hold of his arm and dug in her heels.

"There's nothing you can do right now except get yourself arrested."

Ryder's jaw worked, and he glared at her. Finally he closed his eyes and and inclined his head. Eva nodded to the lieutenant, who escorted them out of the hotel. By Inspector Palgrave's command a carriage was waiting to take them home. Eva refrained from hurling questions at Ryder until they got to Tennyson House. The lieutenant, a young aristocrat with a stiff bearing and nervous manner, asked Eva for her word that she and Ryder would remain at home until officials could take their statements, and she gave it.

Watching the officer leave, Ryder growled, "He didn't want my word, I noticed."

"Well," Eva said, "you're American."

"Aw, hell."

"Ryder, you really must curb your language."

"Sorry. *Sorry*. It's not every day that the cousin I love like a brother is arrested for attempted murder of a queen."

Eva pulled him by the arm into the library, and they sat down on a leather couch.

"I tried to warn you about the attempt. I sent messages. Merciful heavens, why didn't you answer?"

Ryder turned on the couch to face her. "I got no messages." He stared at her in shock. "I came home and found your note. I don't understand." He chewed his lip for a moment. "Mama Gris-gris! Confound that voodoo witch."

"That what?"

"Oh, Mama Gris-gris is a Negro servant of Mrs. St. Cloud's. Been with her since she was a little girl, and she's . . . well, she's an evil old woman. She raised Gabrielle, and the two of them put their heads together and hatch wicked plots. Who knows what they're really up to. Whatever it is, I'm sure it has very little to do with the Rebel cause and much to do with their enrichment." He rubbed his temples and sighed. "Dang, my head hurts. I had port last night, and it must not have agreed with me."

Eva summoned her courage. "About last night. Did you— What were you—I mean . . ." There was simply no delicate way to ask a man if he'd slept with a woman. When Ryder lifted his emerald gaze to her, she blushed, but she blurted out, "What were you doing with that woman?"

"Danged if I know."

"What do you mean? You must know."

Ryder shook his head and winced. "I was going to—how can I put this?—I was going to court the lady, and things were going smoothly until after dinner. We were, um, getting along very well in the drawing room, and then she gave me a glass of port. After that, things are a bit confused. I can't tell if what I remember is a nightmare or real."

"Not a pleasant dream? A nightmare?" Eva asked hopefully.

"A nasty, strange nightmare. I dreamed I was sleeping in a field of sweet grass, and then suddenly I was in a swamp, and Mama Gris-gris was there, forcing some foul-tasting brew down my throat and chanting something unintelligible. After that Gabrielle joined Mama Gris-gris, and they were whispering and whispering until I thought I'd go mad, but I couldn't wake up. I don't know, that part might have been real. Anyway, I woke up alone in a bedroom in Gabrielle's house. I felt pretty bad, so I dressed and came back here. So much for my clever plan to search Mrs. St. Cloud's house while she slept."

Eva rose and walked to the fireplace, where she pulled the bell cord. She was worried about Ryder for too many reasons to be able to sort them all out now.

"You have someone watching her still?" she asked.

He nodded and lowered his face to his hands. "I've got to talk to your uncle about Hamilton."

"He should be home any minute," Eva said. "He

was seeing the prime minister and Lord Russell. I'm sure he'll help. Meanwhile, at least the queen's household is on guard now."

Peering at her through his fingers, Ryder scowled. "And once again you ran off without consulting anyone and nearly got yourself killed."

Eva bristled and stalked over to him.

"I did consult my uncle. He didn't believe me, and then I spent most of the night trying to contact you. But you were with that—that—"

"Don't say it," Ryder said hastily.

Mr. Tilt arrived, and Eva ordered tea and sandwiches. When he was gone, Ryder sighed and looked at her ruefully.

"All right, Eva Sparrow. You saved the day, just like in a novel. Do you mind filling me in on the details? The assassin is still out there, just as you said he was, and we're going to have to do something about that."

Eva folded her arms and lifted her chin. "Very well, but you might start by having Mr. Frye arrest that awful woman."

"I can't," Ryder said, meeting her gaze. "She might be the only one who can lead us to the killer before he strikes again."

# CHAPTER SIXTEEN

꩜

RYDER LISTENED TO Eva's description of the death of Sir Richard Pembroke-Stuart near Threadneedle Alley and the reasoning that had led her to try to interrupt the queen's drive. Through it all he was treated with a prickly English reserve that told him she was furious about his dealings with Gabrielle last night. Before he could broach the subject, however, Lord Adolphus appeared, in a rare fit of anger.

"Eva!"

Ryder winced as the bellowing voice of his host sent a spike of pain through his head. Lord Adolphus stormed into the room, his hair disheveled, his face crimson.

"Eva, what's this about you throwing yourself at Her Majesty!"

Eva sat down beside the fireplace and smoothed her hands over her skirts. "Someone was shooting at her, Uncle."

"I know that. What I want to know is why you

were there at all. You should have informed the proper authorities and allowed them to handle it."

"I did," Eva said calmly. "If you will remember, Uncle, I informed you. You didn't believe me."

Adolphus opened his mouth. Then the significance of what Eva had said dawned on him, and he shut it. Sputtering, he took a moment to recover.

"It's no use," Ryder said with a sympathetic look at Adolphus. "She's got us both. We should have listened to her."

"Does she, by God? Well. Hmm. Well." Lord Adolphus rallied. "Still, the prime minister is most anxious that this awful incident be kept quiet. Neither of you is to speak of it."

Eva stared up at the ceiling and sighed, while Ryder nodded.

"My cousin is innocent."

Adolphus shook his head. "I admire your loyalty, young man, but Inspector Palgrave has made inquiries at Locke's hotel. It seems his breakfast was delivered two hours before the attempt on the queen's life. He could have slipped out and come back after trying to kill Her Majesty, *after* the meal was delivered. Now, Drake, don't look so shocked. None of us knows for certain what's in a man's heart, even a cousin."

"I know Hamilton's been made to look guilty," Ryder said.

"Yes, well, in any case, your cousin is being held at Westminster police station for now. Palmerston said not to take him to the Tower yet."

Ryder stared at him. "The Tower?"

"All state prisoners are held in the Tower," Eva said.

Ryder protested, "But that's where all those kings and queens were beheaded."

"We don't do that anymore," Adolphus said. "Anyway, Mr. Locke isn't going anywhere right now. And the queen is furious, of course. Palmerston told her all about you, Drake, and the assassination plan. She's not so sure the attempt on her life is a Southern plot. Wants an explanation. From you and Eva."

Ryder jumped up and began to pace. "But I can't waste time with explanations. The real assassin is still loose, and he's going to strike again."

"When the queen invites one to the palace," Eva said, "it's a command one doesn't refuse."

"Is that so? Well, you can tell her from me—"

Adolphus took Ryder's arm. "You're going, boy, whether you want to or not."

"There are hundreds of palace guards to watch her," Ryder snapped.

"Not where you're going," Adolphus said.

"Oh," Eva said. "Is she going to Holyhead right away?"

"Yes," Adolphus replied.

Ryder went over to Eva's chair. "What do you mean, 'Holyhead'?"

"Her Majesty's trip to Ireland," Eva said.

"The royal train leaves for the port of Holyhead on the west coast tomorrow, Drake," said Lord Adolphus. "Your audience will take place on the queen's private train. The prince consort insisted on moving up the departure, for safety's sake, and Her Majesty always does what the prince says. Pack a bag, because you'll stay overnight on the train and come back to London the next morning, from Wattsville station, while the queen goes on to Holyhead."

"The queen is going by train," Ryder said. Something was bothering him. "I don't like it."

Without warning, Eva jumped up from her chair. "Oh, dear God, the timetable."

"What timetable?" Ryder asked, feeling more apprehensive as he saw Eva's alarm.

Looking at Ryder in dismay, Eva said, "The timetable for the journey to Holyhead. I'm sure it was in the documents Sir Richard had when he was killed. It details all the stops and the times they're made, everything."

"You're right," he said quickly. "Iago will try to reach the queen before she arrives in Ireland. We have to warn her."

Adolphus shook his head. "Her Majesty has the utmost trust in Scotland Yard, and Palgrave thinks your cousin is the culprit. And even if they hadn't caught anyone, it would be impossible to convince the queen to travel with detectives and soldiers in her train."

"We have to try to persuade Palgrave."

"My dear boy," Adolphus said, "if you do that, you'll end up in gaol like your cousin. Palgrave doesn't like it that you're related to Hamilton Locke."

"In that case . . . ," Eva said.

Ryder gave her a grim look, knowing there was no way to make her stay at home. "It's lucky we've been invited to travel with the queen."

"Will you look at this?" Ryder said. "Just look at this." He and Eva were standing beside the royal train while the ladies-in-waiting were being escorted aboard. Palace guards stood at the station entrance and at the platform gate, but none were boarding the train. Anyone could sneak aboard in the midst of the crowds of servants and railroad employees.

What was the good of all this wrought-iron grill-work, the gilded gates, and the ceremonial guards outside the station? The iron gates weren't locked; the guards stopped no one. Ryder scowled at the train with its shining black paint and emblazoned royal standard on the cars. Even the wheels of the train shone with polish. Steam burst out from beneath the engine, and Ryder muttered a curse.

"At least there are courtiers and servants," Eva pointed out. "Besides, Her Majesty was most adamant that no cowardly assassin was going to make her hide from her own people behind a bunch of guards."

Ryder threw up his hands. "I hate it when people refuse to listen to reason."

"So do I," Eva said with a meaningful look at him. They hadn't had a moment alone to come to any sort of understanding, mostly due to his being busy arranging matters with Noah Frye.

Ryder ignored her comment. "We need to see a confounded timetable. You'd think with all these servants around they'd have one. We need to see where the train will be the most vulnerable."

"I told you," Eva said, "there will be copies on the train."

A royal footman found them and handed them engraved cards. Ryder examined his. It was by the London and North Western Railway Company, and it was entitled "Her Majesty's Train, from London to Holyhead." On the card had been printed a chart representing the accommodations aboard the royal train. Boxes represented the railway cars, beginning on the left with the luggage car and ending on the right with the engine. Before the luggage car came a service car and then one for the servants. After that came a carriage for gentlemen-in-waiting, then one for the ladies-in-waiting. Next came two royal saloon cars for the queen and prince consort. A break car rode in front and behind the royal saloons to provide privacy for the royal couple. After the front break car came the fuel car and engine.

Ryder had gotten a look at the accommodations while he and Eva were waiting to board. The royal train was luxurious indeed. It consisted mostly of spacious saloon and double saloon carriages in which more than a dozen people could dine formally without being crowded by servants. There were carpets, gaslighting and toilet facilities. Each passenger car held heavy, overstuffed furniture and was decorated with velvet curtains, wood paneling and damask wallpaper. Elegant appointments, luxurious facilities, easily penetrated by a clever agent.

Eva had told him that she would be sleeping in the car with the ladies-in-waiting, while he would be assigned to the one with the male courtiers. Since they were to have an audience, the footman escorted them to the vacant break car behind the royal saloons. It held several small sofas of heavy, dark wood and a Scottish tartan fabric favored by the royal couple. They went right to a stack of printed sheets on a side table and each took one.

"Finally, the timetable," Ryder said.

The table showed each junction through which the royal train would pass, those at which it would stop and for how long.

"No wonder Iago went after Sir Richard," Eva mumbled.

"Look," Ryder said. "The first stop is a junction called Braidwood. The train will switch tracks to head northwest out of London."

"Braidwood is a busy place, with horse traffic as well as rail."

Ryder began to prowl the car. "Wouldn't you know there'd be a long stop right away? Seven minutes to make the switch in a congested junction. Too much time, too much."

Eva creased the timetable between her fingers. "Braidwood is the busiest junction on the schedule."

Steam spewed up from beneath the train, and the carriage jolted. Ryder grasped the arm of a chair and caught Eva's wrist. "There's no more time for royal protocol, Eva. We'll reach Braidwood in twenty minutes. You've got to see the queen."

"I'll try," Eva said.

"Don't just try," Ryder said. "Do it. I'm going to search the train."

He pulled a Colt navy revolver from beneath his frock coat. He hurried Eva forward and opened the carriage door. She stepped onto the platform and crossed to the royal saloon car as the train rattled out of the station.

"Hurry!" Ryder shouted over the noise of the engine.

Not waiting for her reply, he crossed the break car, his revolver drawn. He was about to open the door when he realized he was going to make a mistake. The car behind this one contained the ladies-in-waiting. If he plunged in there, even without drawing his revolver, he would create a furor that would delay him. The best strategy would be to start at the end of the train.

Ryder consulted the diagram of the royal train.

From back to front it read: luggage, service car, servants, gentlemen-in-waiting, ladies-in-waiting, break car. That was the one he was in. He would have to go across the roofs of the cars and begin with the luggage. Iago wouldn't be in the cars with the courtiers anyway. Ryder took out his pocket watch. He had fifteen minutes until the train reached Braidwood junction.

Exiting the car, he stuffed the revolver back in his waistband and climbed the ladder that led to the roof of the car. He stood with his feet planted wide apart. Around him lay warehouses and spurs, the unattractive but necessary accompaniment to railroad transportation. In seconds the industrial district gave way to modest houses, but Ryder was too busy jumping from one car to another to pay attention. He tried not to look at the ground speeding by as he leaped across the gap between cars. One misstep and he'd end up being sawed in two by the giant train wheels. He landed wrong and turned his ankle. Ryder dropped to his knees, regained his balance and flexed his foot. Luckily it was fine. One more jump landed him on the luggage car. He quickly went to the end of the car and climbed down to the platform. Easing to the door, he peered into the window set in the top half. Inside lay stacks of luggage, most of it stamped with the gilded royal arms. It was too dark to see much detail, so Ryder turned the handle on the door and slipped inside, with his revolver drawn.

Inside, the trunks and cases creaked and slid against one another in the darkness. He could hear the muted *click-clack* of the wheels against the tracks and the rattling of the car. The whole place smelled like leather. The luggage was stacked higher than his head, in three rows, with an aisle between each row and between the luggage and the sides of the car. Ryder sidled down the left side of the car, listening closely for any strange sound. At the end of the row he heard a brushing sound and pointed his revolver as a large trunk at the bottom of a stack moved. He pulled back the hammer on his revolver and swiftly moved toward the trunk. He stopped when it shifted again, and aimed the Colt. Just then the train hit a bump in the tracks, and the trunk slid back to its original position; its contents must have shifted from all the jolts. Ryder whipped around the end of the row, revolver pointed—at nothing.

Cursing, he investigated the rest of the car, to no avail. He stuck his gun in his waistband again and headed for the next car. It turned out to be the kitchen car, and it was filled with bustling cooks and assistants who were so busy no one noticed that he wasn't a courtier. Ryder walked casually through the crowded car as chefs beat batter and shoved roasts into ovens. He recognized none of the people in the car, so he went to the next one. This was the carriage reserved for servants, who were all men. It was unlikely that Iago would hide in it, but he couldn't take the chance that there was some place of concealment in this car.

Opening the door, Ryder entered the saloon car. "Good day to you. I'm Ryder Drake."

Three men wearing royal livery rose from their seats and stared at him. One who appeared to be the butler stepped forward.

"You're that fellow who helped save Her Majesty. We heard you were on the train. How did you get in the service car?"

"Took a walk." Ryder pointed to the roof.

The butler frowned. "Here, now, you can't do that, sir. You should go back where you were put."

"I will," Ryder said as he glanced around the car. "By the way, is there anywhere in here that a felon could hide?"

"A felon? We've got no felons on board. The idea!"

"Then there isn't?" Ryder asked, eyeing the spaces beneath the furniture.

"Not unless he's three feet tall," the butler replied. "Now I must insist, sir."

"Going, going right way." Ryder hurried outside.

He hesitated before he entered the car reserved for the gentlemen-in-waiting. It was here that he was likely to encounter trouble. These men would probably delay him. He glanced at his pocket watch again. Only five minutes left until the Braidwood junction. Had Eva persuaded the queen of the danger? The train wasn't stopping and there was no sign that the royal couple had called for more protection. What was delaying her? He made a quick decision and ascended to the rooftops again. He leaped from railcar to railcar until he reached the break car between the royal saloon and the fuel carriage. He clambered down the ladder, jumping to the platform of the break car. He glanced into the car and found it empty. He was about to go inside when the door to the royal saloon burst open. Eva stood there, watching him anxiously.

"Mr. Drake," she said loudly, "Her Majesty saw you peeking through the window in the door. She commands you to join her at once."

Ryder glanced past Eva to see a lady-in-waiting hovering nearby. "Good, there isn't much time left."

He entered the royal saloon car, which resembled

a palace drawing room more than a railway carriage. Queen Victoria was seated on a sofa upholstered in blue velvet, and the lady-in-waiting went to stand beside her. Eva gave him an anguished look and mouthed the word "nothing." Ryder glanced at his watch again; they had but a few minutes left.

"Mr. Drake," the queen said as she pointed to a spot on the Aubusson carpet in front of her. "Stand there where we can see you." Victoria was wearing a traveling dress in an unfortunate Scottish plaid over a wide crinoline. Both the fabric and the crinoline served to emphasize her small stature. Nevertheless, this small, plain woman dominated the scene. She had been knitting when Ryder came in.

"Explain yourself, young man."

Ryder bowed and glanced at Eva. "I thought Lady Eva would have done that by now, Your Majesty."

"She has told us a fantastical tale about a Southern agent bent on murdering me and blaming abolitionists. This whole idea of such a twisted plot is ridiculous. Scotland Yard has the person responsible for the attack yesterday, and you have filled Lady Eva's head with nonsense."

"But, Your Majesty—"

"Don't interrupt us, sir. We shall write to your president directly and tell him what a nuisance you've made of yourself. However, we do sympathize with you. Your cousin is no doubt unbalanced."

A knock sounded at the door.

"Come," the queen said.

Another lady-in-waiting came in, with cakes, biscuits and breads, followed by a footman bearing a heavy tea tray.

"Ah, Lady Beatrix, you've been an age," said Victoria.

The queen continued to upbraid Ryder while the refreshments were being placed before her. Ryder hardly listened, because the train was slowing and drawing into the Braidwood junction. His gaze darted from window to window, trying to watch all his surroundings at once. He could see that Eva was doing the same.

"We have no intention of waking the prince consort, who isn't feeling well," the queen was saying. "We will simply see to it that you leave the train here at Braidwood. Because of your service to the Crown, we will not exact punishment for your intrusion, but you must leave England immediately. With our thanks, of course. Now, Lady Eva, you may serve tea. I believe there's time for a cup before you disembark." Victoria waved Lady Beatrix away.

Ryder muttered, "Yes, Your Majesty." All the while he kept up his surveillance of the railroad station they were rapidly approaching.

Eva sat down before the table in front of the queen's sofa and began to pour tea for Her Majesty. The footman was busy lighting candles under serving dishes to keep the food warm. Ryder stood beside the other lady-in-waiting and watched the train pull into Braidwood Station. As he eyed the royal platform and railway conductors standing at attention on it, he glimpsed movement out of the corner of his eye. The train hadn't come to a stop, but a man wearing the blue uniform of the London and North Western Railway had jumped onto the ground and was walking toward the gate that led from the royal platform to the station.

The queen was speaking again, but Ryder ignored

her and turned to the lady-in-waiting. "My lady, who is that?" He pointed at the retreating man, whose face he couldn't see.

The queen stopped talking out of shock at being interrupted. Eva rose and went to the window, then turned to the lady-in-waiting. "Who is it, Lady Warrender?"

Lady Warrender glanced at the queen, then said, "I have no idea, sir. Some railroad man."

Ryder started to leave, but Lady Warrender blocked his way. Before an argument could erupt, Eva pointed at something behind them. "Look!"

Ryder whirled around and saw Lady Beatrix bending over a covered dish, about to serve the queen. The woman swayed, put her hand on the cover of the dish, then choked and fell on the floor. Eva cried out and rushed to the lady as the queen jumped to her feet. The footman, who was carrying another heated silver dish, suddenly dropped it and collapsed.

"Damn it!" Ryder hurried to the tea table as Lady Warrender sprang to the queen's side and began urging her away from the scene.

Victoria was giving orders, and Lady Warrender was pulling her toward the door when Eva began to cough. Ryder grabbed her before she fell. As he bent over her, he caught a whiff of burnt almonds. He carried her across the car to another sofa.

"The candles!" Eva gasped.

Ryder rushed back to the table and picked up the queen's teacup. Knocking aside the heated silver dishes the footman had set up, he poured tea on each burning candle. Then he rushed to the windows and began opening them. Lady Warrender realized what he was doing and began shoving windows open as well. By the time the train stopped in Braidwood Station, everyone was safe, but no one knew how cyanide candles had been introduced aboard the royal train.

# CHAPTER SEVENTEEN

WITH AN UNHURRIED pace that belied the furor he felt, Iago walked out of Braidwood Station knowing he had failed. It has been a frantic morning, what with having to detour on his way to the royal train. And when he'd arrived, the last thing he'd expected to see was Ryder Drake and Lady Eva Sparrow on the royal train. Now Iago was faced not with success but with retreat, with covering up, with escape.

Earlier, he'd boarded the train at the last possible moment, then learned of his opponents' presence from the servants. Seething with rage at Mrs. St. Cloud's failure to distract Ryder Drake, he managed to remain out of the sight of his enemies as they moved through the railway cars. Despite their presence he thought he could succeed in his task. Once Drake had passed through the service car, Iago climbed down from its roof unseen.

The substitution of the poisoned candles for the originals went smoothly. He left the train confident of success and had reached the platform gate when the cry for help sounded. He lingered beyond the gate, expecting to see a great commotion as the dead queen was carried off the train. Instead, he glimpsed Victoria speaking with great animation to the prince consort as they left the royal train unharmed and walked around the platform as if stretching their legs. At the same time Drake leaped from a railcar and ran toward the crowds in the station. Iago had instantly turned and walked away. Even without Drake in pursuit, the hue and cry was sounding, and a search of the station for the would-be poisoner would commence at once.

Now his mind burned with the acid of defeat. His careful planning had been for naught because Mrs. St. Cloud had failed in the task he assigned to her. Drake should have been with Gabrielle still in a stupor from an entire night of lovemaking.

Iago stepped into the men's facilities long enough to change into gentlemen's clothing he had concealed there previously. He could hear the shouts of the searchers on the royal platform, but they hadn't reached the station yet. He stepped outside and hailed a cab. Traffic was heavy; carriages fought with omnibuses and freight wagons as well as cabs and carts. Pedestrians crowded the sidewalks and stepped into the road in front of vehicles, and it took the cab almost an hour to get back across London. It was after noon when Iago dismissed the cabdriver with a generous tip.

Taking a circuitous route, Iago approached the square near his intended destination. There he approached a man loitering beside an oak tree, one of Drake's men. This was a quiet neighborhood, with little traffic. There were few pedestrians, and Iago waited for them to leave the area before he stole close to his intended victim. A quick rap on the head with the butt of his pistol was all it took. He lowered the man to a park bench so that it appeared he had fallen asleep. His hat was set at a jaunty tilt to conceal the bloody knot on his head. Iago left his victim to make a foray to the next block, where he found another watcher and dispatched him.

Returning to the square, he walked up the steps of a detached villa. Without ringing the bell, he entered and looked around. There were signs that the occupant was going on a journey. Several trunks stood in the entry hall. One was open and was being stuffed with cloaks and bonnets. Iago heard footsteps and retreated behind a drawing room door.

Mama Gris-gris was herding several servants down the stairs. "Shoo now. You done been paid, so get along with you." She drove the servants before her, evidently sending them on their way after they'd been discharged.

Once Mama Gris-gris and the others were gone, Iago came out of concealment and ascended the stairs noiselessly. He knew where he was going, having been there several times. He stopped at a pair of doors, touched the gilded handle lightly and gave it a slight push. Through the gap, he saw Gabrielle St. Cloud. Smiling grimly, he slipped inside the room.

Mrs. St. Cloud didn't notice him because she was hurrying from her bedroom to her sitting room, carrying toiletries and jewel cases to several pieces of leather luggage. She dumped the toiletries into a suitcase on a settee, dropped jewelry boxes into a small case and scurried back into the bedroom. Iago drifted silently after her, approaching as Gabrielle swept earrings, necklaces and brooches off a dresser and into a velvet box. Before she could turn around, Iago grabbed her from behind, covering her mouth. The velvet box dropped to the floor, spilling its contents in a bright spray over the carpet. Gabrielle screamed into his palm.

"Shh!" he hissed, his grip tightening as he put his lips near her ear. "You were supposed to seduce him, keep him besotted and immobile for at least two days. What happened?" He released her mouth.

Gabrielle gasped for breath. "He woke before he was supposed to! I was coming to give him another dose of belladonna, but when I got to his room, he was gone."

"You drugged him?"

"He wouldn't go to bed with me. I swear, I tried, but every time I thought I had him close to submission, he drew back. It got late, and I knew the stakes, so I had Mama Gris-gris mix one of her potions."

"That old witch. Her concoctions are more superstition than drug."

"Her magic works, I swear it."

Iago clasped her head in his hands and twisted it so that she was looking at him over her shoulder. "No, Gabrielle, it doesn't. If it did, she would be here to save you." His hands jerked quickly, with a mighty force, and he heard Gabrielle's neck snap.

A low gurgle escaped her lips, and her body went limp. Iago released her, and she flopped on the floor amid her jewels, with her knees bent. Straightening his coat and tie, he returned to the sitting room door and stood beside it. He drew a knife from a sheath on his wrist and leaned against the wall. Only a few minutes passed before Mama Gris-gris entered, pushing the door back so that Iago was hidden behind it. She was carrying a leather suitcase and a long gown on a hanger. She paused not a yard from Iago to set the suitcase on the floor. As she straightened up, she saw Gabrielle. Iago heard her draw in a sharp breath, but instead of going to the dead woman, Mama Gris-gris whirled around, her skirts a black tornado, and spotted him.

"You!" she said, raising a finger to point at him. "Legba curse you. Papa Ghede curse you. Baron Samedi take you." She reached in a pocket and produced a rattle topped with red and black feathers and shook it. "Papa Ghede protect me. I got my gris-gris bag. Papa Ghede help me, I got my juju." Mama Gris-gris touched a small bag suspended by twine around her throat. "I call up Kalfu, who will destroy you!"

Iago sighed, drew his knife back and hurled it. The blade hit Mama Gris-gris with such force that she jerked backward. She stared down at her chest, to see the handle of the knife protruding from it. Wrapping her hands around it, she tried to pull it out, but it had lodged between her ribs. In the next instant, her eyes rolled back, and she fell. Iago walked over to her, kicked the rattle that lay beside her, and turned his back on the two bodies. He left the room, shaking his head.

"Legba, Kalfu. What nonsense." He made his way through the deserted house to the servants' entrance at the back. Shortly, he was several streets away and hailing another cab.

"A pity there's no time to finish dear Ryder," he said to himself. "No matter, he'll come to me."


Eva accepted Ryder's arm and descended from the carriage at Tennyson House on the evening of the second attempt on Queen Victoria's life. Together they entered the house, bone-weary and apprehensive. The search for Iago had been futile, and they had been questioned by high officials of the government for hours before being released. Eva had tried describing the vanished railroad employee, but the authorities hadn't been impressed with "tall, blue uniform and cap."

Ryder guided her into a chair in the drawing room and fetched a glass of water for her. Eva's throat and lungs were raw and burning. A doctor had examined her and the other victims and had her wash her eyes with a saline solution, but some effects of the gas lingered. At least she was no longer dizzy or nauseated.

Standing over her, Ryder scowled. He'd been fuming for most of the day. "*Now* do you understand why I didn't want you involved in this? You could have been killed, and I—"

"You what?" Eva looked up at him with undisguised annoyance, expecting another rant. To her consternation Ryder dropped to his knees in front of her and grasped her hands.

"You could have been killed, and..." He closed his eyes as if in pain, then opened them in resolution. "And I couldn't bear to live in a world without you."

Eva's mouth fell open, and she gaped at him. "But you're always angry at me. I irritate you."

"Why do you think that is?" Ryder said.

Eva threw up her hands. "Because you're a stubborn American."

"I admit that." He smiled tentatively, and, uncomfortable as she was, she smiled back.

They stared at each other in silence. Ryder began to fidget, and then he reddened under her gaze and rose to his feet. Running fingers through his hair, he paced in front of her. Eva watched him in confusion, for he seemed flustered and shy, which wasn't like him. Finally he rounded on her.

"Aw, hell, Eva. Aren't you going to say anything?"

Eva blinked. "Oh. Yes, um, yes. I—I—"

"Confound it, woman, do you think you might be able to care for me?"

Stunned, Eva's mind went blank. "But—but... What about that woman? After all, you've been enchanted by her." She stopped because Ryder uttered a growl, swept over to her and knelt at her feet.

"No more of that," he said, gathering her hands in his. "She's the past, Eva. The poisoned past. You're the future, my future, if you want me."

"Oh, I want you," she said quickly. Then she blushed and looked down at their joined hands.

He laughed softly, and Eva felt his lips on her temple. They brushed her ear, and then found her mouth. The burning in her throat and lungs receded, along with her weariness. She ran her fingers through his soft, dark hair, and he deepened the kiss. She felt the heat of his hand over her breast, but he suddenly removed himself from her. She heard what had startled him; someone was knocking on the drawing room door.

Eva cleared her throat. "Come in."

Mr. Tilt entered carrying an envelope on a silver tray, which he offered to Ryder. Eva watched him read the contents and suddenly drop into a chair. The note fell to the floor as Ryder stared at nothing, pale and stunned. Eva picked up the note, which was from Mr. Frye, and read the news that Mrs. St. Cloud and her maid had been found murdered. One of the men sent to watch her was dead; the other had a serious head wound. Eva knelt beside Ryder and covered his hand with hers. He flinched, but said nothing.

"You were right all along," she said softly. "Mrs. St. Cloud knew the assassin and could have led us to him. That's why she's dead."

A spasm passed over Ryder's features and was gone. "The bastard has been one step ahead of us from the beginning. I should have arrested her."

"But then you would have lost the chance of finding Iago. You had her watched."

"And got a good man killed," Ryder whispered.

Eva ached for him. "Did your man not know his job? Did he not know what to expect?"

"Of course he did," Ryder said hoarsely. "I made sure everyone understood what Iago was like."

"Then what more could you have done?"

"I should have been there," Ryder snapped.

"If you had been, Her Majesty would be dead," Eva retorted. Then she squeezed Ryder's hand. "It's terrible that your man was killed, but please don't take the blame for what only this assassin could control."

Ryder met her gaze, and Eva saw the pain clear a bit.

"Will you tell me about Mrs. St. Cloud?"

At first he didn't answer. After a moment's contemplation, he said, "I will. Later." He rose and helped her stand. "I must go."

Before he could say anything more, Adolphus Tennyson's voice sounded in the entry hall. He came into the drawing room, silver hair wild, his hands full of telegrams and other papers.

Eva said, "Uncle, you've heard what happened on the royal train?"

"Of course, my dear. I'm glad you're unhurt, but the government is in an uproar."

She glanced at Ryder, then turned back to Lord Adolphus. "We hope the government realizes now that Hamilton Locke isn't the killer. He was imprisoned when the attack occurred."

Her uncle was shaking his head. "No, my dear. As you were boarding the royal train, the police discovered that Locke had escaped during the night."

"Oh, no," Eva said.

Ryder drew closer. "How, my lord?"

"With help, of course. Someone drugged the night watch and picked the lock on his cell. He covered pillows with a blanket to simulate a body in his bunk, so no one noticed he was gone until they saw that he hadn't eaten the breakfast they'd provided."

Eva put her hand on Ryder's arm. He'd gone white and seemed at a loss.

"I'm sure there's an explanation," she said.

"I don't know," Ryder replied.

"There's worse news," Adolphus said. "The fools at the police station didn't report him missing to the Yard until hours later. They wanted to search for Locke and bring him in themselves. Now the trail has gone cold. We're searching the docks and checking the passenger lists of the ships that left port this morning, but there seems to be no trace of him."

Eva squeezed Ryder's arm. "Shall I send for Mr. Frye?"

Ryder shook his head, then whispered to her, "I'll go to Mrs. St. Cloud's and speak to him there. I've got to find Hamilton again, Eva, before the police do."

Several days later, Eva was in her sitting room, at her desk, writing a letter to Winnie Eastman back in Natchez. After going without sleep since their adventure on the royal train, Ryder had finally collapsed with exhaustion and was sleeping in his room. He and his American agents had searched for his cousin without success. The authorities had told the public that Mrs. St. Cloud and her maid had been killed during a burglary. They had kept the attacks on the queen as quiet as possible, although rumors were beginning to spread. Eva sighed and continued to write.

*Mr. Drake tells me of the battle at Newport News, Virginia, where there were terrible casualties on both sides. Your description of the Battle of Bethel Church was most upsetting. I am sorry for the deaths on both sides. A friend of mine reports that the Northern troops were green, and that some wore gray uniforms. These were mistaken for Confederate soldiers by the New York regiment.*

*We also heard that General Benjamin Butler commands Fortress Monroe at the tip of the York-James Peninsula. I know you detest him, and no doubt you're especially angry about his latest declaration. As I understand it, when the fighting started slaves fled to Fortress Monroe, and General Butler refused to comply with the Fugitive Slave Law by returning them to their masters. He declared the slaves "contraband" and subject to seizure by the military. For my part, Winnie, I believe that the slaves should be set free. I might as well admit to you now that I have freed Josiah, as my conscience required me to do. I hope you will understand that I did what I felt was right as a Christian and as a member of the human race.*

Eva paused and watched the lines of ink dry on the page. Winnie might forgive her, but Cyrus Eastman probably wouldn't. It couldn't be helped. She finished the letter and addressed the envelope. As she worked, a smile hovered on her lips. It had been there frequently since Ryder had declared his affection for her. They'd come a long way since their first meeting a few short months ago. He'd given up his assumptions about her light-mindedness, and she had learned to admire and trust him. Together they were learning how to love.

Eva was worried about him, though. Ryder had taken the death of Mrs. St. Cloud and the disappearance of his cousin hard. There was something about his relationship with Mrs. St. Cloud that had scarred him deeply. The aftermath of it was still eating at Ryder, but the danger to Hamilton Locke was more urgent.

It was difficult to understand why Hamilton had run away. All he'd had to do was remain where he was to prove his innocence, and the fact that he hadn't tried to vindicate himself worried Eva. Was there a side to Hamilton that Ryder knew nothing about?

Eva took her letter downstairs to leave on the silver tray in the entry hall and was in time to see Mr. Tilt admitting a well-dressed couple.

"Ah, my lady," said the butler. "Mr. and Mrs. Cornelius Bird have called."

"What a pleasure, Mr. and Mrs. Bird. Do come in." Eva led the way to the drawing room.

Cornelius Bird and his wife were making calls before they embarked on a trip to Paris.

"We were going home," Cornelius said. "I'd purchased our return tickets. But Mrs. Bird wanted to buy new gowns to impress the neighbor ladies. Say,

Lady Eva, have you seen Mr. Bedford Forrest? Can't find the devil anywhere, and he was supposed to recommend a good hotel in Lyons."

"No, I'm afraid I've been a trifle preoccupied and haven't gone about in Society for a few days."

Josepha leaned confidentially toward her. "That's quite all right, my lady. I have no interest in going to Lyons. Paris is what interests me. The fashions. The Empress Eugénie is so elegant, quite the opposite of the English queen, don't you think?"

"Perhaps," Eva said diplomatically. The empress was indeed quite beautiful and elegant, but Eva was certain that Josepha didn't care that she was also good and gentle. To her gratification, the Birds didn't stay long enough for refreshments.

"We've so many calls to make," Josepha chirped.

Cornelius was disgruntled. "This extra trip is costing me a fortune."

Eva refrained from telling him it wasn't polite to discuss money. Telling Cornelius rules of etiquette was futile. She walked with the couple back to the entry hall.

"Would have cost me more if I hadn't got rid of our tickets," Cornelius grumbled. "Got almost full price for them from young Locke."

"What?" Eva paused in the hall.

"I wasn't going to just throw them away, now, was I?" Cornelius said with a self-satisfied grin. "Locke bought them a few days ago. Good luck for me."

"Mr. Bird, exactly what were the ticket dates, and what was the name of the ship?" The government had been keeping the incident with the queen quiet.

Both Josepha and Cornelius looked at her strangely.

"They were for the eighteenth, on the *American Freedom*. Why?"

Eva recovered herself. "Oh, I was surprised that Mr. Locke didn't pay us a farewell call."

"Well," Cornelius said, "he's young. Such niceties sometimes escape young men."

Hardly able to contain her impatience, Eva escorted her callers out the front door and ran upstairs to Ryder's rooms. Knocking, she rushed in and found him half dressed. Sitting on a chair, his shirt open, he was pulling on half boots.

Ryder looked up at her entrance. "Eva!"

Eva stopped short and whirled around. "I'm sorry. I had news that made me forget myself."

"What is it?"

She heard linen rustling as Ryder buttoned his shirt. "Hamilton sailed for America the day he disappeared."

"Hold on a minute." Ryder was in front of her, his shirt untucked. "Are you sure?"

She recounted the story of Cornelius Bird and the tickets for the *American Freedom*. By the time she'd finished, Ryder was dressed.

"I don't understand why he'd light out without talking to me. He knew I was defending him. It's not like him to run away."

"I must tell my uncle," Eva said.

Ryder grabbed her hand. "Don't. Please."

"Why not?"

"Because if you do, the prime minister will send someone after him, and that will create an incident. Can you imagine what will happen if my government learns that the British have grabbed one of its citizens and accused him of attempted regicide?"

"Merciful heaven," Eva said. "We might find ourselves in the war on the Confederate side after all."

Ryder went to the armoire and removed a suitcase.

"What are you doing?"

"I've got to get to Hamilton before anyone else does."

"And what about Iago?" Eva asked.

"I had already suspected he might have left the country. It's no use staying here. I'll pick up both trails back home, probably somewhere near Washington."

"You mean *we* will." Eva met Ryder's stern gaze with equanimity.

He studied her for a moment, then threw up his hands. "Aw, hell."

"Your language, sir."

"Aw, hell."

"I'm going, Mr. Drake." Eva walked to the door. "Whoever the assassin is, he tried to kill my queen. I can't allow that. I'm going to find him and call him to account."

"Do you hear yourself?" Ryder asked. "You're just a little bit of a female, and—"

"And we've had this argument before. I'm going, and that's all there is to it."

Ryder came toward her. "Now, listen—"

"Don't even try leaving me behind," Eva snapped. "I'll simply come on my own. If I can get to Egypt, I can get to Washington, even if there is a war going on."

Ryder paused, then shook his head. "You'd do it too. Sail right into the middle of some all-fired battle. So you'd better come with me. That way I can keep an eye on you."

"And I can keep an eye on you."

# CHAPTER EIGHTEEN

❧❧

*Washington, D.C.*

THE DAY AFTER the American Independence Day saw Eva again a guest of the Blairs on H Street. She and Ryder had arrived in the city the day before to find the place much changed. Hundreds of troops marched in the streets. The railroads ran constantly, ferrying supplies and men, and politicians clamored for a decisive strike against Richmond, the Confederate capital. The abolitionist press was strident, castigating Congress and the president for wasting time.

So far they'd found no trace of Hamilton Locke or Iago. At the moment, Eva was waiting for Ryder, who was going to enlist Alan Pinkerton's help in tracking them down. He and Pinkerton were meeting this morning to plan their strategy. If all went well, Pinkerton would commit several of his best agents to the job. Eva was nervous because she expected her uncle and Scotland Yard to show up any day on their own hunt for Hamilton Locke. If Ryder didn't find him before the British, Locke could be in desperate trouble.

In addition to her other cares, Eva was fearful for Josiah. Ryder had told her he'd gone back behind enemy lines with one of Pinkerton's men posing as his master. The young man was proving an innovative and efficient spy. But no one had heard from him in weeks, and Eva couldn't help picturing what might have happened to him.

Eva's tension warred with her newfound happiness. On the voyage to America she and Ryder had finally been able to confide in each other in a way Eva had never suspected could happen between a man and a woman. On the third night out, in the middle of the Atlantic, they had walked on deck after dinner. The moon gleamed its silver-white radiance down on them, bathing the surface of the black water. Ryder guided her to the prow, where they leaned against the gunwale. Eva knew he was going to tell her about Mrs. St. Cloud. She knew it from the white line around his mouth and the tortured look in his eyes. He was wearing a topcoat with the collar turned up against the cold Atlantic breeze. His chin sank into the black wool, and he sighed.

"Eva, I promised to tell you about—about Mrs. St. Cloud. I've been avoiding it. You can't help but know the subject is most unpleasant to me, but we must be frank with each other."

"I shall be," she replied.

Ryder smiled tightly. "Perhaps after you hear my tale you won't wish to be frank. You may wish to end our relationship altogether."

"Impossible."

"My dearest Eva, I hope you're right." Ryder paused, as if gathering his courage. "You know something of my family situation, but no one knows the whole truth about Mrs. St. Cloud. We met in New Orleans many years ago...."

One of the hardest things Eva had ever done was to remain silent and allow Ryder to tell his story without interruption. By the time he spoke about the duel with Villafranca she was glad Mrs. St. Cloud was dead or she might have been tempted to shoot the woman.

"So you see, I killed that boy for nothing. For less than that. I allowed myself to be jealous of that— that—"

"Harlot," Eva said quietly.

"Yes." Ryder refused to meet her gaze. His head bowed, he whispered of his guilt and shame. "Now that you know, I must offer to withdraw from our acquaintance. I know how honorable you are, and my actions must disgust you." Ryder gripped the gunwale with both hands, gaze lowered, silent at last.

Eva knew he was waiting for her to recoil in disgust. She pulled off her glove and placed her hand over his. "I want to tell you a story about my parents and how I ruined their marriage. I've never told anyone else because I was too ashamed." She drew closer to him, and he turned a disbelieving gaze on her. "I was twelve, old enough to know right from wrong, but not old enough to understand that my parents had never been known for their marital fidelity. My father and mother weren't happy together. Mama required music and laughter in her life, and she had a great deal of love to give. Papa was more down-to-earth, and hadn't been brought up to show his love to anyone. Mama begged for attention, and he ignored her. I suppose she was desperate when she fell in love with Papa's best friend, Raphael Meredith.

Mama was so ecstatic that she couldn't control herself. She told me all about Mr. Meredith, you see."

Taking heart from Ryder's honesty, Eva plunged on, describing how she'd given her mother's letter to Raphael to her father. It was cold on deck, but that wasn't the reason Eva began to stutter. "They had an unspoken arrangement, so Father couldn't bear it when he realized Mother had exposed his private affairs to his best friend, and to me too, I suppose. He sent me to a French boarding school, and Mama was exiled to France too. I used to th-think that if I was very good, my parents might forgive me and love me again. That's why I married John Charles. I was being good, you see."

"But it wasn't your fault!"

Eva smiled ruefully. "Do you know how long it took me to realize that? Even now part of me still cringes and blames that little girl for something she couldn't control. The blame belongs to two people who should never have burdened her with confidences and responsibilities that were theirs alone."

"Oh, I'm so glad," Ryder said with a sigh of relief. "I was worried you still felt responsible for the conduct of two selfish people and—" Ryder stopped and eyed her. Understanding seemed to dawn, and he narrowed his eyes. "Eva Sparrow, you're a confoundedly clever woman."

"I was wondering when you would see the similarities."

"You could have just told me."

"You had to come to it yourself. Have you?"

Ryder stared up at the moon, took in a deep breath and let it out slowly. "I suppose it's rather presumptuous of me to take the blame for something that wasn't even in my power. Gabrielle was a

monster. She and that voodoo woman of hers manipulated me, and Villafranca too. But Eva, I could have
controlled myself. Nobody forced me to duel. I'll
never forgive myself for that."

"You weren't much older than Villafranca, Ryder.
Mrs. St. Cloud manipulated both of you, and you
weren't the first. It was horrible, but you must realize
as I have, that we make mistakes. If we're lucky, we
learn from our faults and correct them, as you have."

Speaking so low Eva could hardly hear him,
Ryder said, "Then you don't hate me?"

"Ryder Drake, I'm not even going to answer such
a foolish question." She watched his clouded face
and sorrowful eyes. He set his jaw and turned to
meet her gaze. His eyes widened, as if he was surprised by what he saw. Then he smiled, and the sor-
row vanished.

Ryder laughed softly. "When you had your great
revelation, did you suddenly feel free?"

"As free as an angel in the clouds." Eva gasped as
Ryder swept her up in his arms and whirled her
around.

"We're free!"

Eva almost laughed aloud at the memory of
Ryder's elation. It had been a tonic against the worry
he felt for his cousin. Then her thoughts turned to the
present once more. It was odd that they hadn't found
Hamilton in Washington. Once he'd reached the
United States, he could have stayed in any number of
places unknown to the British. Ryder had checked
them all and found no trace of his cousin.

Eva looked out the windows of the drawing
room, to H Street. She was occupying her time with
embroidery while waiting for Ryder. As she gazed on
the tree-lined road, Eva saw a carriage pull up, and

Lucian Bedford Forrest got out. In moments, he'd come inside and was sitting with her.

"I had no idea you were back in Washington too," he said. He produced a handkerchief and coughed into it. "Pardon, my lady. This humid Washington weather strains my lungs."

"It is quite warm and moist," Eva said. "I understand many people have come down with fevers. Tell me, Mr. Bedford Forrest, have you by any chance seen Mr. Locke?"

"No. Not since London, I'm afraid. I was going to Italy, but my business manager needed me back here. Something about one of my properties being confiscated by the Confederates. Of course, Mr. Lincoln says that they are simply rebels and refuses to recognize the Confederacy. He maintains that they have no rights as a sovereign country. But that makes no difference when their troops occupy one's property, now does it?" Lucian smiled wryly.

Eva smiled back at him. "Perhaps you should thank Providence that you weren't there at the time. No doubt the Confederates would have thrown you in jail for being a traitor to your state."

"Indeed," Lucian said with a chuckle. "They hate those of us who have remained neutral more than they hate Yankees."

"Lucian!" Ryder came striding into the room and gave his friend a rough hug. "I'm surprised to see you here."

Lucian explained his predicament again.

"I wouldn't worry," Ryder said. "The president is planning a strike at Richmond soon. If we're lucky, the Confederates will have to retreat. The whole city is talking about it. So much for military secrecy."

Lucian shook his head. "I know, but what shape

will my fields be in after they leave? They might burn them."

"True," Ryder said grimly. "Oh, by the way, have you seen Hamilton?"

"I was just telling Lady Eva that I haven't seen him since London."

"I need to speak to him urgently." Ryder sat down opposite his friend.

Lucian turned to Eva. "And what brings you back during such an uncertain a time as this, Lady Eva?"

Eva had been preoccupied with the news that there was to be a campaign against Richmond. She stuttered, unable to think of a good excuse for her return.

"Might as well tell you," Ryder said, meeting Eva's gaze. "Lady Eva and I have an understanding, Lucian old fella."

"An understanding," Eva repeated blankly.

Lucian was up and shaking Ryder's hand. "Congratulations. A very fine idea, and a fine match indeed." He kissed Eva's hand before he sat down again. "I wish you every happiness, Lady Eva."

"Thank you," she said as she glared at Ryder. An understanding? No one had informed her of it. Anger simmered to a boil, and her lips pressed tightly together.

"I must go," Lucian said after a few more minutes of conversation. "I'm seeing an officer about a pass through the lines to inspect more property north of the city. I hope you find Hamilton."

Eva accompanied the two men outside. Lucian paused as he descended the front steps.

"By the way, have you thought of checking at Belle Aire?"

Ryder frowned, then nodded. "Oh, yes. I'd for-

gotten about Belle Aire. It's been so long since we've
been there, and the place is shut up."

Lucian shrugged. "If you've tried all his other
haunts, you might as well try that one."

"Neither he nor I have been there for years," Ryder said. "Still..."

"Good day, Mr. Bedford Forrest," Eva said. Still
angry, she turned on her heel and went inside, leaving
Ryder to say good-bye to his friend.

Ryder caught up with her in the entry hall. "I have
to go to Belle Aire."

Eva rounded on him

"An understanding? Just what does that mean,
Mr. Drake?"

"What? Oh." Ryder shrugged. "Had to tell him
something, and that seemed a plausible excuse for
your being here."

"Now everyone will think we're engaged!" Eva
cried.

"We are, aren't we?" Ryder was looking at her as
if she were a little slow.

Eva folded her arms and glared at him. "Not unless I've suffered a loss of memory. You never asked
me to marry you, sir."

"But on the ship—"

"Did you ask me to marry you on the ship?"

"Not exactly, but—"

"Then I haven't been asked," Eva snapped. "I've
had one marriage where everyone assumed my consent, sir. I'll not have another." Eva held up her hand.
"Not another word about it, Mr. Drake. I shall give
you a few days to think about what I said. Then you
may ask for my hand in marriage in a more agreeable
manner. And once you ask, I shall give your request
serious consideration."

"Aw, hell, Eva."

"Mind you language, sir."

Ryder stuck his thumbs in his vest pockets and frowned at her. "I always know when I'm in trouble with you, 'cause you start calling me 'Mr. Drake' and 'sir.'"

"Hmm. Then you may expect to hear yourself addressed thus for the foreseeable future. Sir."

"Maybe you'll have calmed down after I get back." Ryder plucked his hat from the stand near the door.

Eva rounded on him. "Oh, no. You're not searching that Belle Aire place without me."

"But you're riled at me."

"My being 'riled,' as you put it, does not interfere with my wanting to find the assassin." Eva lifted her skirts, preparing to mount the stairs. "I shall change and be down directly."

"Yes, ma'am," Ryder said.

He was smiling at her in a peculiar way, but Eva was in no mood for further arguments with him and went upstairs.

They left Washington that afternoon, riding south with Noah Frye and one of Pinkerton's agents, Benjamin Lovejoy. They left the city and took a road that paralleled the Potomac River, passing plantation after plantation, some of which had been abandoned once Virginia seceded. Eva was surprised to see groups of escaped slaves in carts and on foot, all headed for Washington. She wondered what these poor people would do once they got to the capital, for the white citizens of the city didn't seem prepared to accept them. She would have to see what she could do for them when she got back.

The sun was sinking behind a line of pine trees when Ryder turned down a road that led toward the Potomac. Eva's anger had ebbed somewhat, enough for her to be cordial to him on the journey, but Ryder was preoccupied and distant. She knew he was worried about his cousin again, but there was nothing she could say that would ease his anxiety.

Dusk closed in on them quickly; old oak trees lined the road and arched their branches overhead to form a green rooftop. Crickets chirped all around them, and in the distance Eva could hear the croaking of toads. Eva breathed in the warm scents of old wood, drying grass and bruised leaves and felt the allure of this land. Not for the first time she glimpsed the passion it inspired in Americans of all political leanings.

Ryder turned down another road, which wound toward the river and then broadened into an avenue lined with giant tulip poplars. The trees stretched down to a large house resting in their shadows, a red-brick colonial manor house with a Greek portico supported by eight white columns.

"Merciful heavens," Eva murmured.

Ryder slowed his horse until he was riding beside her. "I know. It's beautiful. Belle Aire has been in the family for one hundred and thirty years. Hamilton's namesake planted those boxwood hedges around the turn of the century."

"But why doesn't he live here?"

"You haven't seen the slave cabins," Ryder said. "Once his mother passed on, Hamilton arranged for the slaves to buy their freedom. It took several hundred of them to farm Belle Aire. It takes thousands of acres to support a place as large as this, and Hamilton wasn't willing to profit from the misery of his slaves. He sold half the land and shut the house. He rarely comes here. I like the place, and I think it could be made profitable with paid labor and the right crop once slavery is abolished. We'll see."

It occurred to Eva that this plantation explained much about Ryder's mother. Having grown up in such splendid privilege, she must have been raised to expect her life to progress in unruffled opulence in settings equally as grand. Ryder's father probably had given her a terrible shock with his carelessness and squandering ways that threatened her ideal existence.

They stopped at the steps leading to the portico and dismounted. In the fading light Eva could see that Belle Aire rested on a gently sloping hill. The river curved past the promontory, and a velvety lawn stretched down to the water at the back of the house. Ryder had described the place as it had been in the last century—a busy plantation with many ancillary structures. There had been a stable, mule shed, paddock and coach house, a wash house, smokehouse, storehouse and clerk's quarters. These buildings lay unused now, along with the separate kitchen, salt house, spinning room, greenhouse, slave hospital and shoemaker's shop. The gardens that lay between these buildings and the house were overgrown and choked with weeds.

"No lights," Eva said as she surveyed the dozens of windows across the front of the house.

"The place is so big fifty people could be in there at the back of the house, and you wouldn't see anything," Ryder said as he tethered his horse. "Besides, the shutters are closed."

Ryder motioned for Noah Frye and Ben Lovejoy to accompany him, while Eva followed the men onto the porch, passing between two of the enormous columns.

Lowering his voice, Ryder said, "Now, remember, no weapons drawn. Hamilton isn't a violent man, and we don't want to scare him into defending himself."

He produced a key and unlocked the mahogany front doors. They creaked open to reveal a gloom so deep they couldn't see more than a couple of feet beyond the threshold. Noah passed out lanterns to Ryder and Ben, and they preceded Eva inside.

The lantern glow revealed a long entry hall with a drawing room and dining room flanking it. Dust cloths covered the furniture. A crystal chandelier hung in the hall. It still bore the burnt candles from its last use. Eva shivered in the unnatural stillness of this forgotten house. Ryder ordered Noah and Ben to search the ground floor, and together he and Eva mounted the elegant curved staircase to the second level.

"Hamilton's bedroom is on the second floor," Ryder whispered. "If he's here, he'll probably be in it."

On the landing Eva noticed that dusty paintings covered the walls. Ryder pointed to a portrait of a handsome man in old-fashioned riding costume holding the reins of a Thoroughbred stallion. "That's my grandfather Julius Caesar Locke. He was an ornery old cuss. Used to go out shooting at poachers for sport until one got him in the hip with a load of buckshot."

Eva smiled, because Ryder bore a distinct resemblance to the ornery old cuss. As she followed him across the landing she felt a breeze. Glancing aside, she saw that the second-floor hall ended at a window, and the window was open. Eva caught Ryder's arm and stopped him.

"Look." She pointed to the window as the sad call of a whippoorwill floated to them on the breeze.

The wind picked up suddenly, and in the distance she heard a muffled clatter. She glanced at Ryder, who had cocked his head to the side to listen. Eva hardly dared breathe. Ryder turned to her, lifting an eyebrow in inquiry. Eva pointed at a closed door, the third from their left. They went to it, and Ryder's hand clasped the lever.

He bent down to her, placed his lips against her ear and said, "Stay here. I'll call you once I've let him know we're here." He handed her the lantern he carried.

Ryder twisted the lever and slowly pushed the door open while Eva watched. Then he slipped into the darkness beyond. Eva strained to see him, but the breeze abruptly whipped down the hall, causing the door to slam shut. At the same time, Eva heard another muffled clatter and a heavy thud.

"Ryder!" She fumbled at the door, but it wouldn't open. She put her shoulder to it and pushed, but it stayed closed. She twisted the lever hard and shoved again. "Ryder!"

Eva banged her shoulder against the door, then stopped to listen. "Ryder?"

There was no answer, and again on the breeze came the lonely call of the whippoorwill.

# CHAPTER NINETEEN

❧

RYDER OPENED HAMILTON'S bedroom door as Eva put her shoulder to it once more. He caught her as she tumbled toward him and caught the scents of lavender, horse and leather that clung to her clothing. Eva righted herself and peered past him into the darkened room.

"He's not here," Ryder said. "But a window has been left open, and a shutter was loose and bumping against the window frame. His things are here, so maybe he's outside."

"Perhaps Mr. Locke heard us coming and retreated to one of the outbuildings."

Ryder glanced up and down the hall and saw no light under any of the doors. He listened for a moment, but heard nothing, not even the whippoorwill.

"This place is too quiet," he muttered, guiding Eva toward the stairs. "Let's see if the others have had any luck."

"But there are other rooms off the landing, and we haven't even tried the wings of the house."

Ryder urged her down the stairs. "I've got a bad feeling."

"But—"

"Damn it, woman, this is no time to come over all cussed stubborn."

He tightened his grip on Eva's arm and ushered her to the ground floor. For once, she stopped protesting and allowed herself to be guided. At the bottom of the stairs Ryder stopped to listen. The breeze had vanished as suddenly as it had appeared, and the hum, whir and twitter of insects and birds had ceased as well. Ryder strained to hear the fall of a boot, the creak of a floorboard. As he listened, his skin began to crawl. Something was wrong. He'd known this house since childhood. He'd been here a few times after it had been closed. It was somehow different. This wasn't the natural silence into which an occasional animal interjected a noise. This was a waiting, tense silence.

Beside him Eva stirred. He still hadn't heard Noah or Ben. They might have gone outside to check the stables. Leaving Eva in the hall, he moved to the dining room, which afforded a view of the front grounds. Seeing nothing but their horses, he returned to Eva.

He took her hand and whispered, "Listen, Eva, I want you to go outside and mount your horse. Wait about fifteen minutes. If I don't come for you, ride back to the crossroads and turn left at the intersection. About two miles farther is a little farm run by an old army veteran Hamilton and I have known all our lives. His name is Orpheus Weems. You tell him I sent you. He'll know what to do."

"I'm not going to leave you!"

Fear for Eva made Ryder grip her by the arms and

raise her to meet his gaze. "Eva Sparrow, you're going to do what I say. This is my territory, not yours, so I call the shots. Now get out there, or I'll carry you."

His determination must have been clear to her, because Eva nodded rapidly. He set her down on the floor, and she let him lead her to the door. He pushed her outside and locked it.

Hearing her test the lock, Ryder growled, "Get on the horse!"

"Yes, sir!"

Ryder could tell she was angry at being excluded, but he could also tell that she knew she had no choice. He drew his revolver and did a quick and silent survey of the ground floor, even going into the rooms of the east and west wings. He found neither his cousin nor his fellow agents. Ending back in the hall, Ryder was about to make a quick search of the stable and decaying outbuildings when he heard the long, low creak of a door swinging open upstairs. He looked up and saw a light issuing through the partially open door of the room next to Hamilton's bedchamber. This was a study and library for the master of the house. It had once held a valuable collection of books of all sorts—rare manuscripts that had come with the family from England, first editions, specially commissioned sets of the great works of European, Greek and Roman philosophers. Ryder frowned as he mounted the staircase. Hamilton had never been bookish, and in any case would have little reason to seek out the empty library.

Reaching the door, Ryder raised his revolver and shoved the door all the way open using the barrel. A lantern had been set in the cold fireplace, and in the shadows at the edge of the light he saw a tall, lean form with its back to him.

Ryder whispered, "Hamilton?"

Lucian Bedford Forrest turned to face him.

"Do you know, Ryder old fella, I think I could forgive Hamilton anything except selling off all your family's magnificent books." He gestured at the empty bookshelves that covered the walls.

Ryder lowered his revolver, his heart pounding. He seemed incapable of doing anything but staring like a beached fish, his mouth working and his eyes glazed.

"At last," Lucian said with a smile, his hands clasped behind his back, "I've succeeded in stunning you speechless. No more dashing elegance, just gawking stupidity. Oh, and by the way, don't expect any help from your two friends. I don't know if I killed them, but they'll certainly be unconscious for a long time."

"What are you doing here, Lucian? You can't be—"

"Iago? Oh, but I am."

Ryder shook his head, and Lucian sighed in irritation.

"You don't believe me. Who do you think arranged all those silly diversions for you in London? Who killed that annoying St. Cloud woman when she failed to keep you distracted? You should thank me for that. She and that demented Mama Gris-gris were a menace to civilized people."

Ryder was having a hard time reconciling his fragile, asthmatic and bookish friend with the murderous Southern agent. "But why, Lucian? You don't hold any strong beliefs in slavery."

"I suppose I have time to explain, since you got rid of little Lady Eva."

Lucian walked away from the fireplace, and Ryder moved to keep distance between them. Going behind a heavy walnut desk, Lucian produced a bottle of bourbon and two whiskey glasses. He poured two drinks and handed one to Ryder. He sipped from his own glass before beginning.

"You're right, I don't care about slavery. In fact, philosophically speaking, I find it distasteful. But what I find even more distasteful is the idea that a pack of moneygrubbing shopkeepers and factory workers is set to march through my state and destroy my whole way of life." Lucian set his glass down and sat in the leather chair behind the desk. "You've lived among the Yankees, Ryder. You know how rabid the abolitionists are. Sooner or later they'll prevail over the moderates, and then they'll burn every plantation from here to Texas. Do you know what that means?"

Ryder shook his head.

"It means no more hot, lazy days spent rocking on the veranda, smelling the gardenias on the breeze. No more long, quiet nights reading Chaucer and Shakespeare to a cicada serenade. Have you thought of these things at all, Ryder? I suppose it doesn't bother you that none of us will be able to travel to Florence or Milan, places where art is the breath of life. We'll never waltz in Vienna or hike in the highlands of Scotland or go to the opera in Paris. That's what will happen if the North wins, you know. They'll bankrupt the whole South."

"It doesn't have to be that way."

Lucian sneered. "Your family is wealthier than mine. And in any case, our wealth is in the land and slaves, not cash or other assets. And the abolitionists have made it clear that they'll see to it that we receive no compensation for our lost property once the slaves are freed. Well, I have no intention of allowing a passel of Yankee barbarians to destroy my home. It's older than Belle Aire and as beautiful, and I love every moss-covered oak tree and azalea bush."

"But what about the Union?"

"What about it?" Lucian sighed. "I'm not going to get into an argument with you about the proper balance of power between the states and the federal government, Ryder. We'll never agree. Besides, it was only seventy-four years ago that Jefferson said the tree of liberty must occasionally be renewed with the blood of patriots and tyrants."

Ryder looked at his whiskey with distaste and set the glass on the desk. "So you decided to become the South's secret champion."

"Can you blame me? Most of my life I've had to sit at home while you and Hamilton and the rest of my friends had adventures." Lucian's eyes glittered as he spoke. "You never thought about that, did you? I used to hate the way you'd look at me with such compassion and then go off with Hamilton or our other friends hunting or riding. The rest of them would come back with stories of their exploits, but not you. No, you made light of the fun. I could see the sympathy in your eyes, Ryder, and I hated that you tried to conceal how much I was missing, *out of pity*!" His breathing grew rapid, and his fair complexion flushed.

Concerned, Ryder moved toward Lucian, but his friend suddenly reached into his coat and drew a revolver.

"Drop the gun, old friend." When Ryder hesitated, Lucian cocked his weapon. "Don't test me." Ryder dropped his gun.

"As I was saying, I hated being less than a man.

But that has all changed. For the last few years my health has improved, and I've recently found that the excitement of stalking an adversary is most invigorating. It's amazing, but I never suffer from asthma while I'm working." Lucian eyed Ryder slyly. "You might say that spying is palliative."

"You enjoy leading a secret existence," Ryder said. "Iago has killed a lot of people, Lucian. I can't believe that—"

"That I'm capable of defending my home and myself as any man might?"

"That you'd commit murder."

Lucian shrugged. "I'm a patriot defending himself. That's not murder. In any case, I find the greatest satisfaction in outwitting the enemy. The South needs someone of my intellect to guide and defend her. She needs someone with great physical daring and equal vision. You should hear my Southern friends talk. They consider me a savior, a king's champion, so to speak, all the more wondrous for the weakness I had to defeat to become what I am."

"Lucian, you sound as if you're creating your own legend."

"What if I am? The South is going to need heroes, and if I'd have succeeded in London, it would have added greatly to my reputation. There was only one flaw in my plans."

"Yes, they were too complicated."

"No, I was referring to my having underestimated you. Had I not been so sure I could mislead and confuse you, I would have simply killed you and gone ahead with my plans to kill the queen. But I was worried that your death would validate the tales you were telling the British, so I left you alone."

"And we ruined your cursed plot to kill an innocent woman and drag a foreign nation into this war."

Lucian passed over this accusation, and looked thoughtful. "My friends in Richmond won't be pleased." He shook his head. "I suppose I'll have to agree to their original target, even though I told them it matters little who leads the North. After all, it's to our advantage that the Yankees take orders from a barbarian and a clown."

Ryder felt his heart suddenly in his throat. His alarm seemed to gratify Lucian, who smiled at him.

"This time I won't mess about. It should be easy to shoot him as he walks from the White House to the War Department. He does it every day, I'm told." Lucian waggled the barrel of his revolver. "But before I do that, I must take care of you."

Ryder tensed, readying himself for a desperate lunge. He doubted he'd be fast enough, but he had to do something before Lucian decided he'd done enough talking. Ryder asked the question he'd been avoiding.

"Lucian, where is Hamilton?"

"Everyone is down in the cellar."

"Is he all right?"

"He's as well as can be expected. This is how it will appear. Hamilton was the assassin, as I planned, and you and your party tracked him here. He saw your party coming and lay in wait, shooting you all. Too late he discovered you were one of his pursuers. Overcome with grief and remorse at having murdered his dear cousin, who he loved like a brother, he killed himself. I shall compose a dramatic letter of confession. Everyone will think Iago is dead, leaving me free to carry on with my work." Lucian cocked his head to the side. "I don't want to kill you, old friend, but you've left me no choice. However, I do regret you brought Lady Eva into this. You realize, of course, that she must die too. The poor little thing must still be out front waiting for you."

"No, I'm right here."

Ryder heard a shot from somewhere behind him as Lucian aimed his revolver. His friend grunted and recoiled from the impact of a bullet. A hole appeared in the flawless white cambric of his shirt, and blood spurted from it.

Stunned surprise swept over Lucian's face as he looked past Ryder. "No, this isn't what I planned. . . ."

Ryder lunged and knocked the revolver from Lucian's hand. His friend didn't seem to notice. He was still staring at Eva, who hadn't moved. His legs buckling, Lucian dropped to his knees behind the desk. Ryder grabbed for him, but missed. He saw the life go out of Lucian's eyes before his body sank to the floor. Tossing the revolver aside, Ryder turned to Eva.

She was frozen, both hands gripping her Colt. The weapon trembled as she gazed at Lucian's blood-soaked body. Ryder gently placed his hand on the gun and lowered it, easing it from her grip. Eva's gaze was still pinned to Lucian's body, so Ryder turned her away and guided her onto the landing.

"Eva? Aw, hell, what possessed you to bring a gun?"

"Y-you sh-shouldn't complain."

She was shaking, and her breath was coming in gasps. Ryder knew what was coming. He shoved her to a sitting position on the stairs and made her put her head between her knees. He instructed her to slow her breathing.

"Breathe slower, honey, much slower. It's over

now. You did what you had to do. You saved my life."

In a few minutes she was able to stand. He supported her with an arm around her shoulders. Still shivering, Eva sucked in great gulps of air in a brave attempt to master her horror. Ryder kissed her forehead.

"I have to look for Hamilton and the others. You stay here."

Eva gripped his arm. "Don't leave me with him!"

"All right, all right." Ryder helped her downstairs. Behind the staircase was a door that concealed another stairway, leading down to the cellar. Ryder retrieved his lantern and preceded Eva to the dark cellar. The place had a clammy, musty smell, and it was cold. At the foot of the stairs he almost tripped over two bodies. Holding the lantern closer, he saw Noah Frye and Benjamin Lovejoy. Both men had been struck on the back of the head, but they were breathing. Eva squeezed his arm.

"Ryder, I'm sorry."

He met her gaze and read the truth in her sorrowful eyes. He closed his briefly, then turned and held the lantern high. About fifteen feet from the agents lay his cousin. He had been tied to one of the support posts of the cellar, but he slumped within his bonds, a bullet hole in his temple. Ryder handed the lantern to Eva and went to Hamilton. Loosening the ropes that bound him, he lowered the body to the floor. He knelt beside Hamilton, trying to reach past a sudden feeling of unreality. Dear, softhearted, fanatical Hamilton couldn't be dead. He took his cousin's cold hand; his vision blurred with tears, and he choked. Thankfully, Eva allowed him privacy and remained silent. He didn't know how long it was before he was able to speak.

"He hasn't been dead long," he said at last. "If we'd gotten here an hour earlier..."

Eva approached him finally, knelt and spoke softly. "Mr. Bedford Forrest would have shot him before we could set foot in the house. Ryder, he set this trap before we even saw him in Washington."

"And I walked into it. Damn all to hell! I should have protected Hamilton. I should have known better than to trust Lucian." Ryder brushed tears from his cheeks in sharp, angry movements.

"No one suspected Lucian," Eva said. She touched his shoulder. "Not even Scotland Yard or Mr. Pinkerton, and they suspect everyone. He was supposed to be in delicate health and with more interest in books than real life. He deceived everyone."

Ryder didn't reply. For him there was no comfort. Hamilton was dead, and Lucian too. He should have figured it out. Lucian had shown up in London at the time Iago was supposed to have appeared there. He moved in the same circles and had the same opportunities for mischief as the assassin, and he had the skills. Of course, Ryder hadn't considered it relevant that Lucian knew how to shoot rifles and revolvers and use a knife, because he hardly ever used those skills. At least, not in Ryder's presence.

"Mr. Bedford Forrest must have gone to the police station, drugged the men on duty and helped Mr. Locke escape," Eva said. "He probably told your cousin you'd sent him to get him out of the country. Heaven knows what lies he spun to keep him in hiding."

"This is all my fault," Ryder said.

Eva rose and looked down at him. "I'm not going

to try to convince you otherwise right now." She stooped and kissed his cheek. "Come. Mr. Frye and Mr. Lovejoy need our help."

Ryder placed Hamilton's hand over his heart and rose. As he went to attend to the two agents, he listened to Eva reassuring him that he'd prevented Queen Victoria's assassination and avoided war between their countries. Every point she made only deepened the grief and remorse that threatened to envelop him. No success, however important, was going to bring back the man he'd loved like a brother.

# CHAPTER TWENTY

❧☙

EVA WAITED AMID the dusty wagons and dilapidated landaus at Beamish and Quick's at dawn on the morning of July 23. Ryder was away on a scouting mission but would return soon. So much had happened that she felt like one of those tiny ships that had sailed to the New World in the sixteenth century, tossed on seas that threatened to swallow them. In her hand she clutched a velvet box and an envelope. She wore a new gown of midnight blue tartan and white lace and a matching bonnet, and over her gown was draped the ribbon of orders given her by the queen and fastened by a diamond broach.

She felt ridiculous wearing such finery in this place, but circumstances made secrecy necessary. At her side stood the secretary to the British ambassador to the United States, Sir George Knyvet, a callow youth whose family connection with Lord Palmerston had earned him his post. Sir George looked like he belonged in a boarding school rather than an embassy, but at least he was dressed in a morning coat and striped trousers.

Eva heard the door open and shut and fussed with the curls that tumbled from beneath her bonnet before turning to stand formally beside Sir George. Threading their way toward her were Mr. Alan Pinkerton and the Union spy, Josiah. Eva smiled when she saw the young man in his new suit. He walked with his shoulders straight, and his gaze lighted on people in a direct and forthright manner. Josiah had found self-respect, no matter what the world thought of his color. When he glimpsed Eva, his pace quickened, and he grinned.

"Miss Eva! Mr. Pinkerton said you wanted to see me. What're you doing here? This ain't no time to be in Washington. You ought to go on home."

Eva held out her hand for Josiah to shake. "I'm fine, Josiah, and I'm most pleased to see you've returned safely as well." Seeing Josiah glance at Sir George, Eva cleared her throat. "Josiah—um—have you a surname?"

"My ma said she forgot our name that came from the old country, so I chose me one. I'm Josiah Henry, after Mr. Patrick Henry. 'Give me liberty, or give me death.'"

"An excellent choice," Pinkerton said. "Now, Mr. Josiah Henry, as a representative of the United States government and the president of the United States, Abraham Lincoln, may I present Lady Eva Sparrow and Sir George Knyvet, who are here on a special commission from Her Majesty Queen Victoria of Great Britain."

Josiah's eyes widened, and he glanced from Mr. Pinkerton to Eva, who winked at him.

"Yes, sir," Josiah replied.

Eva stepped forward. "Mr. Josiah Henry, I have been commissioned by Her Majesty Queen Victoria of Great Britain, Ireland and the dominions, to award to you, for deeds of bravery and service to the empire, the Victoria Cross."

Opening the velvet box, Eva handed it to Sir George, who held it while she removed the medal. She reached up and pinned the cross on Josiah's lapel as he stared in astonishment. His eyes swept to Sir George when the Englishman began to speak in a high, nasal tone.

"Mr. Henry, Her Majesty has given special dispensation for the Victoria Cross to be awarded to you. This decoration is awarded to British soldiers of all ranks and services and is inscribed 'For Valour.' Only men who have faced the queen's enemies and performed an act of supreme bravery and devotion to duty are given this decoration. It is the most highly prized military decoration in the empire. Thus it is a measure of Her Majesty's gratitude that you receive it today."

Pinkerton nodded at Sir George, who handed Josiah the velvet box. Eva then held out the envelope, which had the royal seal on it.

"A lifetime pension of ten pounds per year accompanies the Victoria Cross," she said. "And Her Majesty has added to it a sum meant to show her personal gratitude and that of His Royal Highness, the prince consort." She pressed the envelope into Josiah's free hand.

Josiah stood staring at Eva for a full minute before he could open his mouth. "This here medal is for spying on the Rebels?"

"And for uncovering that plot against Queen Victoria, as I told you," Pinkerton said.

"A queen give me a medal, just like white folk get," Josiah said in a rather disbelieving manner. Then he pulled himself up and assumed his usual expression of youthful dignity.

"Miss Eva, ma'am, Sir Knyvet, will you please tell that queen of yours thank you very much. I never got a medal before, and I'm mighty proud to get this one. And if I can ever help her out again, you tell her I'm ready."

"Well," Sir George said, "I don't—"

Mr. Pinkerton's scowl silenced the secretary. "We'll give your thanks to Her Majesty, Josiah. Miss Eva will write her personally."

Eva held out her hand to Josiah, who fumbled with the velvet box and envelope until he could grasp it. Shaking hands, Eva leaned forward and said, "Do take care, Josiah. I worry about you and your family."

"These are troublous times, Miss Eva, and I thank you for your worrying. But a man's got to stand up for what he believes, or he ain't no man."

Nodding, Eva shook Josiah's hand again, and Alan Pinkerton escorted him out of the building. It had been as Ryder had predicted. His own government failed to recognize Josiah's contribution to its defense. Most likely the Victoria Cross was the only reward the young man could expect.

"Well," Sir George said when they were alone, "I must say, that was extraordinary. Personally, I see no reason for all the fuss. After all, this Josiah person is just a Negro."

Eva rounded on him. "In my presence you will refer to him as Mr. Henry, and if you're not careful, I'll mention your boorish conduct to Her Majesty."

"Oh! I say. No need, Lady Eva. I do apologize."

"Go away, Sir George. Just go away."

Later that morning, escorted by a young infantry captain, Eva stepped inside the White House to the shocking sight of hoards of office-seekers crowding the mansion's halls. The captain brought her to a small, empty room and deposited her on a plain, cane-backed chair.

"I'll tell the president you're here, ma'am."

Left to herself, Eva jumped to her feet and strode about the room. It had been over two weeks since they'd come back from Belle Aire, two weeks filled with unhappy duties. Ryder had arranged for the funerals of his cousin and Lucian, and Eva had helped so that he didn't have to face undertakers and curious friends alone. Speaking to the families of both men had taken great strength, but Eva was learning just how resilient Ryder Drake was. He had to be, because while they were in the midst of tracking Lucian's movements in America and abroad and making full reports to the British government and Mr. Lincoln, the first great battle of the War Between the States opened.

Three days ago, on July 21, General Irvin McDowell attacked the Confederate forces of P.G.T. Beauregard in the region south of Washington known as Bull Run. Ryder had been dreading the confrontation, having sided with General Scott in his opinion that the Union troops were untrained and unready for a major battle. When reports of the battle began to come in, Ryder had ridden out of the city to meet the returning troops. Eva expected to meet him here. A few minutes more, and she was drumming her gloved fingers on the windowsill and looking out on a patch of green lawn where one of the president's boys was leading a goat with a duck perched on its back. Evidently the goat gave rides to the pet fowl in the Lincoln menagerie, for this was the second duck to be given this treat, and several chickens were waiting their turn nearby.

The door opened, and Eva turned to see Ryder enter. He was wearing the uniform of a cavalry colonel. His hat and gold-braided epaulets were covered with dust. He was holding his riding gloves and came to Eva with his arms outstretched. She nestled against his chest and kissed his cheek.

"I'm covered in road dust," he said.

"I don't care. What happened?"

"I thought you'd have heard by now." Ryder sat down on the cane-backed chair and rested his forearms on his knees.

"Everyone says the Union army was routed. Is it that bad?"

"It was bad enough, but most of the ones who broke and ran in the retreat were the ninety-day troops the president first called up, plus some teamsters in their wagons and the fools who went to the battlefield to observe."

Eva shook her head. "I saw several of my acquaintances heading off to watch. Mrs. Blair took her carriage and two friends who brought picnic baskets."

"I don't blame the women," Ryder said, "but I do blame the idiot senators and congressmen who hightailed it at the first sign of trouble. They were squealing for a fight just a few days before."

Eva put her hand on Ryder's shoulder. "Are the Confederates so much better at fighting?"

"That's why I checked the situation myself."

Ryder put his hand on hers. "Eva, you've got to help me get the truth to the British government. Most of McDowell's troops fought well, and we would have won if General Johnston hadn't moved his army from the Shenandoah Valley to reinforce Beauregard. But that idiot Patterson let him slip away, and Johnston put his troops on trains and got to Bull Run in record time. McDowell took too long to march to Bull Run. If he hadn't delayed, he could have attacked before Johnston got there."

Eva sighed. "I just got word from Uncle Adolphus. We sold Confederate purchasing agents eight hundred thousand Enfield rifles."

"Aw, hell."

"When Lord Palmerston hears about this battle and how well the South did, he's going to recognize the Confederacy formally. France will do the same."

"But it was really a draw, damn it."

"I'm sorry."

Ryder kissed her hand. "It's not your doing."

"I'm sure Uncle Adolphus will take my account of the assassination plot to Lord Palmerston and the queen. That will ease matters and perhaps help ensure that Britain stays out of this conflict." She paused as she saw a look of pain cross Ryder's face. "What's wrong?"

"I was just thinking about Lucian and my cousin. They were such friends, and yet Lucian stole Hamilton's rifle, probably made sure he brought it to England just so he could use it to implicate him. And Hamilton was never in the Sons of Freedom, so Lucian had to have planted those abolitionist plans in his overcoat. It's just so hard to believe. Lucian killed that man watching Gabrielle, he killed Zachariah Gordon and Mama Gris-gris, and Gabrielle too."

"Did you ever find out why she became a spy?"

Ryder shook his head. "She never allowed anyone close enough to understand her completely except Mama Gris-gris, but..." His lips tightened for a moment, then he sighed. "There was something strange about Gabrielle's nature. She always had to be causing a sensation or manipulating people. She was addicted to power over men. We found a great deal of her correspondence in a locked jewel casket among her things. It seems she'd been spinning intrigues since she was a girl. I think Mama Gris-gris must have aided her from the beginning. Gabrielle thought of her as a mother, and the two of them hatched plots together. They fed on each other's twisted need for control. In the end, however, they were no match for Lucian. He was the more ruthless killer."

"Merciful heavens." Eva felt a small twinge of sympathy for Mrs. St. Cloud, but only a small one. "And Lucian was working against you all that time in London, encouraging Mrs. St. Cloud to corrupt you."

Ryder shivered. "It's a measure of Gabrielle's hubris that she thought I would ever again become enslaved to her. What's worse is how Lucian manipulated Hamilton into escaping so that he looked guilty. I'm sure it was his idea for Ham to sail to America without contacting me, damn him."

"He was daring, though," Eva said. "Showing up in Washington just to drop that hint about searching Belle Aire. He could have stayed out of it altogether and been safe." She looked into Ryder's sad eyes. "We should be glad he failed and Britain won't be tricked into joining this war, at least for now."

"Speaking of staying out of conflicts..." Ryder stood and took her hands. "Things are only going to get worse, Eva. Mr. Lincoln hasn't found a good commander. McDowell won't do. We can't even put camps very far west of the city without running into Southern pickets. They ambush and snipe at the troops."

Eva knew where he was going with this description. "Ryder, I'm safe in Washington."

"No, it's more than that." Ryder squeezed her hands. "I found out that Confederate spies telegraphed our troop movements out of Washington as McDowell left for Bull Run. Pinkerton and I have a load of work to do if we're going to stop them. Eva, this city is riddled with Southern agents and sympathizers. If the war goes badly, Washington could fall, and then—"

"Then my retreat will be much more orderly than General McDowell's. I'm not leaving."

Ryder dropped her hands and went to the window. Running his hand through his hair, he looked out on the lawn. "I didn't want to say this. I thought I could convince you without it, but I was being too optimistic." He looked down at his boots and said softly, "Eva, I don't know what's going to happen. I have no right to ask you to remain here when there's a good chance I'll be killed in this war."

Eva swept across the room and batted Ryder on the shoulder.

"Hey!"

"How dare you underestimate my character after all these months, Mr. Drake."

"Oh, now I'm Mr. Drake again."

"If you think I'm going to run away from this fight and from you, you're mistaken, sir. I can face danger just as bravely as you can. You ought to know that by now."

"Well, yes."

"Have your feelings toward me changed?"

"Of course not."

"Then, sir, we will proceed as we have been."

Ryder took her hand again and bent down to kiss her. "Are you certain?"

"You're just lucky I don't join you as a special agent."

"Now, Eva—"

"Don't worry, I don't think I'd make a good spy. My accent is all wrong."

"Thank Providence," Ryder said.

He was looking into her eyes and smiling, and Eva cocked her head to the side.

"You're looking pleased with yourself all of a sudden."

"Oh, I suppose it's because I got what I wanted even though I tried not to," he replied.

"What in heavens are you talking about?" Eva gawked at him as he dropped to one knee while holding her hand.

"Dearest Eva, will you forgive me for my prejudices and my bumbling attempts to gain your affections?"

"Um, yes." Eva held her breath, as Ryder suddenly seemed to have lost his voice.

He stuttered a bit, then got some words out. "Aw, hell—I mean . . ." He bit his lip, sucked in his breath and rushed on. "I love you more than my life, Eva. Will you marry me?"

Sinking to her knees before him, Eva kissed his hand and brought it to her cheek.

"I will, my love."

Ryder gripped her shoulders, kissing her hard,

and it was at that moment that the army captain knocked and opened the door. They broke the kiss.

"Oh! Pardon me, my lady, sir."

"Oh, drat," Eva said as Ryder helped her stand.

Chuckling, Ryder returned the captain's salute. "It's all right. Lady Eva and I have just become engaged."

"Congratulations, Colonel Drake. The president is ready to see you now. If you'll follow me."

Ryder offered his arm to Eva. She took it and whispered to him as they left the room.

"By the way, Colonel Drake, I'm still going to find a way to serve the Union cause."

"You're going to make my life hell, woman."

"Nonsense, sir. The devil is much worse than I am."